Key to Yesterday

By

Jonathan Young
and Dennis Houghton.

This novel is a work of fiction. The characters portrayed are fictitious and the product of the authors' imagination. Any resemblance to actual persons, living or dead is purely coincidental.

ISBN 9780955185427

MRA Publishing

Brooke House

Apreece Way

Stilton

PE7 3XG

PREFACE

I started to write this book as I was flying to New York to watch the Republic of Ireland in the world cup in 1994. I had written the teams song "Thank you Jack" as a tribute to their then manager the late Jack Charlton, I had a sister, Ann, who lived there so I wasn't going to let the fact that I was from Northern Ireland stop me. I had written plenty of songs so I thought how hard can it be to write a book?

Having worked on cruise ships I was lucky enough to meet authors who had come to do lectures and all their advice was the same.

WRITE WHAT YOU KNOW ABOUT.

Hence my main character Sean Clarke is a singer/Actor who was born in Belfast and now lives in Manchester, just like me. There the similarity ends and my imagination takes over. He is a person who tells himself that he has made mistakes but he has done his best, still like the rest of us if we had done our best we wouldn't have made so many mistakes and Sean made plenty. It's a story of how extraordinary experiences can intertwine into ordinary lives and believe it or not to say anymore would spoil the story which, I hope you are about to read.

I had more or less written the story with Sean telling it to the reader but I still didn't feel there was enough to make a novel so I took it to my friend and neighbor next door Dennis Houghton.

Unlike me Dennis had already written two or three books so I was not surprised with what he came back with. He had added a few more characters plus a few sub plots and together we finished the book in 2005.

After hearing nothing concrete from publishers I did some rewrites and had a new version by 2008 but still nothing favorable from publishers so back it went on the shelf.

Then came the COVID-19 pandemic and the lockdown of 2020 which is when I really went to work on the book. I listened to suggestions from friends and developed the characters to make them more believable and real.

 I would especially like to thank my wife Margaret for her patience during the 26 years it took to finish this book. Most of the early parts I wrote while on tour as one of the Bachelors with John Stokes and the late Kevin Neil and their encouragement was greatly appreciated. In fact the first draft was printed in Australia on our 2005 tour. My meeting with Roy Baines at a monthly gathering of entertainers called "The Wooden Hut Club" gave me the final incentive I needed to finish the book. Roy is an author himself and his help with getting it published was invaluable. Lastly I would like to thank my granddaughter Megan Clark who did most of the editing and proof reading not to mention designing the cover of "Key to yesterday" the book I hope you are going to buy, or hopefully already have.

Jonathan Young.

Key to Yesterday

By
Jonathan Young
and Dennis Houghton.

Chapter
ONE

The year is 2004, the place, Manchester, England.

Fate is truly fickle. I'd spent a whole day chasing after a story, only to have all the main protagonists refuse to speak to me. I was tired, hungry and thoroughly pissed-off.

As a consolation, I treated myself to a Big Mac, and drove to a quiet road where I could at least assuage my hunger pains. I idly watched the light traffic passing as I munched, and then I saw the long black hearse. Nothing unusual in that, since I'd parked in a lay-by opposite a cemetery. I hardly gave the hearse a thought, and only gave the following limousine a cursory glance … But I did stare at the silver Jaguar XJ6 that sidled through the gates a few seconds after the limousine.

What was Sean Clarke doing at a funeral? Instinct had me start the car and turn into the cemetery, keeping a respectful distance behind the Jaguar. It stopped some distance from the small chapel where the hearse and the limousine had halted, so I came to a halt. Sean stayed in his car until the funeral procession came out and moved into the grounds. He set off and so did I, keeping a safe distance between us. When he stopped, I stopped. He got out and walked to where a tiny group of people had gathered by a grave. He stayed close enough to see the proceedings but far enough away not to be involved. He remained where he was until the priest and the small group began to walk from the grave. I took this as a cue to get out of the way, so I reversed and made my exit.

It was a simple matter to follow Sean's car. He drove quietly into town then pulled into the car park of a restaurant. I parked beside his car and called to him as I closed the door.

"Sean … It is Sean Clarke, isn't it?

For some seconds I thought he was going to ignore me. He stared, but not at me, as if his mind had been elsewhere. Then, he blinked. I expected a quick snarl, a sharp dismissive retort … Instead he nodded. "Yes, I'm Sean. Who are you?"

"My name is Priest, Andy Priest and no I'm not the guitarist with the pop group Sweet. You don't know me…"

"That's right, I don't. What do you want?"

"Would you let me buy you a drink?"

"In exchange for what?"

I hunched my shoulders. "I don't know."

He laughed low and humourless. "You're the first journalist who didn't know what he wanted. You are a journalist are you not?"

"Freelance."

"And you smelled a story?" He held my gaze with his clear blue eyes. His forehead creased in a faint frown. "Have you been following me?"

I shrugged. "I did happen to see you drive into the …"

"And then you followed me." He looked away for a moment then let out a sigh. "OK You can buy me a

2

drink." He turned and walked towards the entrance leaving me to chase after him.

He was already at the bar, lifting a glass when I joined him. He drained his glass and nodded to the barman. "Same again."

I watched the barman pouring a double measure of Brandy into the glass before handing it to Sean.

"I'll have a half of lager."

"Do you know I used to drink in a bar where the landlord Terry refused to serve lager because he thought it attracted a bad element." Sean smiled as he raised then drained the glass.

"Same again." Sean waited until the refill arrived then he turned from the bar.   "Are you ready to eat?"

He didn't wait for my answer, but headed off towards some unoccupied tables beyond the end of the bar. I joined him and took a seat facing him across the small rectangular table. He ignored me, poring over a menu and jabbing his finger at several dishes while a young waitress hovered at his shoulder. I opted for a boring salad.

"Now," Sean smiled at me. "You were going to tell me why you were following me."

"I wasn't following you. I just happened to notice you as you drove into the cemetery."

"And then you followed me, yes, we've already established that. So you thought what?"

"I just wondered what a ..."

"You just wondered what a star like me was doing in a place like that... That's what you were going to say, isn't it?"

3

I hesitated. Sean Clarke was not a star as such. He was a celebrity, pretty well known locally, and I knew he'd had a hit record somewhere abroad, and had appeared on TV a few times. Show Business wasn't my scene, but I knew he'd been around for more years than I'd had shaves, and he was popular with people like my Mum and my Auntie Jean. I nodded.

"Yes, that's just what I was going to say."

"You're a liar, but not a good one." Sean smiled. "It's all right. I know I'm no star ... but I have been known to twinkle at times."

"The funeral ..."

"Ah yes, the funeral." He inhaled and held his breath, letting it out in a long sigh. "You wouldn't know the person."

"But I could find out who it was."

"Yes, you could ... But even if you did it wouldn't help. You still wouldn't know her."

"Someone from your past?" I inquired.

Sean laughed. "Journalists have a one track mind, and it's a dirt track."

"I didn't imply that ..."

"Yes you did, and you were way off target ... Ah, here comes my starter." He grabbed a fork and started eating. During the next forty minutes I learned something new about Sean. He had a great appetite and a capacity for drink that would have left a sponge jealous. Dean Martin once said that he didn't really drink a lot that it was just an act. Well Sean was the real deal.

We talked, but he managed to say nothing of consequence. I also discovered he had a sense of

4

humour, which as I would later find, could be a little bit wicked.

When the bill arrived, he scanned it carefully then passed it to me. I must have gone pale since he started to laugh. He took the bill back from me and carried it to the bar where he paid in full and left a generous tip. As he was heading for the door, he turned to me. "You still owe me a drink."

We stood by our cars and he stared at me for some time before he inclined his head. "Do you want to come back to my place? I'm not working 'til Thursday, so if you want a chat, we can chat."

"Thanks. Will you be all right to drive?"

"No. I'll leave my car and you can drive. Why do you think I invited you back?" He stood grinning at me until I opened the passenger door of my car. Already he was treating me like a chauffeur.

He lived in a semi-detached house in a quiet cul-de-sac only a couple of miles from the restaurant. When we arrived he welcomed me inside his house with a genuine show of friendliness.

We went into a room at the front of the house, and I couldn't help but notice the mass of electronic equipment and the array of guitars resting on stands in the corner. I sat on a settee facing a modern fireplace and he went to a cabinet standing beside an easy chair. He offered me a drink, and I accepted, a soda, while he poured himself a good measure of Brandy. Lowering himself into the easy chair, he stared at me.

"What do you want from me, Andy?"

"Whatever you're prepared to offer, Sean."

"Fine." He sipped the Brandy. "I was born in Belfast, Northern Ireland in November nineteen forty-seven, and I lived there until I was twenty. I'm a professional entertainer and have been since I was seventeen. I tell jokes and I sing - which means that when nobody laughs, I sing."

"So you mainly work the pubs and clubs in and around Manchester?"

"Yes, but I do get an occasional bonus trip. For example I'm off to Australia next week. Four weeks in the sun."

"Sounds good."

Sean shrugged. "It's a living."

"You were once married to Marianne, weren't you?" I saw I'd touched a raw nerve, and for a moment I thought he was going to throw me out. Instead, he took another sip of Brandy, gazed into the distance, and nodded.

"Ah, you're referring to 'The Dancing Queen'? Yes. We were married. "

I took his response to be a rather disdainful reference to the fact that she now owned the Dido Dance Studio - the largest and best known dancing school in Manchester.

I could see he was disturbed, so I smiled. "If you don't want to go on, I'll finish my drink and leave."

"That might be the sensible thing to do." he said as he stood up, and I realised just how big a man he was. I started to rise and he shook his head. "Right now, I'm not feeling very sensible. Could be too much Brandy or maybe not enough." He went to the cabinet and poured himself another.

"Want a refill?"

I declined his offer, but only because I was driving. I somehow felt he'd feel less vulnerable if I was getting pissed with him.

He sat down, cupping the glass in his hands and staring at the amber liquid. "Yes, I was married. I met Marianne at the Winter Gardens in Blackpool. We were doing a Summer Show in nineteen eighty-four. I was the compere, and she was a dancer. My God she was beautiful - still is. I remember thinking she had great legs." He laughed. "Have you ever heard of a dancer with ugly legs?" He smiled. "Until then I'd adopted the Jerry Lordan philosophy."

I hunched my shoulders and gave him a blank look.

"You know - eat when I'm hungry, drink when I'm dry - ain't gonna marry, ain't gonna try?"

"Sorry, I haven't a clue what you're talking about."

"The singer for God's sake. Jerry Lordan, he wrote 'Apache for The Shadows'."

"Sorry you've lost me."

Sean frowned and shook his head. "His hit record was 'I'll stay single'. "My God I thought we might have a generation gap, but this is a generation chasm!" He let out a long heavy sigh, and then went on. "I took one look at Marianne and that was it. It was, as they say, lust at first sight. That was probably why the kids came so quickly."

"Jason, and …?

"Michele." He raised an eyebrow. "I see you've done

some homework?"

I shrugged. Most of what he'd been saying was common knowledge. I looked up to find him staring at me.

"Maybe everything came too quickly." He frowned.

Sean shook his head, looked as if he was about to say something, then he closed his mouth. He remained quiet for several seconds before he spoke again. "How do you pinpoint the moment when a marriage starts to go wrong?"

I stayed silent. Sean rolled the glass between his hands while looking somewhere over my shoulder. "You never know what your partner expects of you, so you don't know if you're letting them down." He gave a deep shrug. "I know I wasn't living up to her expectations - but then again I wasn't living up to mine either."

"When was this?"

"What? Oh, ninety-four I think. Jason was eight, and Michele must have been about nine. I remember I was taking any and every job that came along, telling myself it was a step along the way to better things. In reality, it was just a way to keep a roof over our heads and pay all the bills."

"When did you break up?" It would have been easy enough to check the details, but I wanted to keep him talking.

Sean shook his head before draining his glass. I could see he'd reached a point where he could open up like a ruptured dam, or retreat into defensive silence. I thought it wise to change the subject.

"You said you were working on Thursday, is it somewhere nearby?"

"Why, are you thinking of joining my fan club?" He hadn't replenished his drink, just replaced the empty glass on the cabinet before sitting down. "If you really are interested, I'm doing a country club near Preston. Late night cabaret at the 'Lakeside'. I'll give you a couple of tickets. Bring a friend." He gave me a mischievous smile. "You have got a friend, haven't you?"

"One or two. Thanks I look forward to it." He seemed to have relaxed so I took a chance. "This funeral ..."

"I'll get those tickets." Sean stood up and went out of the room. I finished my soda and took the glass back to the cabinet. On the wall of a small alcove I noticed a picture and by craning my neck I could see it. Tom Jones was grinning at the camera, and on either side of him were Sean and a beautiful blonde girl, who I took to be Marianne. Sean hadn't been lying when he said she was attractive. I heard footsteps coming along the hallway, so I returned to my seat.

"Here." Sean thrust the tickets into my hand then glanced at his watch. "I don't want to rush you, but there are some things I have to get on with."

I got up. "All right. I still owe you that drink, and I'll see you on Thursday."

As I drove home I got the feeling I'd stumbled onto a story. I didn't have a clear picture, but I did get the impression that Sean wanted to unburden himself. He'd come close that afternoon, and I wanted to be there when he did.

9

I forgot about Sean when I listened to the message on my answer-phone. One of the characters in my current project had had a change of heart and wanted to speak with me.

In the thirty five minutes it took me to drive from my flat to the subject's house, they'd changed their mind. When I got to their front door, it was opened not by the subject, but by a solicitor who told me quite bluntly that 'his client' had no intentions of speaking to me about 'the situation' - or anything else for that matter. He also 'advised' me that the other interested parties had all been advised to adopt a similar stance by their legal representatives.

Without my original project, I was at a loose end or more like a dead end. Sean Clarke was my immediate and obvious target, so next morning I began to follow my instincts.

It was a simple matter to discover who had been buried at the plot in the cemetery the previous day. Her name was Sharon Hanson, and as Sean had predicted, it meant nothing to me. A visit to the Registrar's office followed by a trip to the local daily's library provided me with a little more information but it still left me puzzled. Sharon Hanson had been in her car which was involved in a collision with an articulated lorry that had jack-knifed on the motorway not far from Manchester.

With only a name to go on, I tried using the search engine to see if there was any more information about Sharon stored in the newspaper's archives. It came up blank, and left me even more determined to discover how Sean and Sharon were linked.

I went home and spent the rest of the day trolling numerous 'pop' websites to see if I could unearth more information about Sean. What I got was virtually what I already knew, and the additional details I found, dealt with his career. I did notice that there had been a lengthy break during the mid-eighties, and I assumed that was the time when his marriage was heading for the rocks.

Then I tried using Sharon Hanson as a 'keyword' and the search provided a dozen possibilities. None of them was the woman who'd been buried the day before.

I had taken note of her address, so a little legwork was called for. Sharon had lived in Shaw, a one-time village, now a distant suburb to the north east of Manchester. It took less than forty minutes to find her home.

The estate wasn't new, or old, but it certainly was 'select'. The houses were large, detached, and expensive-looking. Each had its own garden and drive, and I parked in the drive of Sharon's house then went to the front door. Several pushes on the bell produced melodic chimes from the interior, but no response. I turned and started to walk back to my car, when I noticed a woman.

She'd crept out onto her own drive, next door, and was eying me with distinct suspicion. I gave her my most winning smile and went towards her. She stood her ground, still regarding me with a stony expression.

"I was trying to contact Sharon Hanson. I believe she lives here?"

"Why? What do you want with her?"

"It's a minor legal matter. Nothing drastic, but I do need to speak to her or a close relative." Fortunately I'd chosen to wear a decent set of clothes that morning, and I could have passed for a solicitor's clerk. The woman studied me closely for some time before her expression softened.

"Sharon died last week."

"Oh dear, I'm sorry to hear that. Is Mister Hanson available?"

"Tom died two years ago. You're not here to cause trouble, are you?"

"Not at all. My firm has been appointed to find Mrs Hanson, or a relative, by a client in America. I'm sorry but I can't divulge any more."

"I see."

"Do you know if either Mrs Hanson or her husband had any close relatives?"

The woman pondered for a moment then shook her head. "Not that I know of.

Sharon and Tom were a quiet couple, but they did mix quite well. When Tom died, Sharon kept herself to herself for a while, and then she started going back to her charities."

"What sort of charities?"

"Everything you could think of - Cancer Research, Underprivileged Children in the Third World. It was her whole life. But she never looked for publicity or credit for herself."

12

"Did she have many visitors, after her husband died?"

"A few. The ladies from our local church used to call round once a fortnight for a coffee morning."

"Did any gentlemen call?"

"Oh goodness no. When Tom died, she was quite happy on her own …"

"Well thank you, you've been helpful." I gave her a smile and turned away. A thought came to me, and I dipped a hand into my pocket. Taking out a photo of Sean Clarke I'd copied from one of the web sites, I held it out. "You haven't, by any chance, seen this man?" The woman glanced at it then beamed. "Of course I have. It's that Irishman, what's he called … the singer."

"When did you see him, and where?"

"The first time I saw him was, let me see, Blackpool, about ten years ago. He was in a show at the North Pier Theatre. I told the ladies' group how good he was then we organised a trip to see him at a club in Rochdale a few years ago."

"Did Sharon go with you?"

"I don't think so. She'd agreed to go, but if memory serves, she was ill at the time."

"Do you recall if Sharon said she knew him?" The woman gave me a puzzled frown. "Knew him? I don't really know. She never spoke of him, if that's what you mean?" Her frown deepened. "What's he got to do with Sharon?"

"I don't know. I honestly don't know." My reply was more to myself than to her but I was now more than ever determined to find out.

13

TWO

On Thursday morning I contacted Amanda, a college friend from the old days. She was unattached and always ready to 'party'. So when I mentioned I had tickets to a cabaret, she agreed to come along. I arranged to pick her up at eight, and purposely forgot to mention where we were going.

She almost went hairless when I did tell her we were going to Preston. At first she refused to go. Then, after some subtle persuasion, she reluctantly agreed, but she spent most of the trip complaining. She calmed down a little when she saw the club, and she was subdued during the meal.

When the cabaret began, Amanda moved into top gear, she sighed so loudly that it sounded as if a force ten gale was sweeping through the place. Then, in a whisper so loud that half the diners could hear, she told me she was bored. The only thing that appealed to her that night was Sean. When he walked onto the small stage, Amanda's eyes lit up. She gazed at him, transfixed as he chatted to the audience.

"He's a dish, isn't he?" This time her whisper attracted some approval. But she reverted to type once Sean started to sing. "It's all old stuff. I don't know anything he's done so far."

Then, as soon as his act had finished, she got to her feet. "Right. I want to go. Now!"

I didn't want to create a scene so I took her back to

Manchester, dropped her off at a night-club where she was meeting some friends, and went home alone. I said to myself, "That went well."

Next morning I drove out to Sean's home. I guessed he wouldn't have risen early so I arrived a little after eleven. He opened the door and smiled at me. "I believe you had a problem with your 'friend' last night?"

"I wanted to talk to you, but she ..."

"It's all right it's that generation gap again. I've been there myself. D'you want some breakfast?" He stood back and allowed me to enter the hallway. I could smell bacon and heard the chuckle of frying eggs coming from somewhere beyond the far end of the hall.

We sat in the kitchen while we ate, and then moved to the room at the front of the house. I took a seat on the settee and Sean sat in the easy chair. We drank coffee.

"I found Sharon Hanson's home yesterday." I'd hoped to startle him.

"I thought you might." He smiled. "Do you want a medal?"

"No. I want a story!"

"I thought that's what you got yesterday?"

"You were humouring me. Playing me along - like you are now."

"You're perceptive, I'll give you that." He glanced towards the door. "You can leave anytime you want, it's not 'Hotel California'."

"The Eagles, now I've heard of that one." I stared into his pale blue eyes. "I know you want to tell me something, and it involves Sharon Hanson."

"Maybe you're right; or maybe I just like your

16

company." He was still smiling, but for an instant I saw a change in his expression.

"Or maybe you're scared?" I held his gaze.

"Of what?" He grinned. "You?"

"Not me, but what I could do if you did tell me your story. You see I'd have your secret then." I spoke softly. "I think you're still in love with Marianne, and I..." I gaped at him as he started laughing out loud.

When he'd regained control, he shook his head at me. "I take back what I said earlier. You're not perceptive, you're guessing - and your guess is totally wrong."

I was totally confused. "But ... the picture?" I pointed towards the alcove to his left. "Isn't that Marianne?"

"Yes, it is. Look behind you." Sean stared somewhere over my right shoulder.

I turned to look at the wall behind. It was filled with dozens of framed photographs. A brief inspection showed that Sean and Marianne were on them all, along with a host of celebrities.

"I keep them," Sean addressed me as if I was a child; "to remember the great people I've had the pleasure of meeting in the business. It was coincidental that she was with me when most of those were taken, what do you think I should do? Cut her out?"

"I noticed the first time we met - you're wearing a wedding ring."

"So?" He gave me a studied stare. "Ah, you thought the only reason I could be wearing it was because I still wanted to remember Marianne. Well Andy your powers of deduction leave a lot to be desired as does your research because I ... Ah never mind. We will deal with that later."

"All right, I was wrong. But I still believe you have … something to … Oh, I don't know. I reckon you have something bottled up inside and you want to get it off your chest."

Sean blinked slowly. He avoided my gaze and stared at some of the photographs on the wall behind me. When he turned to look at me, he gave me a wry smile. "Maybe you're right."

"You'd feel better if you did tell somebody."

"How do you know? Suddenly become a psychiatrist as well as a snoop?" He saw my reaction and gave a quick shrug. "Sorry, I didn't' mean to insult you."

I smiled. "Forget it."

An idea came to me. "Look, if you have trouble talking about - whatever it is, perhaps you could write it down? I know whenever I have worries, problems that prey on my mind, I write them down. I call it 'writing out my devils'."

"Does it work?"

"Not always. But sometimes, when I put the problem down in writing, it seems to clear my mind. I can look at the problem objectively, and do something about it. If I can't do anything, then I forget it. It helps me sleep at night."

"I'm not a great writer apart from the odd song I might write."

"You don't have to be. All you need do, is get the problem down in front of you, on your computer, it kind of makes your thoughts official."

"Let me stop you there Andy, I'm not into computers in fact, a mobile phone is my only concession to modern technology, still maybe I'll try writing it down." Sean got up. "Now, I have a few jobs to do, and …"

"OK. I'll go." I fished one of my business cards from my pocket. "If you do want to talk, call me."

Sean took the card and read it before he slipped it into his pocket. He gave me a brief smile then showed me to the door.

I didn't expect to hear from Sean until he'd come back from his Australian 'jaunt'. I didn't want to hang around waiting for him to get back, so I looked round for something else to do. I managed to dig up some details of a seedy little story that involved a Manchester United player and a young girl. He was married and she was pregnant. Not a thing to be proud of, but I did as good a job as I was able, and sold my effort to the local rag. I even got a bonus when some of the National tabloids took it up. It helped pass the time, and kept me occupied for a few weeks. At least that's what I tell myself, it makes it easier for me to live with me.

Sean telephoned me two and a half months after I'd last visited him. His voice was 'easy' and I guessed he'd had a few drinks.

"Hello Andy. I wondered if you felt like a drink, or two?"

"Where are you, Sean?"

"I'm at the Rose of Lancaster, in Middleton Junction. It's off-"

"I know it. I could be there in about half an hour. OK?"

"Sure. I'll be here."

He was leaning against the bar, an inevitable Brandy in his hand and another at his elbow. He looked leaner than when we last met, and his face was tanned. He finished the drink in his hand and reached for the second. He wasn't aware of me until I stood beside him. He turned and wrapped his free hand around my shoulder. "If it isn't my old trick-cyclist Andy Priest. "

"How was Australia, Sean?"

"How long have you got, my friend? I could talk about the place for hours. I could tell you tales about the scenery the cities and the people … and maybe some time later, I will. You know, you could do a lot worse than go out there yourself. There are a million opportunities for somebody as young and enthusiastic as you."

"I'll bear it in mind, Sean."

He was silent for a considerable time while he just stared at me. Then he spoke. "I tried it, you know - the 'devil writing'. And d'you know what? It didn't work, but I got a hell of a lot of waste paper for my troubles." His expression became grave and he stared directly into my eyes. "It's still here." He tapped a finger against his temple.

"Can I help?"

"You tried Andy. Like I said, it didn't work."

"Not at all? I didn't say it worked every time."

Sean hunched his shoulders which I now noticed he had a marked tendency to do. "Well, maybe it wasn't a complete disaster. It got me through the time in 'Oz'."

"You want to tell me, don't you?"

"Not right now. I couldn't go through with it. But if you could read what I wrote, I'd be grateful. Then, if you still think you can do something, give me a call." He drained his glass then took my arm. "I have it all right here." He led me to the car park where he unlocked the boot of his car and took out a large cardboard box. "That's it, my friend. See what you can make of it." He handed me the box, and before I could respond, a taxi drew up and he got into it.

I watched him go then went to my own car, wondering what had prompted me to get involved with him in the first place. I dumped the box on the back seat and sat staring into the distance for some time before I moved away.

The box remained unopened in my kitchen for most of that day. I walked around it when I made myself a snack. I stepped over it as I went to the sink to fill the kettle, and I skirted it when I carried my coffee into the living room.

It was like an itch I couldn't scratch. I did my best to ignore it, but sometime after eight that night, I grabbed it and carried it into the living room.

I opened the box and found a complete trash-pile of paper. There were scraps no bigger than postcards, pieces of torn envelope, and a great wedge of A4 lined paper. I picked up one of the scraps and began to read, never realizing I was embarking on an adventure even I would struggle to comprehend.

21

The stupid little bitch, she's finally got her way.

I dropped the scrap and tried one of the envelopes. The writing that covered it was disjointed and erratic, and after I'd read it a couple of times I guessed it was about something in Sean's earlier life. The next piece involves me!

He might be onto something, and he has the tenacity to dig deep when he senses a story. I still don't trust him enough to tell him everything and yet what's the point if I don't.

I'd emptied the box scattering the contents all over the room. Then I started to put the individual pieces into neat heaps that had some relevance to each other. In all there must have been a dozen piles when I'd finished. I picked up the nearest pile, made a space on the settee then sat down and started to read each piece thoroughly.

By three o'clock the following morning I'd come to the conclusion that there was no way I could figure out a link between the majority of Sean's scribblings. What he'd given me enabled me to get a much clearer picture of the man, as he was twenty years ago, and how he had changed in the intervening years. But it still didn't give me a complete picture. It was as if he'd presented me with a puzzle, but deliberately kept a few major pieces from me.

I went to bed.

It was early afternoon when I woke, and after a quick

breakfast I began to make my own notes, based on Sean's writing. Putting the incidents into what I thought was a reasonable chronological order; it strengthened my view that Sean really did have something important buried deep in his memory. Even from my brief examination of his writing it was evident that he had omitted certain sections of his tale; and it didn't take a genius to figure out that he'd left out the key aspects. Whether by accident or design it certainly fuelled my interest and made me even more determined to uncover that secret.

I tried to contact him, but all I got was a recording requesting the caller to leave a message. I did, but I wasn't too hopeful that he would answer my call. I was wrong.

Sean telephoned me shortly before midnight, dragging me out a particularly pleasant dream involving … I snatched up the phone and grunted.

It was Sean and he was cheerful enough for both of us. "Hey, did I wake you? Sorry Andy. I got your call and figured you wanted to talk." He continued in the same effervescent manner. "I'll be finished here in about thirty minutes and we could meet up …"
"Jesus Sean! I'm in bed, and…"
With your lack of charm and charisma I bet you're on your own, so as I'm not interrupting anything how about a meet somewhere in town."
We briefly discussed the location and agreed to meet at ten thirty that next morning.

I was late, by only a couple of minutes, but Sean was already at the café when I arrived. He grinned after glancing at his watch. "My old grandad used to say that punctuality was the pride of kings. You're obviously a commoner." He indicated the chair opposite and ordered coffee and a fry-up, for both of us."

"Fine." I'd collected the notes I'd made on Sean's scribblings, and tucked them into a well-worn briefcase which I slid onto the table. Sean eyed it then me. "You're serious about this, aren't you?"

"Of course"

"Have you read my notes?" He raised an eyebrow when I nodded. "All of them? My, you certainly don't hang about, do you? What do you think?"

"If you wanted to intrigue me, you succeeded. I'm intrigued."

"You told me to write down my thoughts, as they came. So, that's what I did. I never intended it to be a 'manuscript'."

"Don't flatter yourself, that, it most certainly isn't."

"Look. If I wanted your literary criticism, I'd have asked for it." His pale blue eyes locked onto mine for a moment, and then he smiled. "You want the full story, don't you?"

I let out a long sigh, interrupted by the arrival of breakfast. I waited until the waitress had gone, then I nodded. "That's the only reason I'm here Sean, as Sinatra sang, "All or nothing at all." I hoped to appeal to his love of quoting the lyrics of songs.

"Ha! I would have thought Frank was before your time." Sean laughed. "First we'll eat, then we'll have a drink, this place is licensed, and then we'll make a start."

24

It was almost an hour before we retired to a small booth at the rear, where we'd carried our drinks. Sean gave a contented sigh and rubbed his stomach. "Makes you ready to 'face the world', does a good breakfast."

I merely gave him a bloated smile.

Sean nodded towards my briefcase. "Got my stuff in there?"

"No. Just some quick notes I made. I had problems getting them into any sort of sequence. I didn't know which notes referred to which incidents."

"I do." Sean gave me a broad grin. "Would you like to dig some of those notes out, and I can tell you where they fit in the order of things?"

"I have a better idea. Why don't I keep your notes for referrals and you just tell me the story - the whole story."

"How long do you have?"

"I've nowhere else to go and nothing else to do."

Sean pulled a face. "Well I have. I'm due at a recording studio around half-two."

"Then we'll have to do it by instalments."

"In that case I'd better order some drinks to keep us going." He grinned impishly. "Thirsty work, storytelling."

"Do you always drink before going to the studio?" I called to him.

"It's alright. I'm making a 'tribute to Dean Martin' album" was his reply.

Was he serious? I have no idea but I wouldn't put anything past him...

Once he was settled with a supply of drink, I took out my miniature recorder. At my suggestion he started at the earliest significant point of his story, and I promised not to ask too many questions, leaving him to decide which incidents were relevant. Sean began.

In December 1964 I was seventeen years old and still living in Belfast. I earned a few quid playing and singing with a 'beat group' I'd formed along with three of my old school friends. We weren't fantastic, but we were good and getting better.

We'd finished an engagement at a semi-classy hotel in the north of the city, and we started packing up our gear when I began to feel odd. My head was 'muzzy' and my throat started to get dry. Before we'd stowed all our equipment in the van, I'd started to shiver.

It got worse as we drove towards the area where we all lived, and by time we reached my mother's house I was on fire. I had a headache to crown all headaches, and I was sweating so much that my clothes were sticking to me. Teenage lads are not the most sympathetic people, but when my mates saw how much worse I'd become during the drive, they helped me out of the van and almost carried me across the pavement. I showed my gratitude by vomiting over them while they held me upright at the door.

My mother took one look at me and had them

carry me up to my room. By that time my legs had refused to work and I was in no mood to protest when they stripped me, bundled me into my pyjamas and slid me into bed.

I don't remember much about that night, but I do recall my mother's face when she came into my room the following morning. She stomped downstairs, calling out to my younger brother as she went. I heard his footsteps on the stairs, then a muffled conversation in the hallway shortly before the front door was opened and closed.

The doctor went through the motions with an air of someone who would rather have been somewhere quiet and indulging in a spot of fishing. He checked my pulse, looked at my throat, and then pronounced that I had a 'bad cold'. Twenty seconds later, he was gone.

You have to bear in mind this was forty years ago and people like my mother would never have thought to question the diagnosis of someone as 'important' as the doctor. So, she left me in bed, and did what she could to make me comfortable, even though her ministrations had no effect.

Fate, or God, then played a part. The lads had decided to call in to see how I was, and on the way to my mother's that evening they met Pat Maguire who came along with them.

Pat had been a great help to us. In the early days, he worked for the Corporation and would take us to engagements in his dustcart. He would always joke that we were rubbish - and he was always ready to lend a hand whenever we needed a strong right arm.

Pat came into my room along with the others, but it was his voice I remember. He called out loud enough to shake the fillings in his teeth.

"Jesus, Agnes. Your boy has more than a bad cold. He should be in hospital right now." He ran out of the room and I heard his heavy boots clattering down the stairs.

I was taken to the Royal Hospital where I was diagnosed as having pneumonia. In all I was in there for about a month, and not long before I was discharged I was told that my first week there had been critical. I'd been close to death a few times, and I lapsed in and out of unconsciousness like a yo-yo, apparently the parish priest was on standby. Anyway while I was in that daze they told me I began shouting what appeared to be delirious nonsense, and I kept on crying out no matter what they did. They said the strange part was that I didn't appear to be in any discomfort - apart from the 'bad dreams'.

Anyway, I recovered but not completely. I still suffer with chest problems, but at least I'm alive.

Sean lifted his glass in salute. "Here's to good old Pat Maguire."

I nodded in agreement. Then noticed Sean's expression. He must have seen me looking at him and he shrugged. "I was just considering how some people seem to be 'God's workers'. There's no doubt about it, Pat definitely saved my life; and yet, a month later he was dead.

He was killed in a car accident, drove off the road and smashed into the corner of a house not far from where we lived. According to the post-mortem he'd had a massive heart attack at the wheel. But it didn't end there. I heard later that a number of witnesses had said it was a miracle that his car narrowly missed a group of young women taking their kids to school. Not a scratch on them. Maybe he was 'working for God' that day too?"

I hunched my shoulders in response, and Sean gave a sad smile, I even thought I saw a hint of a tear which didn't surprise me as I was beginning to notice that his emotions were always in tune with his recollections.

He then glanced at his watch and stood up as if a hypnotist had snapped his fingers for him to wake up. "See what you can make of that before I see you again. I'm working away for the next couple of days but I'll be free most of next week."

"Next week it is then. I'll give you a call."

"Do that." Sean said as he started towards the door.

I decided not to wish him well with the Dean Martin tribute.

It was a week to the day when Sean called me. I was asleep when the phone rang, and I was still only half-awake when I heard that he was coming home that night and would be free to see me in the morning. In a half-daze I agreed to his coming to my flat the following day.

He arrived a little after ten, and after giving my flat a cursory examination, he accepted my offer of coffee then followed me into the kitchen.

"You were right," he said as I filled the kettle. "I really do have to get all this off my chest. I couldn't think of anything else this week, and all I wanted to do was to tell somebody just to stop myself 'cracking up'."

I didn't see the point in gloating which Amanda says is my specialty, so I asked him about his booking for the previous week. He told me he'd had a good reception and an offer of another booking later in the year. He then described the boarding house where he'd stayed, and the 'showbiz' characters lodging there.

We carried the coffee into the living room and he sat on an easy chair facing me across my only table - a once fashionable coffee table that had seen much better days. My notes were neatly stacked on the settee beside me, and Sean nodded towards them.

"Have you been able to arrange them properly?"

"No. I can see where some of them are heading, but its better, and easier, if you 'steer' me through them." I picked up a couple of sheets I'd been working on. "I guessed that the next incident of any real note is your divorce ..."

Sean shook his head. "That's important, I agree, but it doesn't quite fall into the pattern of things just yet."

"All right, so tell me, what did happen after you recovered from pneumonia?"

"Not a lot. The group split up, and I came over to

30

England, to try out my luck. I got some bookings, found myself an agent who did very little to help, still I got better at my profession." He sipped his coffee and I saw a faint smile on his lips. "I told you how I met Marianne? Well, that was one of the better times in my life. For some years after we got married I was happy, or I suppose as happy as I could be. There were bad times, and really bad times, when Marianne went out to work just to keep the bailiffs from the door. But I just sailed through it like Micawber, believing that something would eventually turn up."

"So, your relationship with Marianne was getting worse, without you realising it?"

"More or less. When I think back, I realise she tried to talk to me about it, but usually at times when things were going well for me." He shrugged. "When I was in work, and the audiences were loving me, I couldn't see further than the next performance. Everything else was just immaterial, something to be tolerated until I was on stage again." Sean then looked at me with sad eyes. "I didn't intend to hurt her, I just didn't.'" He gave a heavy sigh. "Well that's all gone, and I can't change it."

"Would you want to, if you could? "I couldn't help but ask.

Sean grinned. "Wouldn't anyone want to change something in their past? The problem is, the thing you might change could eventually leave you in a worse situation than you are now, something like the butterfly effect."

I smiled back at him. For a few moments there was an easy silence, and then I glanced at my notes. "What *was* the next incident of note?"

"Oh," Sean gave a small start as if awakening from a reverie. "That would be the American booking."

I placed the notes back on the pile and reached for my recorder. Showing it to him I raised a questioning eyebrow and he nodded before I turned it on and placed it on the table. Sean let out a long sigh and closed his eyes as if picturing the scene as he spoke.

It was mid-October nineteen ninety four, Marianne and I were arguing, about money, or should I say, the lack of it. She kept going on about how little I was doing to keep the house 'running' and I was trying to explain that my next big opportunity was only just around the corner.

"Which corner?" was her sarcastic reply?

The kids were upstairs, playing some music, far too loud and we were forced to raise our voices.

Marianne started to shout, and I shouted back. Her tone rose half an octave, so did mine, and before we knew it, we were screaming at each other. Then, something snapped inside my head. I was on the point of grabbing my coat and heading for my local pub, The Circus Tavern, my usual cop out when losing an argument. In fact, I had started walking towards the door. Then the phone rang and as I was nearest I picked it up.

"Hello, Sean. Ronnie here, have I got you a fabulous booking in 'Frisco or what?"

Ronnie London was the agent I told you about. He

hadn't done a thing for me for in years, in fact, I thought he was dead.

"Sean … are you there, Sean?"

"Yes, Ronnie, I'm here."

I looked round and Marianne was mouthing something not very pleasant at me. I gestured to the telephone whereupon she gave me an acid grimace and stormed out of the room.

Ronnie shouted at the other end of the phone. "Didn't you hear what I just said?"

"Yes … I heard."

"What's the matter? Is something wrong Sean?"

Even though I hadn't spoken to him for years, I knew Ronnie of old. He was never blessed with a great deal of patience, and 'understanding' and 'sympathy' were not in his vocabulary.

"Nothing wrong Ronnie just surprised at hearing from you."

"Then, how about it?"

"Let's have the details first."

"Oh, Sean, you always was a cautious bugger. You know, I wouldn't go to this trouble for anybody else? OK, this is the deal. I got a booking for an entertainer. Three solid months' work compering a floor show on a liner cruising out of San Francisco. "

"Is there an Equity contract?"

"The cruise starts in November, and runs for three months, into January with options."

"Ronnie! I asked you if there was an Equity contract."

"Equity - shmequity. Look Sean, do you want this booking or not? I don't have the time to hang around.

The people 'Stateside' are waiting for an answer, and if you don't want to go, then say so. I can always get in touch with-"

"I'll take it!"

Right then I was ready to do anything to get away from the pubs and working men's clubs around Manchester. In addition, my funds were getting pretty low and in need of a hefty 'transfusion'. A three month booking would bring in a sizeable fee.

Ronnie responded in his smooth silky voice. "Good boy. I'll get in touch with you with the fine details later this week."

"What about-" I found myself speaking into the dead end of a telephone.

Marianne was 'busy' in the kitchen when I found her. She was taking pans out and putting them back in different cupboards. She always used to rearrange things when she was annoyed. At least she put the pans back on the shelves. But the look I got from her made me feel she might rather have tried to retexture my head with one.

I moved, only a pace towards her, and she instinctively took up a defensive pose. Her arms were raised in a sort of protective attitude, and she was looking at me as if she expected me to ... Let's say, she was tense.

I stayed where I was and tried to keep my voice level and 'normal'. "That was Ronnie London on the phone."

"What did that bastard want? "She said with her usual

charm.

"He … he offered me a job, a good one."

"Him. He's never offered you a good job in his life, if we had depended on him we'd have starved." Marianne had a dead sort of expression in her eyes as she looked at me and her voice was full of venom.

"No, I'm serious. He said he could get me a three month contract …"

Her expression didn't change. "What's the catch?"

"No catch. It's straightforward." I avoided her gaze. "He's phoning me later with all the details. But three months' money will do nicely."

"You're hiding something, and don't say you aren't." Her eyes bored into me like hot pokers.

I shrugged and huffed a bit before I spoke to her. "Well ... the engagement is in the States - on a cruise liner."

"Oh fucking great! And you expect me to be delighted that you're going to be a missing link for the …" She frowned. "You are going to be here at Christmas?"

"Well I …"

"Don't faff about. Are you? Yes or no?"

"The booking starts in November, and ..."

"Oh Christ! You're leaving us on our own - At Christmas of all times. Well thank you very much you selfish bastard! Oh yes Ronnie, I'd love to get away for three months … swanning around on some bloody great liner doing sod all while your wife is forced to…"

"Look Marianne, it's not like that."

"Then what is it like? Go on, tell me!" Her eyes were

35

wild and her face was set in a vicious grimace. "What the hell have we been talking about for the last hour? Your input into this marriage. And your response is to fuck off to America?!"

At one time, not long after we first met, I used to tell her she looked beautiful when she was angry but something told me this was not the time to use that line.

Sean was now back. He let out a long sigh, looked at me and lifted his cup to his lips. "I suppose that was the beginning of the end. He shrugged. "I could have turned down Ronnie's offer, and stayed at home, but the prospect of three months solid work was too much to refuse."

"So," I said, "you went, and Marianne got even angrier?"

"That's the funny thing - she didn't. She sort of slid into a shell. She spoke to me, polite and correct. But it was as if she was talking to a stranger. No, that's not quite right. She'd have been far more attentive to a stranger. It was almost like, well like I didn't exist for her." Sean's face softened in a wistful smile and for a moment he spoke with a very strong accent. "Hindsight's a marvellous bloody thing don't you think Andy?"

It wasn't a question and I didn't bother to answer. I just waited a few moments then spoke. "So, you didn't change your mind - about the decision to take the engagement in America?"

"No. I went full steam ahead. Like I said, things were strained at home. The atmosphere was like wafer-thin glass, and to be honest in a way I was glad to be out of there. Of course there were a few tears, especially from Jason and Michele. Marianne went through the motions. I suppose it was for the benefit of the kids, but I could tell she didn't mean it when she told me to have a great time. I remember stepping out of the house and closing the door then just standing there for a second. The taxi was waiting at the end of the path, and I just stood there ... I won't say that I had a feeling that everything had finished between Marianne and me, but I did sense that things might never be the same when I got back."

He hoisted his cup and drained it. Setting it down on the table he stared at me then gave me a wickedly cheerful grin. "Life's a bit of a bitch at times' I even forgot to pack my new mobile phone which of course Marianne will say was on purpose." Cocking his head towards the kitchen he asked, "Any chance of another coffee?"

It was some time before Sean resumed his story. We'd had more coffee, and a snack by the time he seemed ready to continue. We faced each other across the small table, and he appeared to be quite relaxed as he spoke.

The journey from Manchester to New York, then on to the west coast was a long one, and it gave me time to think. I came to terms with my situation and decided that once the cruise was over, and I'd made enough money to pay all our bills with whatever was left over, I would take Marianne and the kids on a long holiday. I had not decided where I'd take them, but it would be something unforgettable - to make up for not being there for them at Christmas.

It was my first visit to America, and when I stepped off the plane in New York, you can't imagine the emotions it generated. There I was stepping onto the home soil of all the greatest artists the world has ever seen. If you're an entertainer, it really is the place to be. I just stood there and dreamed of topping the bill at Las Vegas. The mere act of placing my feet on that tarmac gave me the feeling that I really did have a chance. To a dreamer – and I certainly was then - anything was possible. The atmosphere there made me think of all those great stars, Sinatra, Streisand, Diamond, and Presley. I was absolutely full of it, and right then I felt as if I could have done anything.

By the time I got to the west coast some of the confidence had worn off, but when the taxi dropped me off at the dockside and I walked along the quay to where the liner was moored, I felt a new surge of optimism. The boat was enormous, and I can remember craning my neck to look up the great white-painted sides to the name on her bow. 'Pacific Princess', that's what she was called, and my first impression was that here was a great floating palace where I would soon become king.

I did the usual cruise check in and when I had completed all the formalities I was allowed to proceed to embarkation. As I carried my bags up the gangplank I met an officer who regarded me with pure indifference.

He told me to report to the 'Cruise Director', but didn't tell me where to find him. It didn't matter right then. I can tell you, I was so keyed up nothing mattered, I was *there!*

After about a half-hour, I did find the hotel manager, Arnold Weischmann. He was short, fat, bald, and he smelled of garlic and expensive aftershave. His palm was soft, fleshy and sweaty when I shook his hand, but he did seem pleased to see me. He also told me I would be reporting to the Cruise Director; a man called Webber, and advised me to find the man before dumping my bags in my cabin.

I met the assistant bars manager, Patrick Flynn, on my way out of Weischmann's office, and he gave me a wide beaming smile. I recognised his Belfast accent straight away, and he recognised mine.

"Patrick Flynn, a good Catholic boy from The Falls Road I suppose?"

"I don't know about good but how did you know I was from The Falls?"

"With a name like Patrick Flynn you would hardly be from the Shankill now would you?"

"That's true; you seem to have lost a bit of the old twang along the way."

"Yeah I've lived in Manchester quite a while and done a bit of acting which might explain it."

"I thought your name sounded familiar, I have a sister who lives in Manchester and I stayed with her for a while." Anyway Sean it's nice to meet you and by the way everyone calls me Flynn or Paddy so suit yourself as I answer to either preferable if there is a tip involved."

He then told me to ignore the director's advice, and get my 'gear' stowed rather than carry it around the ship. He scanned some sheets on a clip-board he was holding, and told me where my cabin was - somewhere below the waterline and deep in the bowels of the vessel. I had the feeling that this could be the start of a beautiful friendship.

I was really glad of Flynn's advice, since it took me almost two hours to find Webber, who I discovered, had the ability to make himself scarce without much effort. Several times during the cruise he managed to disappear completely - especially when there was some kind of crisis. I don't know how he did it. Searches were organised, but nobody could find him, then he magically re-appeared when the panic had been sorted out.

Anyway, I did manage to find him on that first day, and he chewed me off for being late. He told me the passengers would be arriving soon, and that my duties included being part of the 'welcoming party' waiting to meet them as they came on board. He directed me to one of the three main gangplanks and said I should make myself 'amenable'. I looked at him like a 'gone-out' streetlamp, and he explained it as if I was retarded.

"Your job is to make sure that all our clients are totally satisfied with the service we provide. If that means carrying their cases to their cabins, then do it. If they want you to serenade them while you're carrying their bags, then serenade them … got it?"

That first meeting with Webber set the tone for all our other meetings. Needless to say I made sure those future meetings were as few and as brief as possible.

Anyway, I did as he'd asked, and went down to the boat deck where I performed like a seasoned campaigner. I smiled until my teeth ached, I carried bags with a joviality that must have made most of the passengers think I was off my trolley, and at the end of embarkation I retired to my cabin to take a hasty shower and get changed into my 'entertainer's' outfit.

The first cruise took a week, and once I'd resigned myself to the fact that, in the eyes of the officers and crew, I was little more than a singing lackey, I settled down to a sort of routine. In addition to acting as an unpaid porter while the passengers came on board, I was told that I was expected to be present at breakfast when I was to mingle with the guests and indulge in 'cheerful conversation'. You can imagine how cheerful I was at eight in the morning after finishing the late-night cabaret somewhere around two.

Still I made a good fist of it, and received some pretty complimentary comments from some of the guests as they were leaving. The ship stayed in port for a couple of days before the next set of passengers arrived. Thankfully I was allowed to take a couple of trips ashore and take a look around the city. I thought about ringing Marianne, to see how she and the kids were getting on, but I kept putting it off. I think I was afraid of what I might hear ... and the longer I left it, the harder it was to make the call.

Just before we set sail for my second cruise, Paddy Flynn came looking for me. He found me on the boat deck where I'd been painting new lines on the shuffle-board court. He took me to his cabin and treated me to a couple of glasses of decent single malt while he offered me some sound advice.

"Most of the entertainers don't last the course. Webber sees to it that they quit before the end of their contract, so the company don't have to pay them their full fee. You seem to have worked out a good way to deal with him."

"Yes. I just keep out of his way. I've been wondering about the man. Just exactly what does he do?"

"As little as he can. It helps that his father is on the board of directors, so he can get away with pretty much anything. You'll never make a friend of him, but as long as you don't antagonise him you'll be all right. And if you do need a 'safe haven' to make sure he can't find you … see me, and I'll let you stow away here for a while."

I followed Flynn's advice, and was able to shut out the anger and resentment I felt whenever I was asked to do some menial task that was considered too low for a member of the crew. Most entertainers have what they call "passenger status" which more or less means that when you are not working you are treated like one of the passengers. A proper agent would have made sure this clause was in the contract but we're not talking proper agent, we're talking Ronnie London. Still I smiled my plastic smile and adopted a duly deferential manner to everyone, and it worked. I didn't enjoy it, but at least I had the satisfaction of dreaming about the big fat fee I'd get once the contract was over.

November slipped away, and December came in, warm and pleasant. I was totally into the ship's routine by then, and even some of the crew had started to speak to me as an equal. Paddy Flynn had been as good as his word, and had hidden me in his cabin a couple of times when I needed to avoid Webber. He even provided me with decent alibis when the 'cruise director' did finally find me.

It was the week before Christmas. The latest cruise was scheduled to end on December twenty third, and all the passengers who were boarding brought a sense of anticipation with them. I'd accompanied a couple of families to their cabins and had made my way back to the boat deck where I stood with my Barbie doll smile fixed on my face. It slipped a little when a lithe blonde-haired young woman came up to me and drooled at me in full view of her middle-aged husband.

"I want this one to take our things to the cabin." Her voice was loud enough to attract everyone's attention, and I could see Webber trying to smile while making mute signals encouraging me to act like the model servant. I could sense trouble right from that first moment, and I wasn't wrong.

I soon discovered that the husband was in fact a Senator, and his wife was a former model almost twenty years his junior. On the first night out, Webber made a point of talking to me about them, and stressed that the Senator's party should receive preference over everything else. Whatever they wanted, we were to oblige them. I'd already got an uneasy feeling about Shawnie, the Senator's wife, and I voiced my concern to Webber. I told him that I had the suspicion that she was after far more than a few 'cheerful conversations'. He merely repeated what he'd already said, that the Senator's party were to be given preferential treatment.

For a couple of days the woman made it plain that I was the focus of her attention - when the Senator wasn't in evidence. Fortunately for me, he was with her almost every time I came across them. But at the late-night cabaret on the third night out, she was alone except for one of the 'aides' I'd seen in their party.

I'd finished my act and was making my way back through the lounge towards the doors, when Shawnie intercepted me. She stood right in front of me and just stared at me, licking her lips as if she was anticipating a meal. I suppose she was, and she'd got me down as the main course.

She told me quite openly that the following night she expected me to join her in her bed, as a 'Christmas treat'. Expecting me to be a willing partner in her scheme, she told me that her husband would be deep in slumber long before I arrived, and there'd be plenty of time for 'fun'.

I was as polite as I could be when I told her I wasn't interested. But it didn't seem to have any effect. She just looked at me from beneath half-lowered lashes and said she'd meet me the following night.

That night, before the cabaret, I joined Paddy in his cabin. He grasped the situation at once, and put all my fears into words.

"Sean, you've got yourself one hell of a problem. Webber is going to crucify you if you don't play lap-dog to that little 'lady'. You must know what she's after, and if you give in, and the Senator finds out, you're dead meat." He gave me a sad smile. "Thank God I'm not in your shoes. I wouldn't have a clue what to do ... The only thing I can suggest is ..."

"What?!"

"You know, just don't get found out."

I wasn't exactly 'full of the joys' when I left Paddy's' cabin. He obviously thought I was going to give in to Shawnie and let her have her way. It was I admit, not a fearful prospect. The girl was a stunner and no mistake, and any right-minded, red-blooded boy would have jumped at the chance. But at that time, I wasn't your average red-blooded boy. With things being as they were back home, I knew that if I even thought about taking Shawnie up on her offer, I'd more than regret it. I just wanted to finish the cruise, collect my money, and then get home to Marianne and the kids.

Sean looked at me over the rim of his cup and hunched his shoulders before he took a drink. Andy he said "Don't get me wrong, I love the ladies to a fault, and I'll flirt with them, as its all part of the show

45

business thing. But I'm not the sort who'll come running after any girl who whistles… and I'm definitely not anybody's lap-dog."

"Are you saying that you're not a one-girl man?" I couldn't disguise the curiosity in my voice.

"That's a leading question my friend." Sean gave me an impish grin. "You don't expect a direct answer, do you?
"

"I don't really suppose I do."

"Let's just say that I don't let anybody manoeuvre me into a relationship; and that went double for Shawnie. All right, I knew she was the wife of a very powerful man, and was used to getting her own way…"

"So, let's say you were in a bit of a predicament?"

"That's a concise way of putting it. I would have said I was up to my neck in the brown stuff and somebody was about to drop a bloody great rock in the pond." Sean grinned. "Whichever way you look at it, I was walking a tightrope, and the crocodiles below were sharpening their teeth ready for a feast."

"So, what happened?"

"I carried on as usual. I smiled my smile and acted out my role of the genial gofer like I was born to it. Then came the time for the early evening cabaret. I was in a muck-sweat right from the start."

Sean shook his head and grinned at me across the table. "I've had real villains 'in my face' but I can tell you I never was as apprehensive as I was that night. But as the show began and none of the Senator's party had turned up, I thought she might have been joking. You know - teasing me."

"Was she? "I enquired.

Sean gave me a wry smile. "You know what thought did."

I frowned at him. "I don't follow you."

"I said I thought she was teasing ... And 'thought' followed a muck-cart in the belief that it was a wedding. It's an old saying, Andy. Maybe before your time."

I thought it wise not to reply and let him get on with his story, which thankfully he did.

She turned up at the late show, on her own. She took a table right in front of the stage and leered at me all through my routine. It was so bad I could hardly concentrate on my act. It was probably the worst performance I'd ever given in my life and I was glad to get off stage. I hurried off backstage but she intercepted me on my way to the cubby-hole I used as a dressing room.

I won't say I got the 'come-on' but she was practically inside my suit, right there and then. I just didn't know what to do. She had my tie off and was unbuttoning my shirt when I heard a noise at the far end of the corridor.

Paddy appeared as if by magic. He ignored what the girl was doing and came straight to me. He told me I was wanted by the Cruise Director right away and practically dragged me away from her. I didn't argue and we almost ran along the corridor and out of the lounge.

Once we were sure she wasn't following us, Paddy slowed down. He gave me a great big smile then

47

shook his head. "I couldn't think of anything else … but I doubt if I could get away with it again. From now on, you're on your own."

Next day I tried to keep myself occupied with the 'ordinary' passengers, keeping to the lower boat deck where I was sure not to bump into any of the Senator's party. I thought I'd made it, but a little after mid-day one of the cabin crew came to me and told me I was 'requested' to report to the Senator's suite. I did some 'panic' thinking and persuaded the crewman to come with me.

I convinced him it was some kind of joke that the Senator and I were party to when I got him to knock at the door of the Senator's cabin. Shawnie called out, asking who it was, and as the crewman was about to answer I signalled him to keep quiet. I answered her, saying it was me. Then I shoved the crewman in front of the door just before it opened.

I'll never forget the look on the man's face as he gaped at her, and then took a couple of paces backwards. Shawnie was wearing little more than a smile, but it vanished when she saw the crewman. And I won't forget the very un-ladylike abuse that she screamed at him before she slammed the door in his face.

She found me on the lower boat deck about an hour later. She smiled at me and linked her arm into mine; ignoring the people I'd been talking to at the time. She steered me round the corner of the lower lounge, then spun to face me. Her eyes reminded me of a predator as

48

she spoke.

"Neat trick back there, but don't think it's got you off the hook. I've decided that I'm going to have you before I leave - or you're going to regret it for the rest of your life. I'll see you at the 'end of cruise' dance tonight, and be ready to give me what I want. Think about it, big boy."

I spent the rest of the day going through the motions. I couldn't get out of the 'last night dance' - short of throwing myself off the ship, or breaking a leg. On previous cruises, the dance had been something of a change for me. The women I'd danced with had been friendly and understanding, especially when I trampled all over their feet. They all said how much they'd enjoyed themselves, and how glad they'd been to have met me. That night, I knew it was going to be different.

It was an accident, honestly. I know it was the answer to all my problems, and you probably think that I really did stage it, but I didn't.

I turned up at the dance ready for the worst, but for an hour or so I got away with chatting to people and occasionally putting them through purgatory on the dance floor. I was talking to a pleasant young couple about their home in Wisconsin when I saw the Senator's party arrive, and I noticed that Shawnie was wearing her 'hunter's outfit.' If I hadn't been so concerned about myself, I'd have said she looked stunning in a shimmering gold dress that clung to her like a second skin. It must have cost her husband far more than I was earning for my three month's work on the ship.

They ignored me for a while then Shawnie and

her husband came to me as I was standing by the open bar. Her words were quite innocent, when she asked the senator if he minded her dancing with me. He offered no objections and she smiled sweetly at me as she took my arm and led me on to the floor.

I was almost knocked out by the perfume she was wearing. It was subtle yet powerful and obviously expensive. I couldn't help but look at her as we prepared to start dancing, and I had to admit that she really did look gorgeous. She moved in close, and moulded herself to me like a great gold sticking plaster, and then we started. I don't know what dance was being played - not that it would have mattered since I have absolutely no sense of rhythm when it comes to dancing. I suppose I could have warned her, but what the hell she was in the driving seat.

We set off and within a few seconds I'd stood on her foot. She grimaced but smiled and carried on as we jostled and bumped into the other dancers as if we were running interference on a Football field. I'll give her credit for persistence. She stuck it out far longer than I'd expected while I barged into her and positively trampled her shoes to tatters. Then I suppose she decided that enough was enough. She stopped and glared at me right in the middle of the floor.

"All right. You win. You have the co-ordination of a dead penguin. Let's get out of here." She turned and started to thread her way through the other dancers, half dragging me behind her.

It was an accident. Honest and truly it was. As I was following her, one of the dancers in front of me flicked out a leg backwards only slightly, but enough to catch my foot. I stumbled, and since Shawnie was still pulling me, I fell forwards. I instinctively made a grab for some support - which turned out to be the back of her dress. Everything happened in a split second, and yet I saw it all as if in slow-motion. I heard the sound of the dress ripping, and I saw Shawnie spin round with a look of panic-stricken disbelief on her face. Her mouth was open in a startled gasp, and her eyes were wide and horrified. She flailed her arms, like a demented windmill, for a second before she had the presence of mind to cover herself.

I hit the floor holding a great gold duster in my hand, and I was aware of the crowd around me, jostling and ogling at the spectacle I'd created. Most of all, for one brief instant, I was conscious of the humiliation on Shawnie's face. She was, still vainly trying to hide her nudity while looking around desperately as she tried to shy from the tightly-packed crowd around us. I recall that the air was filled with chaotic babbling noise. Then she screamed a wild high-pitched sound that shocked the onlookers into stunned silence.

Less than two hours later I was called to the office of the hotel manager. Weischmann looked at me as if I was something that had crawled out of a gutter.

"Clarke. The *Pacific Princess* is an institution founded on extremely good service, and the ability of our staff to create a happy atmosphere for all our guests." I wasn't going to answer, but if I had, he wouldn't have given me time. "We have a pride in our work, and I believed that when you came to join us that you too would share our feelings. Each member of this crew has dedicated himself to the concept that our guests are to be given the highest consideration in any circumstances." He'd been talking to the ceiling somewhere above my head until then, but he lowered his gaze to snarl at me. "It would appear, however, that you have your own personal view about your relationship with our guests. There is no need to speak!" His face twitched in the semblance of a sarcastic smile. "I have already had complaints about your disgraceful behaviour, from one of our most respected visitors who said you have been making a nuisance of yourself ever since they came on board. This has been corroborated by several of her associates. I can accept no excuse, and will not tolerate any member of my team acting in such a way as to bring major discredit on my ship. As from this moment, you are no longer a member of my staff, and you will confine yourself to your cabin for the remainder of the cruise. Now get out of my sight!"

Needless to say I didn't see Shawnie again, but I did see Weischmann. He called me into his office not long after the ship came to port. I could tell the news wasn't going to be good.

He was in a quieter mood than the previous night, but he still regarded me with distaste. It seemed to give him some pleasure to tell me that my services were no longer required, and that I should leave the ship as soon as possible.

I accepted his decision without an argument, since there was no point in arguing. However I did ask him about my salary, and he looked horrified. I knew that, without the security of an Equity contract I couldn't really expect much, but I stood my ground. He told me I was lucky not to have been prosecuted for my 'assault' on a member of the Senator's party, and might still have found myself the subject of a private law-suit. He added that 'the person in question' after some long and serious deliberation, had decided not to sue the cruise company for the damage to a pair of shoes, a dress, and 'personal dignity'.

I wasn't impressed, and showed it, and he did concede that I should receive something for the work I'd done until the previous night. But from his tone, I guessed that it would fall far short of my full salary. He agreed to arrange the payment, and added that in order to minimise any possible 'bad publicity' I would be given air tickets to take me back to Manchester with the minimum possible delay. He advised me to 'get back to England' as quickly as possible, and then dismissed me.

I managed to see Paddy Flynn before I left. He gave me the name of a boarding house where I could stay if I couldn't get a flight. He reminded me that Christmas in the States was the worst time for travel since everyone was going to stay with some relation or other. We wished each other well, and said goodbye. You know, he was the one good thing I remember from the whole experience.

I came down the gangplank onto the quay wiser, and not much richer. True enough they'd given me the tickets for my flight to Manchester, but in terms of hard cash they'd been, well let's say careful. By the time I got home I would hardly have enough left to take the family to McDonald's. Still, I had the feeling that might be the least of my problems.

*   *   *

THREE

Sean stayed silent for a moment as his mind came back to the present and I saw a look in his eye that spoke of the anguish he must have felt as he traipsed off that ship and stood on the quay. I then stood up and nodded towards the kitchen. "Would you like something to eat?" "What?" He gave a start as if coming out of a reverie. "Er..." He looked at his watch then got to his feet where he stood slightly hunched for a second. "Sorry, I didn't realise it was so late. I'll have to be on my way. I'll give you a call later to fix up another meeting - if that's all right?"

 "No problem."

I walked to the door with him and noticed the slight droop of his shoulders had gone. He turned to me with a great beaming smile. "You know, I think there might be something to this amateur psychology."

I cleared the cups and made myself a quick snack before going back into the living room where I spent the next half-hour replaying some of the recording I'd made. I checked it against the notes Sean had given me, and saw that while speaking to me, he'd gone into far greater detail than he had on paper.

I felt I needed a breath of fresh air, so I left the flat and drove out to Heaton Park. I walked for an hour or so, looking at the grass and trees, and smiling at the ducks and geese wallowing around on the lake. I felt refreshed when I got back to my car.

It was as I was driving home that I realised how much Sean was beginning to monopolise my time. Since meeting him I'd spent very little energy on anything else, and even though I was eager to hear the rest of his story, I felt that I couldn't afford on principal to concentrate all my efforts on him alone. The principal being money, so when I got back home, I called the editor of the local rag and asked if there were any 'loose ends' I could work on. He hesitated and I guessed there wasn't much news about. Then, after a long pause, he said I might try to interview Sean Clarke, a local singer who was releasing a new album sometime within the next week. He told me it was low priority, but if I supplied decent copy, there was a chance that it might be used as local interest 'filler'.

Sean phoned later that evening to say he was off to do a show in Bradford that night, but would be free to see me again the following day. We agreed that I should go to his home about eleven.

"Are you sure you have the time to keep seeing me?" Sean asked as we sat in the living room. "You must have other things to do - not that I'm complaining, mind you, I'm starting to enjoy our little 'sessions' together."

I told him about my new assignment, and he laughed. "Talk about killing two birds ...OK. We'll start with the album. What do you want to know?"

I began. Whenever I did a 'general' interview, I always tried to put myself in the place of the readers. I tried to ask the odd-ball sort of questions that they might ask, and endeavoured to keep away from the run-of the-mill queries that must have bored many an artist. In all we spent about half-an-hour talking about the new album, and when we'd finished, Sean smiled and nodded.

"In future I want you to do all my interviews." He cocked his head on one side and stared at me for a moment. "You're pretty good at your job."

"I like to think so … Now, should we get back to 'your story'?"

"In a minute. All that talking has given me a thirst. Want a drink?"

He poured us two good measures of Brandy and we sipped as we spoke…or should I say, he spoke. I just sat there with my little recorder and listened. He didn't start right away, he hesitated - as if he was casting his mind back and re-creating the situation that faced him as he left the cruise liner back in 1994. His eyes lost some of their sparkle, and his expression became quite sad as he started.

The first and only thing I could think of after I'd left the ship, was to call Marianne to let her know what'd happened. I found a telephone 'booth' not far from the quay, and I called. I knew it'd be the middle of the night in Manchester, but I didn't care. I just wanted to speak to her.

Her voice was sleepy when she finally answered and I had the presence of mind to apologise for the poor timing…

"Couldn't you have waited 'til later?" There was no edge to her voice and certainly no sound of welcome.

"I suppose so, but, hopefully, I'll be on a plane within the next hour or so. I'm coming home."

"Oh."

That was her only reaction and I felt uneasy as I clutched the telephone. "Is there a problem?"

"Well …"

The uneasiness became a leaden weight which fell to the pit of my stomach. I tried to sound cheerful. "I suppose you've gone and planned something?" There had been a few Christmases when Marianne had gone to stay with one of her sisters, and I guessed that was what she was about to tell me.

"I'm sorry, Sean, but we're going away later this afternoon. I'm taking Jason and Michele to Switzerland for Christmas."

"Switzerland! …" I was stunned and I must have looked it as I just stood there staring at the telephone. "I suppose I could …"

"We were quite lucky. We got the last reservations on the plane, and just managed to get rooms at the hotel in Geneva."

"Oh … Right. I …er … I hope you have a good time. Give my love to the kids, and I'll see you … When are you coming back?"

"The eighth of January … We're spending New Year over there."

I didn't answer -'cause I quite simply didn't know what to say. Marianne paused then carried on. "I'll be taking the car to the airport - so you can pick it

58

up when you get there. I'll leave the parking ticket with the people at the information desk and tell them you'll be collecting it."

"Fine."

"There are things we need to sort out which we can talk about when I get back. Enjoy yourself at Christmas - Jason and Michele send their love. I'll ring off now. I don't want to be too tired tomorrow. Bye."

I must have stood in that booth for a good couple of minutes after the phone went dead. Going over what Marianne had said made the lead weight double. I couldn't have imagined her and the kids going off to a foreign country at Christmas. What was more depressing was that I couldn't believe that they would have left me to spend the holiday on my own - not after what had just happened to me. Still when I think about all the phone calls I never made did I really have the right to expect she would cancel her Christmas plans for me? All the same New Year 1995 wasn't looking to promising, to say the least.

I jumped when something hammered on the glass outside and I turned to look at a very ugly seaman who was glaring at me.

"Hey, buddy, have you taken a lease on the booth - or can anybody use it?"

I started to pick up my luggage then became aware that someone had joined the seaman outside the booth. When I turned I saw Flynn gently shepherding the angry sailor away from the door. Flynn shook his head as he caught hold of one of my bags and took it from me.

"It seems like I've spent the last few weeks doing

nothing but get you out of trouble. What was that about?" He glanced back towards the phone booth.

"Oh, nothing. I just called Marianne to tell her I'd be home earlier than expected."

"Was she pleased?"

I hunched my shoulders. "I don't know."

Paddy Flynn stared at me then let out a soft sigh. "I think it'd be a good idea if we went for a wee drink, and you can tell me about it."

We were close to a taxi rank positioned at the end of the quay, and Paddy climbed into a cab and I followed.

The bar he chose was close to the dock and fairly quiet when we entered. He aimed me towards one of the long bench seats running along the wall, while he went to the bar. He joined me, bearing a bottle of Bushmills and a couple of glasses.

After pouring the drinks, he lifted his glass. "Here's to the future. The past is history, and the present is barely tolerable."

"Didn't know you had a degree in philosophy." I mumbled as I saluted him then drank.

"All right. Let's hear what happened when you called your wife - Marianne, isn't it?"

"That's right, Marianne."

Paddy frowned as he stared at me. "You sound … upset. I take it the phone call wasn't exactly a success?"

"Not much. I was going to tell her how I planned to take her and the kids out for a meal as soon as I got home … But I never got the chance. She told me she's taking them to Switzerland today, and they won't be home 'till sometime in January."

"Who is taking them?"

"What?" I gaped at Paddy and felt as if he'd hit me in the guts with a telegraph pole.

He then blinked slowly, looked down at his glass then stared into my eyes. "Have you not considered the possibility that she's got someone else?"

"It never crossed my mind."

"Didn't she give any inkling when you phoned her from the ship?"

"I er ... I never actually called her during the cruises. I was going to, but I didn't get round to it ..."

"You haven't spoken to her ... for weeks? Oh Jesus, what sort of man are you Sean?"

"You know how it is, we parted under bad terms so I thought I'd give it a few days for her to cool down then the days become weeks and the call gets harder to make."

I was aware of my face flushing. It was uncomfortable, sitting there under his gaze. I took a drink from my glass before I looked back at him. He was still staring at me and shaking his head. "Sean, Sean my friend, you're living in a dream world." He filled his glass and sipped it calmly before he spoke again. "How would you have reacted if your wife had gone away for a couple of months and not taken the trouble to speak to you?"

"I'd have understood."

"Like hell you would you. You're still dreaming, Sean." He fixed me with a strong serious stare. "Think about it! She's at home, doing all the routine shitty jobs, while

you're swanning around on a bloody great luxury liner
…"

"It wasn't exactly a holiday. You know that, you know
what I had to put up with-"

"That's not the point I'm trying to make. As far as
Marianne's concerned, she was up to her neck in chores
while you were up to your neck in slinky seductive
blondes. You neglected her for God's sake!" He let out a
long heavy sigh. "I'll spell it out for you. You came away
expecting her to sit at home like an old-fashioned dutiful
wife, doing nothing and just waiting for you to come
home. Bollocks! If she has any self-belief, like a normal
human being, she'll have found somebody to pay her
some attention. It's pretty obvious she hasn't had any
from you … Oh yes, you thought about giving her a
call." He shook his head. "How long have you been
married?"

"Over ten years."

"I'm surprised she didn't find herself somebody long
before now. Or maybe she has for all you know."

"I don't know, do I?" God I was starting to feel very
sober.

I picked up my luggage and Paddy walked beside me
out of the bar. He gave me a smile tinged with concern
as he held out his hand. "Take care of yourself, Sean."

"You too," I tried to smile back at him. "Thanks - for
everything."

We shook hands then Paddy Flynn just turned and
walked away. He looked back and gave me another

smile before he vanished round the corner of the block. I had only known him a short while and yet I had the feeling that I had just said goodbye to a good friend. I then hailed a taxi and threw my luggage inside then flopped onto the back seat.

"What line are you in?" The driver asked over his shoulder as he forced his way into the traffic.

"I'm an entertainer." I forced myself to answer.

The driver turned briefly towards me, ignoring the honks of the surrounding traffic. "Guess you just got off 'The Princess' - don't need to answer, I can see it in your face." He let out a loud sigh as he turned to face the front. "I'll never understand you guys and I see plenty of you, sloping back from the boat with your hip pockets draggin' - bet you thought you were going to make your name, or your fortune on that floating gin palace - and all you got was the bum's rush ... Am I right, or am I right?"

"Sorry. I'm not in the mood right now."

"You ain't the first, and sure as hell. You won't be the last ... Er, you got the fare, haven't you?"

"Oh yes, I have the fare and not much else."

The driver took my hint, and remained relatively quiet for the remainder of the drive. He dropped me off outside the airport terminal, a long low building which reminded me of a garden centre. I picked up my luggage and went inside. As soon as I stepped into the hall I got the full Phil Spector sensation ...

"Hold on Sean!" I stopped him in his tracks. "What are you talking about? What's a Phil Spector sensation?"

Sean grinned and shook his head. "Have you never heard of the Phil Spector sound?" He hunched his shoulders in response to my blank expression. "He was probably one of the greatest music producers of the last thirty years ... 'was famous for his *Wall of Sound*.'"

"I didn't know that ... oh - wasn't he involved in a dubious shooting - or something?"

"Yes ...something like that. " Sean smiled at me. "Should I carry on - or do you want another musical history lesson?"

"Sorry for interrupting ... Yes, carry on, please."

The wall of sound hit me like a punch to the ribs. Everywhere I looked there were people bunched and hunched in an almost solid mass. I gripped my luggage firmly, and started to shove my way towards the Pan Am information desk. I was never into sports like rugby or wrestling, but I certainly got introduced to a number of 'moves' while I tried to force a path through to the desk. As I stood there, I could hear in the background Frank Sinatra singing 'Have yourself a merry little Christmas'. I thought 'you must be joking, Frank.'

I was on the point of calling it a day when a couple of gorillas took a firm hold of my arms, and tried to take my luggage from me. I'm quite a big man now, but I was much fitter then, and far stronger, but those two men manoeuvred me as if I was a baby. I was angry to begin with, but when a third man forced his way up to me and grinned into my face, I really lost my temper. The man in front must have seen that I was about to go ballistic, so he held up his hands.

"Take it easy ... We're here to help you sir. Now If you'd let go of your bags, my men will take you to the departure lounge."

"What is this?" I looked around at the people who were staring at us as the three men barged their way through the crowd. I was held firmly, as I said, and I glanced at the men on either side. I suppose you could have described them as muscles wearing suits. I'd seen their sort before, but these specimens seemed to be a cut above the average 'bouncer' I'd been accustomed to. They were very well dressed with their dark suits and immaculately groomed hair, but they were still bouncers ... and they were effective. They cleared a path right through the hall and bypassed a long queue waiting at the Pan Am desk where they spoke to a young woman while my luggage was taken from me and dumped at the desk. The 'leader' of my escort politely asked me for my passport and handed it to the girl behind the desk. In less than a minute I saw the woman hand a ticket and boarding pass to one of the 'suits' and our little party was on the move again, carrying on as before, carving a path through the crowd until we were at the entrance to the departure lounge.

There was another long queue waiting to pass through the barrier, but we swept right to the gate where 'leader' handed my passport to the official. I could hear more than one disgruntled voice as I stood flanked by my two escorts, but the grumbling subsided when my gorillas both turned to stare at the waiting passengers. Next thing I knew I was guided into the departure lounge and steered towards one of the boarding gates where another mass of people were waiting to go through to the plane. Once again we ignored the queue and went straight up to the pretty stewardess who was collecting boarding cards and tickets.

I was close enough to hear something of what was said …

"… Must be somebody special to have the State Capitol arrange this for him…"

"I don't know about that ma'am. I was ordered to make sure he was on the first flight to New York…"

" … It is irregular, but I guess everything's in order."

The stewardess handed the man a ticket and he in turn gave it to me. He pointed to the door leading to the boarding ramp. "Your flight to New York sir. We've arranged a connection to England and the ticket will be waiting for you at the Pan Am desk. Have a nice flight sir."

My passport was handed back to me and I was gently propelled through the door and onto the boarding ramp.

I was bemused to find that I'd been given a seat in first-class and I attracted a few curious stares as I made myself comfortable. In the few minutes before the plane started to move I was able to figure out what had happened … I knew that Weismann had been upset by the prospect of possible adverse publicity, but I could think of another person who would have been even more annoyed. I guessed that Shawnie, or the Senator had taken steps to see that I was removed as quickly as possible, and given little opportunity to speak to anyone from the local press.

Since I had no intentions of talking to anyone about the incident, I sort of thanked them. At least it got me onto the New York flight...and first class too! So whatever their reasons I certainly wasn't bothered I just wanted to get home as soon as possible.

What I hadn't considered was that either the Senator, or more probably Shawnie, would not be satisfied just having me 'escorted' to the plane. The first surprise had been when I was shown to the first-class section of the plane, the second and more disturbing came when one of my 'escorts' slipped into the seat beside me. He glanced at me briefly, giving me the sort of look reserved for some extreme low-life, and then he took out a magazine and started to read.

If you've ever spent several hours in the company of someone whose only interest in you is to make sure you do not speak to anyone, then you might be able to imagine how interesting the flight was. I was 'allowed' to talk to the stewardess in a manner of speaking. Truth is that she did most of the talking. Not long after we were in the air, she came to us and gave me a particularly brilliant smile - it matched the rest of her. She handed me a glass of Champagne, which I refused in favour of a soft drink. As she handed me the glass of Perrier, she frowned.

"We haven't seen you before, sir. You must be one of

67

the Senator's more recent friends?"

"I suppose you could say that."

"You wouldn't believe the hassle we've had re-arranging the ..."

"That'll be all for now, Miss. Go and have a nice day." My strong, relatively silent, companion gave her the sort of stare that would have snapped the spine of a lesser mortal. She took it in her stride, ignored him, and gave me another beaming smile accompanied by the usual "Have a nice day." and left.

She did come back a couple of times whilst we were in the air, but I didn't manage to say more than a dozen words to her. For the remainder of the flight, I was left alone, with my thoughts and the feeling that my conversation was being censored.

My first reaction to the whole situation was one of self-pity. I was upset and angry that everything had gone wrong, with the cruise, and with my relationship with Marianne. Why me? What had I done to deserve such diabolical luck?

I pondered about my dismissal from the 'Princess' and reasoned that Weismann would have found some other excuse for getting rid of me before the end of my contract. He was probably quite glad that I'd 'fouled-up' the night of the end-of-cruise-dance. It had given him the perfect opportunity to dismiss me, and at the same time left me with no hope of any appeal against his decision. I reluctantly accepted that the incident was closed. Thinking back to what taxi driver said I can only assume that Weismann's fiddle was the difference between what percentage he paid the act and what he charged the Company …

Then I started thinking about Marianne.

When Flynn had taken me to the bar at the port I'd been angry with him. They say the truth hurts; well by God it certainly hurt me. I don't suppose he realised how close I was to hitting him as he delivered his home truths. Nobody had ever spoken to me so bluntly before. I'd been used to the sycophantic fawning of fellow entertainers who made sure they made as few 'open enemies' as possible. That wasn't a criticism. I'd done the same myself on more than one occasion when I felt that a few honeyed words might help me 'up the proverbial ladder'. In other words tell them what they wanna hear.

Believe me; it came as a great shock to my system when Patrick talked to me honestly without any attempt to soften his message and now that I had the time to consider what he'd said, I was able to think about it calmly.

The idea that Marianne might have found herself a lover was preposterous … that'd been my instinctive reaction. But now, I began to accept that not only was it not preposterous, it was logical, in fact even probable.

I started to think about the hundreds of times she'd been left alone while I was away working only to have me swamp her with my tales of wild audiences and fantastic reviews when I got home. I could see her expression as she patiently listened to my endless

69

monologues.

At first she'd tried to join in with my celebrations, showing pleasure at my pleasure. But as time went on, her reactions became more muted, until she finally reached a point where she didn't react at all. The stupid part is I was so wrapped up in me that I never noticed!

"What sort of man are you?" Patrick had said. Now I was beginning to realise what had prompted his words.

I'd never really thought of myself as being selfish. I'd given Marianne two wonderful children, a decent home …I'd shared some chores when I was home, and I never once raised a fist to her. Now I began to accept that I'd let her down far more badly than I'd thought. I'd provided enough material things, but I'd not given her the one thing that would have outweighed all the others - understanding. I'd starved her emotionally. I'm starting to realise that it's not enough to tell someone you love them, it's how you show that love. What's that they say about hindsight?

I sat quietly in the plane seat trying to imagine how desperate she must have felt, wanting nothing more than a simple conversation where she had the chance to tell me how *she* felt, how *she* had spent her day. I suddenly felt a great sadness as I pictured her looking at me with her beautiful sad blue eyes while I strutted around telling her how 'wonderful' I'd been on stage. I had never really considered her feelings, not allowed her to disturb my private cocoon of self-aggrandisement. The only time we really communicated was on the few occasions when she'd blown her top at me - and then I hadn't listened to her as we screamed at each other.

It's painful to realise that a relationship has ended, and even more so, to know that you have personally brought about its demise. I stared at the cabin roof and finally admitted that my marriage was dead, and that I'd killed it. If not murder, I was certainly guilty of manslaughter....

My strong silent companion finally broke his vigil as we were coming in to land at New York. He turned to me and placed a very firm hand on my arm.
 "It would be better if you stayed in your seat until all the other first class passengers have disembarked."
From his expression, I gathered that he was not just offering me a piece of friendly advice. I shrugged at him. "Whatever you say Qui no save." I gave him a cold smile and he responded by staring at me with the same dead-pan face he'd worn throughout the flight.

With the same cold efficiency that I'd experienced at Frisco, I was eased through the arrival lounge and taken to a secluded waiting area furnished with several comfortable chairs, a couple of sofas and a decent table loaded with magazines. The room was empty when I and my strong silent companion arrived, but within a few seconds, a waitress appeared and asked if we would like refreshments. I expected my companion to refuse, but he surprised me by asking for a sizeable selection of food and drink.

He filled a large plate with an assortment of cold and warm meats, along with a few vegetables, and started eating as soon as the waitress had gone. I just selected a small piece of fried chicken and a couple of rolls. He wolfed, and I picked for a few minutes, then he took a bottle of Californian white wine and poured himself a good glass. He offered me the bottle but I declined, picking a glass of orange-juice instead.

He raised his glass to me, and I raised my orange-juice. I watched him as he took a slow sip then let out a long satisfied sigh, obviously savouring the wine. A slow smile came over his face and he shook his head as he stared at me.

"I don't know what you did, and I don't want to know. But I'd just like to say it's been a pleasure taking care of you."

"Thanks." I must have sounded surprised, since it was. The last thing I'd expected from him, was civility. "What happens now?"

He shrugged. "We wait. Your flight doesn't leave for an hour or so, and I wouldn't like you to go wandering around on your own." He frowned as a young woman came into the room and, following his gaze, I turned to look at her. She was tall and slim, with a mane of golden-blonde hair. Dark brown eyes stared at us from a tanned, and very pretty face. She was smiling as she came straight towards us.

She glanced at me then faced my companion. "I've come to relieve you." She took something out of her handbag and displayed it to the man. He shrugged and turned to me. "Well, it looks like I'll have to leave you ..." He got up, nodded to me then turned and walked to the door.

I stared up at the woman, who was looking at me with a sort of mild curiosity. Before she could say anything, I sighed. "Yes, I know. You haven't any idea what I'm supposed to have done, but you have to make sure that I leave the country. Right?"

She gave a slight smile. "More or less. I'm Caroline, and I'll be 'looking after you until your departure."

"Aren't you flying to Manchester with me?"

"No. My brief is to make sure you get on the plane, and make sure you don't speak to anyone from the press."

"I don't know anyone from your press. So what do we do until my flight leaves?"

She gave a slight hunch of her shoulders. "I don't know. What would you like to do?"

"I'd rather not stay here, pleasant though it is. I thought I might buy myself a book to read on the flight. I'm starting to feel a little jaded, but I don't sleep well on planes. Reading helps to get me relaxed."

"I know what you mean. I'm not a great flyer myself." Caroline glanced at her watch. "OK, we'll take a walk."

The main concourse was, just like Frisco, filled with people. Unlike there, this time I didn't have a 'bodyguard' to force their way through the crowd. So we just made our way as best we could, pushing here, being pushed there, avoiding the battering-ram luggage whenever we could, and cursing faintly when we couldn't.

Finally we made it to the bookstore. Like the concourse, it was crowded, but I was able to look around and notice that the books were stacked neatly on shelves under general, or specific headings. A large banner high on one wall indicated the 'fiction' section, and an equally large sign on another denoted the 'non-fiction' works.

Caroline looked at me. "Do you have any particular preference?"

"Not really. I'll just wander around to see if anything catches my eye."

Caroline looked up as she read the rear cover of a book. "Didn't you say you lived in Manchester? This might interest you. 'Brothers in Harm' written by someone called Jeff Sommers. It's a sort of documentary about some murders ..."

"I've read it, more than once. The 'Manchester murders' caused a lot of interest, and anger - even in Belfast where I was living at the time."

"Why don't you tell me about it? We have time to kill, if you'll pardon the pun. She gave me a crooked smile.

"I'm not just saying that. I really would be interested to hear about those murders. "

I shrugged. "All right. But let's find somewhere a little less crowded."

We moved from the aisle to find a quiet spot away from the general flow of browsers, where I began to relate my condensed version of Jeff Sommers' book.

"The killings took place in the early sixties and the victims were all children. They were aged between five and nine. In total, seven were murdered. When the first one disappeared, a young boy called Brian, it was thought maybe he'd run away or at worst been kidnapped. That was until his body was found. It was discovered in a shallow grave on a deserted patch of moorland on the outskirts of Manchester by an elderly couple who had got out of their car to walk their dog. The old lady never got over it, which I suppose, is hardly surprising."

"As you can imagine, I 'vet seen some pretty awful things in my job." Caroline gave a sigh. "But I can never get used to the death of a child. Sorry to interrupt."

I nodded, sharing her sadness for a moment before I went on.

"The killers were two brothers, twins in fact, called Tom and Peter Boswell. They lived on a housing estate in Wythenshawe on the outskirts of Manchester. At the time they were in their twenties and on the face of it just seemed like ordinary people."

"Doesn't it ever make you wonder?" Caroline held me with her eyes.

"What?"

"Why God, if he exists, lets this sort of thing happen, especially to children."

"Funny you should say that. Both of them professed to be particularly religious. You know, going to church regularly with their mother ... They even claimed to read 'The Good Book' as they called it, every single day. At their trial they said God told them to torture then kill the children … Apparently for their eternal salvation can you believe? I suppose that's why the bodies were laid out in the cruciform position."

"Jesus!"

"Another pun Caroline?"

She gazed into my eyes then shook her head silently.

I continued. "Would you believe the killers quoted from the Bible in their defence? 'Suffer little children to come on to me'… It would appear they took the passage too literally."

"It's the same over here. We've had countless murderers admitting that they only killed because some voice was 'guiding' them." She gave a humourless laugh.

"It's the standard cop-out."

"What makes this case different is the fact the Boswells were never together after their arrest, yet when interviewed separately, both claimed to have 'heard the voice' at the same time. When they were compared their statements were identical in every way- as if written by the same person."

"How was that explained?"

"It wasn't nor was the unusual circumstances of their deaths."

"What do you mean?"

"Two years into their sentences they managed to hang themselves at precisely the same time."

"They'd made a pact?"

I shook my head. "It wasn't possible, Caroline. They'd not been in contact since the time of their arrest, and they'd been incarcerated in prisons more than two hundred miles apart."

"Fascinating." Caroline murmured as she flicked through the book.

"Why not buy it if you're so interested?"

She laughed." I don't need to buy it now. You've told me everything."

"No I've just given you a synopsis. Sommers book is an in depth study of the whole case. It gives names, dates. The author even interviewed Martha Boswell, the twins' mother, who incidentally was the one who turned them over to the police. They might never have been brought to justice otherwise. They were sentenced to life in prison and the judge recommended that it, should mean, Life. In his summing-up he described the brothers as 'the embodiment of an evil that was beyond comprehension.' My guess is that Sommers tried his damnedest to understand it."

"Did he succeed?" Caroline flourished the book.

I grinned at her. "Buy it and decide for yourself."

She paused, frowned at me for an instant, and then nodded. "O.K. You sold me."

She took a deep breath. "Now let's see if we can find you something to read, not too serious, I'd say a bit of light reading for the flight. How about something funny?" She held out a book and turned it so I could read the sleeve. *How to get rid of your wife without trying.*

"Right now," I felt a small lump in my throat. "That's the last thing I want to read about."

"Oh?" Caroline frowned for an instant before her eyes lit with a spark of cognisance. She hunched her shoulders in an expression of apology. "I think I'd better leave it to you. OK?"

She stayed close to me, but said very little as I sidled my way along the aisles, picking up a few random titles, inspecting them, then putting them back. I finally settled on a couple of contrasting works. I chose *My view of 'The United' phenomenon* - an account by an American author of his experiences while staying in Stretford, close to Manchester United football club; and a paperback *Made in The USA* by Bill Bryson.

Caroline studied my choices while we were standing in the queue at the checkout. She frowned. "I don't understand 'soccer'."

"And I don't understand your 'football', so that makes us even." I managed a faint smile and was rewarded by quite a pleasant response. She placed a hand on my arm and looked straight into my eyes. "You know, this is just a job for me. It isn't anything personal. I have my orders and …"

"Don't worry about it. Compared to old 'laughing boy' who flew with me from Frisco, you're doing great. If you ever need any references, just call me."

After leaving the bookstore, Caroline checked her watch and decided we might just have time for a 'farewell' coffee before she escorted me to the departure lounge. We managed to get back to the private salon where we'd met, and she ordered coffee for us.

Sipping her drink, she stared at me with a friendly thoughtful expression. "I've met a few unsavoury characters in my job, but you just don't strike me as being 'an enemy of the State'. I don't usually get involved with my 'clients but you are not at all like anyone I've had to escort. You're normal."

"Thank you." I stared back into her eyes and saw a faint blush tinge her cheeks. "If things had been different, I would have liked to have met you … socially."

Her blush became a deeper red and she covered her embarrassment by taking a long drink. "If things had been different, we'd never have met at all."

"That's true. Well there's something to thank Shawnie for. I mean, meeting you." I raised my coffee in salute. I saw Caroline frown and her stare became quite intense for a moment. "Someday, somebody is really going to hammer that scheming, gold-digging, lying bitch, and I want to be there when it happens." She averted her gaze for a second and I could see her body becoming tense. When she looked back at me, she was composed and she stared straight at me. "I never said anything. Right?"

I looked directly into her eyes. "I have this unusual medical condition. Don't know what it's called, but it makes me completely deaf on occasions." I gave her a quick conspiratorial wink.

She relaxed and gave me a warm smile, put down her cup and got to her feet.

"OK. I think it's about time to go."

I gave a very long reluctant sigh as I rose and followed her to a door close to the corner of the room.

We bypassed much of the crowd leading to the departure lounge, and Caroline walked with me until we reached Passport Control. Delving into her handbag, she produced my passport and handed it to me along with a flight ticket and a boarding pass. She showed the uniformed inspector at the desk some sort of official credentials, and he gave her a curt nod then gave me a long hard stare before waving us through.

Caroline stayed with me, keeping close as I went into the departure lounge; and she walked by my side when I joined the queue at the boarding gate. I suddenly realised I hadn't seen my luggage since I was 'picked up' at Frisco airport. I asked her about it, and she tapped my flight ticket folder. Stuck inside was the perforated half of a luggage label.

When I reached the front of the queue, she held out her hand.

"Well. This is where we part."

I took her hand and held it for longer than I should. "Thanks, Caroline. Before you came along I was treated like a parcel. But you've looked after me like a VIP. I won't forget you."

"I hope you won't think too harshly of our country. Not everyone is like … you know who." She gave me a warm smile. "Merry Christmas and have a good safe flight."

Impetuously, I leaned forward and gave her a quick kiss on the cheek. Before she could react, I went into the boarding tunnel. I halted just before I got on the plane, and saw that she was still standing at the end of the tunnel. I gave her a big smile and a small wave. She waved back to me then turned away and left my life just as quickly as she had entered it.

FOUR

Sean stretched in his chair then got to his feet as if a hypnotist had snapped his fingers bringing him out of a trance.

"I think it's about time for another drink. How about you?"

"Yes, I'll join you." I switched off my recorder and held out my glass while he poured the Brandy. I watched him replace the bottle and I reflected on what he had told me. The man had gone through more than his share of trouble, yet had maintained a kind of dignity throughout. To me, it seemed that no matter what happened he had some natural gift of bringing out the best in most of the people he met.

Another thought came to me and I posed my question as he returned to his seat.

"Did you ever see Caroline again?"

"I wanted to, but I didn't get the chance and looking back I think she was just a pleasant respite from the home truths I was having to face up to." Sean then grinned. "Me and the Senator sort of moved in different circles."

I nodded in response. "I'm curious about Shawnie, and I wonder if you ever enquired as to what happened to her."

"What?! After what she did to me, you're right, I certainly did want to know." He looked at me with a guarded expression. "In fact, I found out."

I couldn't read him as he stared at me. Then, he hunched his shoulders and took a sip of Brandy. "I'll tell you about it later. I don't want to break the sequence, or I'll get confused." He looked at his watch. "Are you ready for the next instalment?"

I turned on my recorder. "I'm ready." I raised my glass.

Sean took a long slow breath, exhaled softly, and began again.

When I got on the plane at New York, this time there was no 'preferential treatment'. I was just an ordinary passenger, and you just can't appreciate how good it felt.

I was directed to a window seat about halfway along the plane on the port side, and when I slid into my seat I got a good view of the port wing. A middle-aged couple filled the seats to my right, and after a brief nodding exchange they settled into their seats.

Once we were in the air and the air crew started on their rounds, bringing hot meals, the lady to my right spoke to me. Her face was homely and weathered and her eyes were bright with excitement.

"Is this your first trip to Europe?"

"Sort of." I answered.

"You're … Irish, aren't you?" Without waiting for my reply, she went on. "We've been saving up to visit my daughter. She married an Englishman and is living over there, and we're visiting for Christmas. Do you know the country well at all?"

"I live in Manchester."

"Oh. Is that anywhere near Sandbach?"

"Not far, about twenty five miles."

"Then you might know her?" She produced a photograph and thrust it into my hand.

I looked at the snapshot of a family group smiling out at the camera. The daughter was quite plain, as was her husband, but their children were beautiful. Unlike their unremarkable parents, both the young boy and girl had something more than just appeal. They showed a kind of vivacity that made me think of Jason and Michele, my own children. "Very nice." I said as I handed the photo back to the woman,

"You don't recognise her?"

"Sorry."

The woman shrugged. "I'd have thought - living so close, you'd have come across her. Our next-door neighbours live thirty miles away and we see them quite regular."

"Where do you live?"

"Sconsett - that's in Iowa."

"Things are a bit different in England ..." I went on to explain how the areas around any city were densely populated, and she listened with growing disappointment. When the food appeared, she concentrated her whole attention on feeding.

When I finished the meal, and the drinks were being brought round, I took a couple of bottles of mineral water, opened one and drank half of it, then settled down to read. The book was entertaining. The author, who had lived almost in the shadow of Old Trafford for two years, had given a new and different slant on life in and around the football stadium, and I was engrossed and amused to read his reflections.

Even though it was still only mid-afternoon, and was quite light outside, I began to feel sleepy. I suppose it could have been a reaction to everything that had happened, but I really did start to feel drowsy.

I hadn't slept much after the incident on the ship, and I'd gone through a fair amount of nervous energy during the previous eighteen hours. I slipped the book into the seat pocket and reclined the back of the seat. With the gentle roar of the engines and the soft babble of voices around me, I closed my eyes...

I dreamed. At first my dream was incoherent and appeared to be a montage of the events leading up to my present state. I was somewhere in Switzerland, standing at the lower end of what I took to be a ski-slope which ended not far from a typical 'Swiss Chalet'. Four shadowy figures came swooping down the brilliant white track and came to a halt only a few yards from where I was standing.

I recognised Michele first, then Jason, and finally Marianne. The fourth figure remained indistinct, but I knew it was a man. My wife and my children clustered around him, and I could hear them laughing as he put his arms around all of them, and they hugged him in return. I called out, but they ignored me as they took off their skis and started to walk towards me. The children passed so close I could have touched them, but they were intent on reaching the door of the chalet and walked past me as if I wasn't there. In the meantime

Marianne had taken off her helmet and goggles, as had the man with her. She slipped her arm into his as they strolled towards the chalet.

They were about to pass me when Marianne came to a halt. Deliberately turning away from me, she gave the man a passionate kiss on the mouth then turned to look directly at me.

"Are you going to miss me, Sean?" She half turned away as the man caught at her arm and tried to pull her towards the chalet. She resisted for a moment while she stared straight at me. "I'm not going to miss you."

Marianne's eyes were cold and hard. They softened a little and she half smiled. "I'm through with missing you ..." She gave in to the insistent tugging at her arm, and joined the shadowy man. She slid her arm around his waist and he did likewise, leaving me standing alone and cold on the bleak snow-covered mountainside. I started to shiver, and looked down at myself. I was wearing my 'performance kit' - a tuxedo with a pristine white frilled shirt and satin bow tie. What had been a desolate mountainside suddenly turned into the promenade deck of the *Pacific Princess* and the end-of-cruise party was in full swing.

I was, as before, dancing with Shawnie. This time, however, I *was* dancing. I was a cross between Fred Astaire and Gene Kelly, and it was Shawnie who stumbled and stuttered as we moved across the floor. I could see the frustration on her face as she stepped away from me then turned, dragging me with her. I didn't trip as she dragged me right into the heart of then revellers.

She stopped and turned to face me. The music had died, and everyone was circled around us, watching. She deliberately slipped the dress from her shoulders and allowed it to fall to the ground, and the onlookers began to applaud while she slowly held up her arms and did a graceful pirouette. Facing me again, she spoke in a loud voice so everyone could hear.

"I wanted this ..." Her lip curled in a sneer as she stared at me. "I was willing to give myself to him, and allow him the supreme pleasure of fucking me ... But what did he do? He turned me down - as if I was some ten-cent common whore!"

The crowd around us started to mutter their disapproval as they closed in on us. I could feel their growing antagonism as Shawnie goaded them on.

"You all know me. Most of you men have had me. What should we do with this piece of shit?"

A woman behind me shouted, "If he's a piece of trash, let's treat him like trash. Throw him overboard!"

There was little I could do as a score or more of them closed in on me. Strong hands grabbed me and even though I struggled for all I was worth, they picked me up. Kicking and shouting I was carried bodily to the guard-rail at the side of the deck. Weismann was standing aloof, watching the proceedings with an amused smile on his face. He looked directly at me and grinned.

"This will solve all my problems at once." He turned to the mob that had hoisted me over the rail and were dangling me over the dark rushing waves.

"Drop him."

86

I screamed as I fell, arms and legs whirling until I hit the water. I have never felt anything so cold and so hostile as the waves closed above my head. I started to sink, and no matter how hard I struck out of the surface, I continued to plunge deeper and deeper into the black icy water...

"I don't want to die. I don't want to die!" I heard a thin high-pitched voice screaming, and I realised it was me.

"Don't worry, my lovely lad. We won't let you die." I felt a cool soft hand on my brow, and I looked up to see a pair of honey-golden eyes looking down at me with a fierce tenderness. "You were having a bad dream, but it's over now. You need to rest, and get your strength back, so don't go having any more dreams. D'you hear?"

"Yes, nurse O'Malley." I responded instinctively. I was in the ward at Belfast Royal hospital, and I was seventeen - and yet somehow I knew I was forty-seven. I lay in the bed and watched the night-nurse, O'Malley, I'd only seen her a few times, during my rare bouts of 'clarity'; but I thought she was the most beautiful woman I'd ever seen in my life. I wondered if she had any idea how I felt about her as I lay weak and almost lifeless in that bed. I was still watching her as my eyes started to close and everything became misty.

It was cold again, so cold I could feel a great numbness creeping through my body. I started shaking and I wrapped my arms around myself to try to keep some warmth. I looked around and could see nothing for a moment, nothing but an endless expanse of impenetrable darkness.

I heard, or felt a wind spring up. It tugged at my clothes and my hair as I became aware that there was tough springy grass beneath my feet. A pale moon was in the sky and cast a chilling light on the desolate expanse of moorland where I was standing. Somewhere to my right I heard the sound of a distant car engine, then I saw the twin spidery beams of headlights moving towards me. The lights rose and dipped as the car negotiated the undulating curves of the moorland road, getting brighter as they approached.

I no longer felt cold. I felt nothing at all. I turned and watched as the car came to a halt and three figures emerged. In the faint moonlight, and the reflected glow of the car headlights, I saw two of the figures, one large one small, moving away from the car, heading roughly towards where I was standing. As they got closer I could see it was a man dragging a young girl with him. He was carrying a spade over his shoulder and he was whistling tunelessly as he strode carefully over the peaty ground.

They vanished from sight, hidden by a deep gully, and when they didn't reappear, I moved forward. The man was standing some six feet below my feet and the young girl was lying on the ground beside him. He was still whistling as he repeatedly jabbed at the earth with the spade. He toiled for I don't know how long before he was satisfied with his work, then he hoisted the spade onto his shoulder and turned back towards the girl.

"Leave her alone! Let her go!" I heard myself screaming as I opened my eyes. "Do as I say. Leave her alone!" Strong hands held my shoulders, and for an instant I stared into nurse O'Malley's eyes. She continued to press down on my shoulders and I struggled even more. I had to get up.

I forced myself upright with a tremendous surge, and I let out a wild yell as my head came into contact with the overhead luggage compartment. I flopped back into my seat to find the lady from Iowa staring at me white-faced and obviously shaken. She removed her hands from my shoulders and gave me a tremulous smile. She placed a hand on mine.

"My goodness, you're freezing, young man. For a minute, I thought you were going to hit me. I guess you had a real bad nightmare? Clem's called for the steward."

"Thanks, but I'm all right."

"You don't look all right to me." She shook her head. "You were thrashing about in your seat something awful, I thought you might hurt yourself, so I tried to wake you, but you just didn't want to wake."

"I'm sorry. Did I hurt you?"

"I've had far worse from the hogs on our farm. Now you just rest easy and we'll get the steward to bring you something soothing."

"Thanks, but I'm fine, really." As if to belie what I'd said, a sudden and vicious spasm coursed through me, and I started to shake. The lady from Iowa shook her

89

head disapprovingly.

"If that's fine, young man, then there are plenty of healthy people lying around in cemeteries. You look like you seen a ghost, or maybe two." She reached out and took my hand. "Mm. Palm's clammy." She released my hand and placed her hand on my forehead. It felt cool and comforting. She inhaled noisily. "Your head's a bit warm too. You could be coming down with something."

"No. Honestly. I'll be all right in a couple of minutes. The dream shook me up a bit it seemed so real."

"I could see you were upset. How's your head? It looks like you're going to have a bruise."

I gingerly touched my head where it had struck the luggage compartment and I could feel the beginning of a swelling. I raised my eyes and looked into the lady's face. Her expression was calm yet concerned. She frowned and turned away. "Where is that- Oh, he's here." She turned to the steward and started to explain what had happened while the steward's gaze alternated between her and me. I interrupted, half-rising, "There's no real need for any panic. I had a bad dream and hit my head when I woke up. Perhaps ..." I paused as I was gently pushed back into my seat. "... An Aspirin?"

The steward seemed relieved. He smiled cautiously at me. "Certainly sir. I'd suggest you see your doctor after we land."

"Mm." I made a non-committal grunt as he turned away. The lady from Iowa was still staring at me, but with less anxiety than before. She gave a gentle sigh. "You do look better than you did."

"I am. Thanks ...?" I posed the question without

90

speaking, and she responded.

"Olga. My folks originally came from Poland, and I was named after my Grandmother. That's my husband, Clement."

I acknowledged them both. "I'm Sean." I glanced up to see the steward holding out a couple of tablets and a plastic cup. I took the tablets but reached for the Mineral water I'd stowed in the seat pocket.

The steward waited until I'd taken the Aspirins then smiled. "If you need anything, just press the call button." He indicated one of the buttons on the overhead panelling.

When the steward had gone, Olga patted my hand. "I can see you don't want any more fuss. So you just sit back and relax." She turned away and picked up a magazine from the seat pocket.

The Aspirins hadn't started to take effect, and my head was starting to throb. I glanced out of the window and saw that the sky was becoming darker as we headed steadily eastwards. I closed my eyes and tried to relax.

I was not feeling too good, and I wanted to be home. Then I realised that 'home' was no longer a haven for me. It would be just an empty house. I started to feel sorry for myself. I'd been kicked off the boat with less than half my expected salary, discovered that my wife no longer cared for me, I'd just had the most disconcerting dream of my life, and almost bashed my brains out … Believe me I'd lots of reasons not to feel good.

Olga and Clement stayed with me after the plane landed. I didn't really appreciate them fussing around while we waited for our luggage, but after her kindness on the plane, I didn't want to dismiss them out-of-hand.

My luggage, for some reason, was amongst the last to appear on the conveyor, but Olga and Clement waited patiently with a spare trolley they'd commandeered until I'd collected my cases. We walked together along the disembarkation corridor until we reached the immigration hall where we were forced to part. I halted.

"Thank you for all you did on the flight. I hope you and your family have a lovely Christmas." I leaned over and kissed Olga's cheek.

"Oh my!" Olga raised a hand to her cheek, and I could see a faint blush rise. She covered her embarrassment by adopting a faintly severe tone. "Now don't forget what the steward told you. Make sure you see a doctor as soon as you can."

"Yes." I smiled at her, knowing that I'd no intentions of seeing a doctor. I watched them head for the 'Non-Resident' section of immigration as I pushed my trolley towards the UK Resident section. They waved to me and I returned their wave before they got lost in the queue.

Marianne was true to her word, she'd left the car keys and the parking ticket at the general information desk, along with a short note.

Dear Sean,

You'll find the car in section K of the long-stay park. I had some trouble with it when I was driving here, the engine kept cutting out. It might be a good idea if you took it to a garage to get it sorted out. See you when we get back.

Marianne.

The assistant behind the desk gave me a quizzical look. "I see you've just got back from America, sir. Do you have any English currency?"

I glanced down at the parking ticket, and realised I hadn't thought about paying the parking fee in English pounds. I opened my wallet, and to my relief found that I did have around seventy pounds in notes hidden away behind a small wad of American dollars.

I turned around and started pushing my trolley into the exit foyer, avoiding folk whenever I could, and barging into them when I couldn't. I glanced at my watch and saw it was already after five o'clock. The light was fading as I emerged and the sky was an unbroken blanket of lead-coloured cloud.

Section K of the car-park was almost as far from the terminal as it could be, and by the time I found my car, I was glad the floodlighting system was working. I stowed my luggage in the boot, left the trolley in a 'trolley-bay' and climbed into the car.

I wasn't surprised when the engine didn't start right away. After all, the car had been standing for a while in the cold dampness. Eventually the engine did fire, sluggishly I'll admit, but it started.

After re-mortgaging the car - I thought I'd bought shares in the airport when I paid the parking fee, I joined the steady stream of traffic heading along the M56. Before I'd driven half-a-mile, I noticed the petrol gauge was very low. I gave a sarcastic laugh when I thought that Marianne had typically assumed I'd put the petrol in.

When I filtered into the flying rank of traffic heading into Manchester, I put my foot down to match the pace of the swiftly moving cars. At first, the engine responded and the car accelerated smoothly until I was moving as fast as my fellow travellers, then, after a mile or so, the engine sort of coughed and the car behind me almost ran into my back-side. The driver gave me an angry blast on his horn and I responded with the accepted Christmas motorist's greeting - signalling to him as he flashed past me and indicating that I hoped he got two mince pies.

Fortunately there was a garage not too far ahead, and I chugged into the forecourt and grunted to a halt at one of the petrol pumps. I filled the tank then went into the small cabin. A youngish man with long matted hair, coiffured in the 'Alice Cooper' style was reading a girlie magazine behind the counter. He reluctantly tore himself away from the naked ladies and looked at me.

"Do you have a mechanic?" I asked as I handed over my credit card.

"Oh, yeah, we got a mechanic."

"Great. Could you ask him if he'd take a look at my car? It's not running very well."

The young man shrugged. "I would ask him to look at your 'motor' - if he was here, but he went home ages ago. It *is* Christmas eve you know."

"Yes, I had noticed. Do you know of any other local garage where I might get somebody to look at my car?"

"Sorry. I don't live round here."

I had a sudden and deflating thought. I was on my way home to a cold empty house. I'm not a great one in the kitchen, and the prospect of making a meal definitely did not appeal to me.

There was a tray half-filled with pre-packed sandwiches lying on the counter, so I examined some then selected a couple of turkey and stuffing with mayonnaise and handed them to the young man. He punched the details into the till then ran my credit card through the machine and gave me the slip to sign.

He handed my card back to me and grinned. "Merry Christmas."

"And to you." I gave him a sardonic smile, but he didn't notice. He had already gone back to his magazine and the seductive ladies.

Having a tank-full of petrol helped, but not much. The car was moving with the power and speed of a three-wheeled tractor, and beneath the bonnet the engine sounded as if it was made from a collection of scrap iron and elastic bands.

I chugged along, ignoring the hoots coming from the motorists who flew by me. At least I was still moving. It's funny, but on recollection, I noticed that, as the car slowed down, I leaned forward in an aggressive posture, gripping the wheel tightly and thrusting my head forward as if I could encourage the engine not to give out on me.

I eventually made it into the centre of Manchester, attracting a few amused glances from the pedestrians who overtook me as I tortoised my way up Portland Street. I kept praying that the lights ahead would remain on green, since I now felt that if I was forced to stop I wouldn't get started again. Fortunately they did remain green, and I was able to negotiate my way to New Cross and turn onto Oldham road. It was then that luck deserted me. The first set of traffic lights on Oldham road turned to red while I was still a good twenty yards from them, and eager traffic coming from the left was already filling up the junction. I had no choice, I braked gently and came to a halt.

No sooner had I stopped the car than the engine gave up the ghost. I turned the ignition key in desperation, but inside I knew it was a waste of effort. When the lights changed the surrounding traffic surged forward, passing me like a mountain stream flowing around a half-submerged rock.

I had no option but to get out and push. I don't know if you've ever pushed a car, but if not I can tell you it's a damn-sight harder than it looks. The first problem is to get the thing started, and since I was stopped on a slight upward incline it took a great deal of effort to get the wheels moving. I slowly shoved the car through the lights, ignoring the fact that even before I was halfway through they had changed to red and I was blocking off all the traffic trying to cross Oldham Road.

The Christmas spirit was in full flow. By that I mean that a number of pedestrians slowed to watch me labouring, and a few offered sarcastic comments, but not one of them offered to help. I continued to shove, moving at little more than a snail's pace, then suddenly the burden seemed lighter. I turned my head and saw a young man at my side. He was pushing heartily and he grinned.

"I'm at the head of the queue waiting to go across Oldham Road. I thought you might need a hand."

Short of breath, I nodded my thanks as we trundled the car slowly up the road. My new companion was far fitter, or younger than I, and he was able to speak. "There's a garage a few yards ahead. Steer closer to the kerb..."

I tugged at the steering wheel and guided the dead-weight car onto the forecourt of the garage. The young man gave a final heave then stood up. "Got to get back ... causing a jam." He gave me a quick wave and ran back down Oldham road to where I could hear a wild hooting of stranded cars. I never found out who the young man was, but I'm still grateful for his help.

I eased the car into a space where it didn't block the entry, then I wobbled on shaky legs over to a small brightly-lit cabin.

"Hello!" I called as I opened the rickety wooden door. There was no answer so I stepped inside. The interior was warm and smelled of old oil. Beyond a narrow counter was a small passage at the end of which was a door. I went to it and knocked hard.

A tousled head appeared. The man was about my age and his face was streaked with oil and grease. He frowned.

"You shouldn't be here. It's restricted."

"Sorry. No-body came when I knocked at the door. I need some help. My car's conked out and I wondered if somebody could take a look at it?"

"Right." The man emerged, rubbing his hands on a dirty rag. Let's have a look then."

I followed him onto the forecourt and stood anxiously watching as he unfastened the bonnet, lifted it, then leaned over and peered inside. "Could you turn the ignition on?" His voice came from beneath the bonnet.

I obliged. Sitting in the driver's seat and praying as I turned the key.

"All right. That's enough." The voice called out.

I stepped out of the car and looked at him hopefully. My hope faded when I saw his expression.

"Don't think we could do anything right now. It looks like your alternator has packed up."

"Is that bad?"

"Could be worse. But it'll be a three or four hour job to replace it - if we had a replacement. These Japanese cars are fine while they're running but they can be a bastard to fix when they break down. Leave it with us, and we'll try to get it fixed as soon as we can - but it'll be after New Year."

"What?!"

He shrugged. "You can't expect us to do it now. It's Christmas Eve and by rights we should have closed already. If it hadn't been for an awkward crown gear job, we would be. We will be shutting up in the next ten minutes." He stared at me for a long moment. "Have you got far to go?"

"New Moston. I just got in from America, and I'm at the end of my tether. Everything that could go wrong today, has gone wrong with a vengeance. I know it isn't your fault, but can't you do something?"

"Not until we get a new alternator, and it's too late to go to the stockist. They'll be closed 'til after the holidays, like I said." He half turned away then paused. He looked back at me. "I'm sorry, mate."

I gave a despondent shrug and turned towards my broken-down car. I'd only taken a couple of paces when a voice called out.

"It's you, isn't it - it is you?"

I turned back and saw another man standing at the open door of the cabin. He was short, thick-set and had a dirty flat cap on his head. He walked quickly over to me and stood grinning.

"Sean Clarke as I live and breathe." He turned to his companion. "Do you know who this is, Tony? It's Sean Clarke, the singer I told you about." He held out a grubby hand and I absently shook it as he continued. "Me and the wife have seen you about six times, and she reckons you're the best thing since tinned tuna. You ... wouldn't give me your autograph, would you? The name's Charlie."

"Sure ..." I found a pen and signed the piece of paper he thrust under my nose. "Now, I'd better get my things out of the boot."

"Things? What things?"

"My guitars and my luggage. I only just got back from America and I need to get home."

"America! Did you hear that Tony, he's been to America."

"That's right, and I'm tired and I just want to…"

Tony, who'd been watching with a bemused expression, butted in. "Mister Clarke has a problem. His alternator's gone bust, and he's stranded. I told him we were ready to pack up…"

"I suppose I could get a taxi, but at this time …"

"Hold on. Don't let it be said that I didn't try to help Sean Clarke, and at Christmas too." He stared at me for a moment then gave a quick nod. "I got an idea."

"Yes?" I said eagerly or a better word might be hopefully.

*   *   *

FIVE

Sean let out a long sigh as he finished his drink and brought me back with a jolt to the present. I looked at him and smiled as he gave me a wry grin.

"I suppose you could say that 'the luck of the Irish' deserted me that Christmas."

I nodded. "It sounds as if things couldn't have been worse."

"Don't you believe it? My old daddy used to say that 'when one door shuts another opens'."

"Was your father religious?"

"No he was a cabinet maker."

"Sean be serious."

"Sorry, where was I ...? Oh yes, my Father always said that God had a very warped sense of humour." Sean got to his feet and walked past me to the door. "Get yourself another drink, and fix me one. I shan't be long ... just going upstairs."

I refilled our glasses and set Sean's down by the side of his chair. I sat down and as I waited, I turned to look at the photographs mounted on the wall behind me. I couldn't help but stare at Marianne. The photo was black-and-white but even so I could guess that her hair was a soft golden blonde and her eyes were sparkling blue. She was smiling out at the camera with an expression that made me feel protective and desirous at the same time. She certainly was beautiful, and I could imagine how crushed he must have felt when he realised he'd lost her. That Christmas Eve, ten years ago, must have been one of the most wretched times of his life.

I heard Sean's footsteps on the stairs and I turned away from the photo and idly swirled the drink in my glass as he came through the doorway. He hardly looked at me as he went across the room to his chair and picked up his drink. He didn't sit down right away, but instead turned to gaze at the photograph I'd been looking at. He regarded it gravely and silently for some time before he gave a sad shake of his head. He glanced down at me and gave me a wry smile before he returned to his chair.

Lowering himself gently, he still had a hazy expression in his eyes, and he didn't say a word for several seconds. Then, as if snapping out of a reverie, he grinned.

"Bet you think I'm a melancholy sort of bloke?"

"Right now, reliving painful memories I can understand why and if you would rather not carry on I would certainly understand."

"No no, the telling helps to focus my mind and take the edge off the way I felt back then, even though it was a long time ago ... I can recall each incident in pretty good detail, not exactly, but near enough to be accurate. The rest is just artistic licence."

Sean paused for a moment before continuing the story.

Now where was I...? Oh yes I was waiting for Charlie's good idea so I stared at him with a kind of desperation, trying to hide all the mixed up feelings that were making my stomach churn. He looked at my car then at me. He frowned.

"I don't suppose you'd consider … No …"

"What?"

Charlie shrugged slowly. "Well, we could, sort of, lend you a car 'til after the holidays. It isn't any great shakes in fact it's a bit of an antique, but it's mechanically sound even though it looks like a shed."

"Brilliant! I don't care what it looks like as long as it'll get me home and help me do a bit of shopping."

"All right, follow me." Charlie turned and walked past the cabin to a corrugated door on the side of the main workshop building. He opened the door and stepped inside with me close behind.

"What do you think?" Charlie pointed to a battered Mini-Traveller standing close to a large roll-over door. "Like I said, it looks worse for wear, but the engine and brakes are in good nick … only one small problem. We haven't got an M.O.T. certificate for it. You can borrow it with pleasure, but if you get stopped by the police, it'll be your responsibility."

"Fine. How about I sign some paper to say I bought it from you, as seen … Then legally the responsibility really will be up to me."

Charlie considered my proposal for a second then nodded. He went through to the office and made out a mock 'bill of sale' and I signed it. He gave me a copy and shoved the original into a desk drawer. "I'll get you the keys. Just be careful with it, and come back the day after New Year's Day, and we'll see how we're getting on with your car."

103

"Fine." I accepted the keys he gave me, and took my front door key from the keyring and put it in my pocket before I handed him the keys to my car. After he'd raised the roll-over door, I started the engine and eased the Mini-Traveller out into the yard. I looked at my watch and saw that it was almost seven o'clock, and a faint mist was beginning to descend. It took a few minutes to transfer my luggage into the rear of the Mini-Traveller. When we'd finished I opened the door and held out my hand. "Thanks for all your help. I won't forget it."

Charlie shook my hand. "You just go and have yourself a right good Christmas." He and Tony waved to me as I steered out onto Oldham Road.

I hadn't driven more than a hundred yards when the mist became a fog. I mean fog - the really thick 'pea-souper' kind where you could hardly see a hand before your face.

I shivered for a moment, feeling as if a sudden cold draught had blown straight through the car. The heater was on but wasn't giving out much warmth, so I turned it to maximum as I peered into the grey gloom outside.

The fog was sort of patchy and, as I drove, I caught glimpses of some of the buildings I passed. I thought I was seeing things when I caught a glimpse of *The Pack Horse* pub, then a few minutes later *The Ram*. I wasn't absolutely certain, but I thought that neither of the two pubs was still open, and I had a vague recollection that

The Ram had been demolished some years earlier. Obviously I must have been mistaken.

I rubbed my eyes, blinked and tried to concentrate on the road while the thick grey fog swirled and billowed around me. Some way ahead I saw the fog was lighted by a harsh yellow-white glow close to a set of traffic lights, and my mouth fell open as I approached the junction.

The *Playhouse Theatre* had been derelict when I left for America, now it was lit up like the proverbial Christmas tree. What's more, the doors were open and there was a mass of people making their way into the cinema. As I drove slowly past, I saw the illuminated sign over the entrance ... They were showing *The Unsinkable Molly Brown,* a film that was at least thirty years old. I then remembered that some cinema in Stockport had started showing old films making me think it must be a trend.

I craned my neck, staring at the crowd, and then I gave a start as I looked ahead. I wrenched at the steering wheel and narrowly missed driving into the near-side pole of the traffic lights, mounting the kerb then bouncing onto the road. I steadied the car and slowly started to accelerate, and then I braked hard when a dark coloured van shot past me then cut in sharply and jammed on his brakes.

I was forced to stop, and I was ready to give the driver a big piece of my mind, when I saw someone step out of the van and march towards me. It was a policeman. Yet when I say it *was* a policeman, he was wearing a uniform that seemed oddly out-of-date. There was no iridescent yellow waistcoat, just a plain dark blue uniform with a plain blue hat. He leaned over and tapped on my window. I opened the window and peered up at him. He didn't look friendly.

"Good evening sir. Is this your vehicle?"

"Yes, officer. Is there a problem?"

"We noticed that you drove onto the kerb just now. We've been following you for the past mile or so, and your driving is erratic. Have you been drinking, sir?"

Thankfully I could reply honestly. "No, officer, I haven't had a drink all day."

"I see, sir. Would you mind stepping out of your car, and walking a straight line for me?"

"A straight line?" I almost laughed. "Tell you what, get your little bag, and I'll blow into it for you."

For some reason this seemed to annoy him. "Do you have your licence with you, sir?"

"Yes I do." I fished in my jacket, found my wallet, and took out my driving licence. I watched him as he stared at it, and he became even more annoyed. "Right, sir. That's it. Would you go to the van, please."

"Why?"

"I don't want things to get 'nasty', sir. So would you please just walk to the van?"

I got out of the car and did as he asked. He stayed close to me, and when we reached the van, he called out. "Bill, we got a real joker here. I think we should take him down to the station."

I started to protest, but they ignored me as they caught hold of my arms and frog-marched me to the rear of the van then unceremoniously bundled me

106

inside. I gave a deep sigh and called out to them. "What about my car? It has all my luggage and equipment in it. We can't just leave it here - surely?"

"Don't worry about that, sir. It'll be brought to the compound at the station." The door slammed with a hollow sound and left me in almost total darkness. I found a narrow bench-seat running along the side and I flopped down as the van set off.

The suspension must have been almost non-existent, since I was thrown about like a cork in a bucket every time we hit a bump. By the time we came to a halt I was punch-drunk. I blinked when the door was opened, and I stepped down with the 'help' of the policeman who kept a really firm grip on my arm. I couldn't help but gape when I saw the entrance, and I was given an extra hard push towards the steps.

I frowned as I momentarily looked around. The surroundings were old, yet not old, and I vaguely recognised the area. I was in Willet Street yet it looked different. Then I saw the old-fashioned blue lamp hanging on an ornate wrought-iron support over the door of the station as I was assisted towards the steps. I gasped as I saw the interior. It looked like the set from a very old Police TV series - *Dixon of Dock Green*. The drab imitation tree and the sparse decorations all looked like a token gesture to Christmas. Everything about the place was antique, from the leaded glass in the doors, to the polished wooden counter behind which stood a tall well-built sergeant. He had a florid face and dark hair slicked down and parted in the middle. He was writing in a heavy looking leather-bound book, and he didn't look up as the young policeman who must have followed in my car, came in and leaned on the counter.

"We got a comedian here, Sarge. Driving like a drunk, but said he hadn't had a drink, didn't want to walk a straight line and said something about blowing into a bag. When I asked for his driving licence - look what he gave me, is he taking the piss or what?"

Having finished what he was writing, the desk-sergeant put down his pen then looked past the young constable to stare at me. As the pale eyes held mine, I had the strange feeling that he was 'reading me'. After a couple of seconds he turned his gaze away and spoke to the constable.

"Right, Harry, let's have a decco at the ... What the heck?" The sergeant glanced at my licence then beckoned me over to the counter. Tapping the document but staring at me he shook his head. "I know it's Christmas, and a lot of folk are playing jokes, but we don't think it's funny when somebody tries to act the goat with us." He handed the licence back to me and gave me a sour grin. "Now if you'd show me your real licence we can be done with this, and I can get on."

I looked down at the licence, trying to see if there was something wrong with it. I couldn't find anything obvious and I was about to say so when the sergeant spoke.

"I suppose you don't have it with you, sir. Then you'd better come back within five days with the real one. Now, my constable says you were driving a bit oddly..."

The constable butted in. "That's right, Sarge - nearly knocked the traffic lights over at the Palace junction on Oldham Road."

The sergeant turned to the constable. "All right Harry! I will take it from here." He turned back to me. "Now, sir, what have you got to say?"

I hunched my shoulders and gave him a sheepish smile. "The constable's right. I did drive over the kerb at the junction - but it was pretty foggy, and I was distracted."

"Have you been drinking?" His pale eyes studied me.

"Not a drop."

"Well Harry 'ere thinks you have, so we'd better send for a doctor and have him do a blood test."

"What?" I gaped. "Why don't you just get a breathalyser or an intoximeter and give me a test?" I couldn't understand why the sergeant and the constable started to laugh.

The constable leaned on the counter. "Sarge, this bloke's been watching too much *Doctor Who*. Don't get him a doctor - he needs a psychiatrist!"

"That's enough, Harry. I've said I will deal with him now. You'd better get back to your vehicle. I'm sure there's plenty to do."

"Right, Sarge." Harry gave me a frowning sort of smile, shook his head, and then went to the door. "Are you going for a pint after duty, Sarge?"

"Not tonight. The wife wants to watch *Holiday Inn* on the telly." He waited until the constable had gone then he turned to me. "Now, sir. Go and sit down while we wait for the doctor. You can keep that young girl over there company."

I turned from the counter, disillusioned and

puzzled. I'd had a few brushes with the law before but I'd never been treated this way. They were acting a bit odd towards me to say the least. In fact if I didn't know it was Christmas Eve I would think it was April fool's Day.

I walked to a long wooden bench were a young girl was sitting. She was about sixteen or seventeen, and had a mass of shining brown hair which curled over her shoulders. She wore a dress that could have come from the sixties beneath a dark coat. She was, to my eyes, very attractive. Don't get the wrong idea. She was the sort of girl I would have fancied when I was a teenager.

I sat next to her and gave her a smile. "I suppose you think I'm crackers as well?"
 "Yeah, I do. But if you want to get drunk at Christmas that's your affair." As she looked at me, I was startled by the deep golden-brown of her eyes.

I shook my head. "I'm not drunk at all." I started to explain what had happened to me but she cut me short. "Mister, you're quite nice - for an old man, that is. But right now, I got enough troubles of my own." She spoke firmly and then turned away, making it obvious she didn't want to talk. I leaned back and thrust my hands in my pocket.

The desk sergeant caught my eye and gave me a quiet smile before he went back to writing in the heavy book. He started humming quietly to himself, and I caught the strains of *Silent Night* as I stared into space.

We all stayed quiet for some minutes, then a weird

sound broke the silence. My stomach started to rumble. I looked up and saw that both the girl and the sergeant were smiling. I fumbled in my pocket and took out one of the sandwiches I'd bought at the garage. As I was unwrapping it, I noticed the girl was watching me with an intensity that gave me an idea.

"Would you like one?" I held out a half of the sandwich."

"Thanks." She grabbed it off me and took a huge bite. "Didn't have any tea." She said after she'd finished. "I'm famished."

"I have another - if you'd like it?"

"Oh, lovely. Thank you, I was always told not to take sweets from strangers but no one said anything about sandwiches."

I fished the second sandwich out of my pocket and handed it to her. She took it and frowned as she stared at the wrapping for a moment before she tore it open. We sat contentedly munching for a few minutes. Then, when we'd finished I took the wrappings and went to the desk.

"Have you got a bin, or wastepaper basket?" I held out the Cellophane.

"Yes, sir." The sergeant took the wrappings from me and turned away to deposit them somewhere behind the desk. When he straightened up he was frowning. He stared at me for a long moment then gave a slight shrug. He nodded towards the bench. "If you don't mind, sir."

I went back to sit beside the girl who smiled at me. "Nice sandwich. Thanks."

"That's OK. I hate eating alone." I grinned. I hesitated

then took a chance.   "What are you doing here?"

"Oh," She shrugged and pulled a face. "If you must know, I was caught trying to sneak into the Playhouse without paying. The rat-bag of a manager called for the police and kept me in his office 'til they came." She looked across at the desk sergeant. "They won't let me go 'til I give them my address."

"Why won't you? Sorry, that's your business."

"It's all right. For some daft reason, I trust you - even though you are crackers." She laughed and her whole face lit up for an instant.

I was starting to like the girl. I held out my hand. "I'm Sean Clarke, and I'm an entertainer. I do a cabaret act …"

"Are you famous?"

"Have you ever heard of me?"

"Not that I can remember."

"Then I'm not as famous as I thought."

We both laughed for a moment then she took my hand. "I'm Elizabeth - but my friends call me Betty. Betty Walker."

"I'm very pleased to meet you Betty. If there's anything I can do to help you-"

"I think you should be helping yourself." She glanced towards the door way. I followed her gaze and saw a smartly-dressed elderly man holding a medical bag. "Looks like the doctor's here for you." Betty smiled.

"We've got a live one for you tonight, doc." The desk sergeant grinned.

"Never mind all that frivolity. Let's get this over with. I don't need this on Christmas eve." The doctor stared at me as he walked past to a door to my left. "Come with me."

I followed him into a small room whose walls were painted an uninspiring drab green. A plain table and a couple of chairs were the only furnishing, and the walls were decorated with several fading posters. One of them caught my eye.

MISSING. BRIAN THOMPSON.

"Sit down." The doctor waved me to the nearest chair.

"What's with all these ancient posters?"

"Just take off your coat and jacket and roll up your sleeve." The doctor ignored my enquiry. "There now, that didn't hurt - did it? I'll have the sample analysed in a couple of days and you take this one to your doctor and have him do the same." He leaned over me and smelt my breath then shone a light into my eyes. "You're as sober as a judge if I'm not mistaken." He lowered his voice and winked at me, "Which is more than I can say for myself. I'll have a word with the sergeant, and if you keep your mouth shut and don't say anything daft you'll be on your way in no time."

I waited and a few minutes later the desk sergeant called out to me. I went back into the reception area and up to the desk where the desk sergeant was smiling.

"Right then, sir. The doc reckons you're sober, so you're free to go. But don't forget to bring your *real* documents in as soon as you can."

"Thank you. But what about the girl?" I turned to Betty and she gave me a tentative smile. "I've had a little talk with her, and I'd like to help her."

"Oh Yes?" The sergeant gave me a raised-eyebrow look.

"Oh, come on! It isn't anything like that! I'm a married man with kids of my own. Like I said, I've been speaking to her, and I just want to help her if I can."

"Sorry, sir. I'm a pretty good judge of character, and I reckon you're all right. I didn't mean to imply that you're -'twisted'. No offence."

"Non taken, sergeant."

"Good." The sergeant glanced towards Betty. "You're welcome to try. All we want is her address, so we can contact her parents. She says she's seventeen, but she might only be fourteen or fifteen. You just can't tell with young girls nowadays, what with all that make-up and such. If you know what I mean?"

"Just let me have another talk with her to see if we can sort this out. You don't want her staying here all night, I wouldn't have thought?"

"I'm tempted to agree. She doesn't seem like a 'bad-un' and like you say, it'll be hard on her to keep her in a cell on Christmas Eve. I'd prefer it if she wasn't here when we get all the drunks piling in later on when the pubs have closed."

"I'll see what I can do."

I went back to where Betty was sitting and sat beside her. I smiled. "They've told me I can go. Apparently being 'crackers' isn't much of a crime."

She smiled. "I'm glad for you."

"Thanks. Now I'm concerned for you." I looked at her gravely. "A police station can get really ugly at night - especially on a night like tonight. When they start to bring all the drunks in they could cause you a lot of trouble. I don't like to think of you being here when that happens ... Why won't you give them your address so you can get out of here?"

She gave me a long hard look as if assessing me. Then she let out a deep sigh. "I'm seventeen, so they've no right to treat me like a kid."

"I agree. So why won't you just tell them what they want to know?"

"It's not that simple. I left home, in Ashton and I've been dossing down wherever I can 'til I get a job and a place to live." She took a deep breath and closed her eyes before she went on. "If I do give them my address, they'll bring my mother and step-father here to collect me. I don't want that!" She clenched her lips and stared at me, her eyes were moist and she blinked rapidly. I found a clean handkerchief and held it out. She took it and dabbed her eyes before going on. "The trouble started not long after my real dad died. I was with him when it happened, and I wanted to call a doctor for him, but he said it was just bad indigestion. It was a heart attack and it killed him." She sniffed and dabbed her eyes again. "You know, at times like that you think that things just can't get any worse. But they did. His name

115

was Bill Jackson, and he was a friend of my dad. At least that's what my dad thought." She shook her head sadly. "It's funny how a man can think another man is great, because he shares drinks with him in the pub, and tells jokes and supports the same football team. It takes a woman to see them for the dirty lecherous swine they are." Her expression was taut as she went on. "Bill Jackson was a real bastard. I lost count of the times he'd tried to fondle me, not to mention the filthy things he said to me when my dad wasn't around. I got sick of my 'groping Uncle Bill'."

I gently placed a hand on her arm. "We aren't all like him, you know."

She gave me a tearful smile. "Yeah, I know. Anyway, things got worse a few months after my dad died. My mother came and told me she and Bill were in love and were going to get married. I just couldn't understand her. How could she have loved a lovely man like my dad then go and say she was in love with an animal like Bill Jackson?" She brushed the tears from her eyes and took a shuddering breath. "Anyway, I thought it would be better for me - you know. He'd leave me alone if he had my mother. Huh, what I fool I was to think anything would change. He got worse. A few nights ago, while mother was staying with my gran who wasn't very well, he came into my room. I was getting ready to go out with some friends and was going to put on my good dress, and I only had my knickers and bra on. He didn't knock, just came straight in. He'd been drinking and he stank. He sat on my bed and started holding his you know. Then he said 'this is for you darlin' and started to get up. I told him to get out, and that I'd tell my mother but he just laughed in my face as I put my dress and shoes on. I shouted - told him to get out, but he just grinned at me. He told me it was a waste of time to put my clothes on since he'd be taking them off again soon. He laughed and told me not to act so innocent, since I was just like my mother, a slag - then he told me how he'd been 'shagging' her behind my dad's back.

He sort of stumbled towards me, making a grab for me. I dodged him and kicked out, hitting him in the groin, and he sort of groaned and fell down. I kicked his horrible face while he was lying there, then I grabbed my coat and ran out.

I ran all the way to my gran's, and when I got there I told my mother what had happened. All I got was a slap across my face and a load of insults for 'dressing up and encouraging Bill like a slut'."

Betty slumped and sobbed for a moment then she forced herself upright. Her eyes were tear-filled as she looked at me. "I realised in that moment that not only had I lost my dad, but my mother as well."

I gave her a sympathetic look. "Why didn't you go to the police?"

"Oh yeah, a typical man's reaction. If my own mother didn't believe me - what chance would I have stood with the police? They'd probably have charged me with assault. I just thought that since my mother was happy with him she could have him. I left my gran's and I've not been back home since then."

"I can see why you don't want them to come here. But -

117

why did you go to the Playhouse and try to get in without paying? That's what has got you in here."

Betty shrugged. "I'd run out of cash, but I really wanted something nice at Christmas. My mother and my dad took me there last Christmas eve, and I suppose I just wanted to remember some happy times." She let out a great sob.

I put my arm around her and held her gently until her sobs subsided. "Don't worry. I'll sort things out, and get you out of here."

I went up to the desk and attracted the sergeant's attention. He'd been sitting in a hard-wood chair staring at something. He dropped it into the waste-basket then leaned against the counter.

I told him Betty's story and he listened with some sympathy until I'd finished. He scratched his head and glanced over to where she was sitting. "You know, if she wanted, she could press charges against her step-father."

"She'd rather not - for her mother's sake."

"All right - but I don't think she's doing her mother any favours."

"What about the entrance money for the Playhouse?" I reached into my pocket and put some pound coins on the counter.

"Oh I don't think we need worry about that." The sergeant handed the coins back to me. "Anyway, those foreign things wouldn't be much use." He gave me a grin. "The manager at the Playhouse is a bit of an Ass - so I wouldn't worry about him. What is worrying is that girl. Where's she going to stay - at Christmas?"

"I could take her home with me. My wife will look after

her 'til she can find somewhere to stay after the holidays."

I didn't mention the fact that Marianne wasn't at home. Even though he seemed a reasonable man, for a policeman, I didn't think he'd look too kindly on my offer if he thought I'd be alone with the young girl.

The sergeant hesitated for some time then he slowly nodded. "All right, sir, since I do trust you."

I went to Betty and told her she was free to go and that she was welcome to stay with me at my house, or anywhere else she might want to go. I went back to the counter then noticed that same old poster about the missing boy - Brian Thompson. Why should they have had a poster that was over thirty years old?

"Just one moment, sir." The sergeant was writing something on a slip of paper. "You have five days to produce your tax and insurance certificates."

"And MOT?" I said.

He frowned at me. "No sir. There's no need for an MOT for a car that's practically new. It's parked round the back and you can collect it whenever you're ready."

"Thank you, sergeant." I joined Betty who was waiting at the door. As she opened it to go out, I turned back to the sergeant. "By the way, what was wrong with my licence - it wasn't out of date, was it?"

"Out of date!" The sergeant grinned at me. "Go on with you - you know darned well it wasn't even *in* date."

We stood on the pavement outside the station for a

moment. The thick fog had dissipated a little, but the air was still quite heavy with a thick mist. I started towards the corner of the building and Betty followed, walking sharply to catch me up. As we turned the corner, I glanced at her.

"I have a confession to make before we go any further. I told a little lie to the sergeant."

"Oh?" Betty half smiled at me. "And what sort of lie was it? Aren't you married, or something?"

"Well, yes I am … but my wife and kids aren't at home right now. They're taking a break in Switzerland."

"Lucky them." Betty stopped and as I turned to her, she stared hard into my face for a long time before she smiled. "No, I don't think you're like Bill. I suppose you lied so you could get me out of there?"

"More or less. I didn't want to think of you spending Christmas Eve in that place. Now, have you decided where you want to go?"

"Yes. I'd like to come home with you - if that's all right?" She stopped and so did I. Again she looked at me directly. "I trust you, Mister Clarke."

We'd reached the gate leading to a small compound where a few cars were neatly parked. A lamp fastened to the rear wall of the building cast enough light for me to see the Mini-Traveller. It looked different, and as we got closer I could see that it appeared to have been cleaned and polished. The paintwork was glistening and the chrome was shining quite brightly.

"Nice car." Betty stroked her hand along the nearside wing. "Have you had it long?"

"No," I answered as I opened the door, "I only got it

recently."

I was confounded when I climbed into the driving seat after letting Betty into the car. It was as if someone had done a complete and very thorough cleaning job on the interior and again there was that strange sensation, the one I had when I first entered the car

"Is something wrong?" Betty looked at me warily.

"Did you feel it?" I stared at her.

"Feel what?" She half smiled then frowned. "What're you talking about?"

"When I got in the car - didn't you feel ... something like a very cold draught?"

Betty shrugged. "It is cold ... but I didn't feel anything like a draught. Are you sure you're all right? You look a bit pale."

"I'm all right, really. No ... No, everything's fine." I started the engine and coaxed the car out of the compound and onto the street. I headed back towards Oldham Road and was startled to see so little traffic. What was more disturbing was that the cars that I did see in the gloom were 'out-of-date'. I felt the hairs on my neck rising, and again I had the sensation of an icy cold breeze blowing at me from behind. I glanced at Betty and she was sitting quite unconcernedly smiling to herself. It was obvious everything was quite normal to her.

She turned to me after a few quiet minutes. "You said you were a singer?"

"That's right. I mostly do the local clubs, but I sometimes get special bookings. I arrived back from

America today."

"Wow! Did you meet anybody famous while you were there?"

"Not really. I was working on a cruise liner all the time. I did meet a Senator and his wife."

"Oh, I'm not into politicians. They're all old, and boring."

"A bit like me?"

"No. You're not boring." She gave me a broad smile. "You remind me a bit of my dad. He was sort of easy going, and would help anybody in trouble."

"You really liked him, didn't you?"

"Yeah, I really did. I mean, he wasn't always 'soft', if you know what I mean. He'd give me a right belt when I'd done something really bad. But he didn't do that very often. Most of the time, he was more like a friend than a dad. I could talk to him - not like my mother. She thought I was farcified, and she never believed anything I told her."

I could see she was getting a little emotional, so I changed the subject. "You said you were looking for a job. What kind of work would you like to do?"

"What I really would like, is to be an airline hostess, and fly to all those wonderful places. But I'm not clever enough, and I don't look good enough to stand a chance."

"Don't belittle yourself. You can do anything you set your heart on - providing you're willing to work hard enough."

"D'you think so?"

"I know it. It all depends on what you truly want out of

your life."

"I just want to be happy. That's all." She stared at me as I started to smile. "What's the matter with that?"

"Nothing at all," I answered. "I think that's what all of us want. The main problem is trying to find out how you can do it."

We had reached Broadway and I turned left and headed up towards the Broadway Hotel. "Not far now." I gave her a reassuring smile then concentrated on the road.

I turned onto Bathhurst Road, then after a few hundred yards, right into Sefton Avenue and parked up outside my home. "Here we are."

Betty peered at my home and smiled. "It looks nice."

"Right. Let's get inside out of this mist." I stepped out of the car and locked the door, doing the same with the passenger door, then led Betty up the path to my front door. It looked different at close range, but I didn't think anything of it. All I wanted to do was to get into the house and shut the door on the outside world for a few hours.

"What's the matter?" Betty frowned at me.

"My key. It doesn't seem to fit the lock." I gave a heavy sigh and tried again, pushing and twisting the key with some force. I gave a start and stepped back when the hall light came on and a figure loomed through the frosted glass panel in the door. As far as I knew the house was empty!

The door opened and the doorway was filled by a short, thick-set man whose ruddy face was contorted in anger. His tiny dark eyes were no more than slits as he thrust his jaw forward aggressively. "What the hell do you think you're doing, pal?"

"I was trying to get my key in the lock, I might ask you the same question. What are you doing in my house?"

"Your house!" The man almost shouted at me. "What are you - some kind of looney?"

I held out the key. "Look… I was just…"

The man took an almighty swipe and knocked the key from my hand, and it went spinning out into the misty darkness. He took a step forward and glared at me. "Look, pal, I've lived here for twenty years, and I don't know you from Adam. You're obviously drunk, and if you don't clear off right now, I'm going to call the police."

I looked past him into the hallway, and I could see that everything was different. I didn't recognise the wallpaper, and there was a small narrow table halfway down the hall that wasn't there when I left. I suddenly remembered the dream I'd had on the plane, and I could only guess that I was dreaming again. I started thinking about all the crazy things that were happening to me and if I wasn't dreaming there was only one other explanation.

I gathered my senses and composure before I looked back at the man who, by now also seemed less angry, maybe he thought I had a mental problem. I hunched my shoulders and tried to smile at him.

"I haven't been too well lately, and it's left me a bit confused, probably the onset of dementia. I'm sorry if I upset you."

124

"Well, it's all right. But I do think you'd better be on your way I'd see a doctor if I were you."

"There's just one thing you could do for me before I go … You don't happen to have a copy of tonight's Manchester Evening News, do you?"

"What?" The man stared at me for a moment then nodded. He closed the door then came back less than thirty seconds later. He opened the door and thrust the newspaper at me. "Here, you can keep it, now piss off." Before I could respond, he'd closed the door.

I stepped off the porch and turned right. Betty stood quite still and called to me.

"Where are you going?"

"I'm trying to find the key…"

She joined me and we searched for some minutes along the path fronting the house and beneath the thick privet hedge bordering the garden, but could find no trace of the key. I realised there was little chance of finding the key so in the end I gave up.

Beckoning her, I led Betty back to the car. She seemed hesitant when I opened the door for her, but after a long pause, she climbed inside.

I turned on the interior light and started to scan the paper, starting on the back page. I gaped as I stared at the headline. **WOLVES BID £40,000 for MANCHESTER CITY'S DAVID WAGSTAFFE.** Further down the page I saw another headline.

United unchanged for their league match with Sheffield United on Saturday.

I turned some pages and blinked as I read a notice advertising the Christmas pantomime at the

Palace. *Sleeping Beauty - starring Morecambe and Wise.* I was now getting flashbacks of all the strange events of the last few hours, in fact I was shaking when I turned to the front page and stared at the date.

24th December Nineteen Sixty-Four.

*   *   *

]

SIX

Sean looked at me and I stared back at him during a very long awkward silence. His expression was bland at first, and then it changed. He started looking at me with a disturbing intensity, his eyes fixed on mine with a sort of searching gaze - as if he expected me to challenge him. I stayed completely silent and it was he who spoke first.

"I wasn't dreaming. It was a nightmare all right, but don't you see it all added up. I really was there, back in nineteen sixty four."

Sean seemed quite calm and I tried not to show the turmoil going through my head. I didn't want to offend him by saying outright that he was lying. Obviously he did seem to believe what he'd told me, and from experience, I knew that I would have to choose my response carefully or risk having him throw me out. I took a slow breath and smiled at him.

"It certainly did sound like a nightmare."

"Don't patronise me, Andy." He didn't seem angry.

"I wasn't." I lied.

"Oh no?" He stared past me, chewing absently on the corner of his lip. Then after a few seconds he got to his feet. "Right, that's all for now. I have to get ready for tonight."

"I thought you didn't have ...?" I saw his expression and decided it would be better if I left. I put my glass down and went to the door of the living room. "I'll give

127

you a call-"

"No! I'll call you. And when I do, I expect you to be a little more receptive - if you know what I mean."

I nodded silently then made my way to the front door. I paused, hoping that he would call me back. He didn't.

I didn't sleep well that night, and I woke up feeling 'frowzy' and ill-tempered. I felt as if Sean had been leading me along, laughing at me as I hung on his every word like some entranced school kid. Well that was it! Sean could call as often as he liked, I was finished with him. Did he really expect me, a professional journalist to honestly believe that he actually went back in time...It was like something straight out of "The Twilight Zone"

God, I was still annoyed after I'd spooned down a cereal breakfast and washed the bowl and spoon. The idea came to me as I was hanging up the tea-towel. I would challenge Sean, yes that's what I'll do and I look forward to seeing his face when I did.

I spent a disturbing hour in the archive at the Central Library where I was advised to go by the receptionist at the Manchester Evening News. It didn't take much effort to have the archivist point me in the direction of 'The Sixties' microfiches, and it took only a few minutes to find the relevant film covering 'sixty-four'.

I got side-tracked a couple of times when I saw the reports of incidents that, to me, were only history, and I indulged myself for a while. Then I turned to the Christmas Eve issue, and scanned the back page...

128

WOLVES BID £40,000 FOR MANCHESTER CITY'S DAVID WAGSTAFFE.

A few inches below was the headline that Sean had told me he'd seen - that Manchester United were hoping to field an unchanged team for Saturday's game against Sheffield United. It was all there, exactly as he'd said - Morecambe and Wise at the Palace Theatre. *The Unsinkable Molly Brown* at the Playhouse cinema.

For a few minutes I was unsettled, and then I started to think without emotion. Sean must have a good memory - how else could he recall the lyrics of all those songs he sang. So - why couldn't he have done exactly what I was doing? I know he doesn't have a computer so he is not online but he had enough spare time to visit the newspaper offices and collect the information. He certainly had the imagination to weave that information into a weird tale.

I gave myself a mental pat on the back. For a few moments I'd been on the point of swallowing his story. Now I was ready to unmask him for the charlatan he was. I wasn't playing devil's advocate, I was trying to prove him an outright liar and I would be ready for him when he telephoned.

He didn't phone that day, nor the next. In fact when a couple of weeks had gone by, I began to think he realised I'd found him out, and he'd cut his losses and run. I was in the shower that Thursday afternoon when he did telephone me.

I wasn't well pleased when the phone rang, and I was definitely not pleased when I heard Sean's voice.

Before I could say anything, he began.

"Andy just hear me out. I know what you must have been thinking after our last meeting. I swear I never went to the newspaper to check out those details which is going to be your first thought. As God is my witness, everything I told you no matter how unbelievable is the truth … and you've only heard the half of it. Just remember it was you who came to me. Just think about that"

He didn't give me the chance to reply. He hung up.

I've never been able to resist an unfinished 'puzzle'. Even when I was a kid I infuriated my friends with my stubbornness, and I never grew out of it. Either Sean was an exceptional psychologist, or he was lucky. He hit on exactly the right means of stirring my curiosity.

I resisted the urge to call him back straight away, but I did call later that evening. I forgot that evenings were his working time, and all I got was the answer-phone. Having to speak to a machine did nothing to help my mood, and I guess Sean would hear the underlying annoyance in my voice when he got my message, telling him that I would call him the next day.

Sean's answer phone was on all the following morning, and with each unsuccessful attempt to contact him, I grew more angry with him. He did finally answer my call a little after one o'clock.

"Hello, Andy. How are you?"

"I'm as mad as hell, that's how I am!"

"And why's that?" His voice was light, jovial.

"You know damned well why."

"Now, how would I know why you are angry?"

"This isn't getting us anywhere."

Sean laughed out loud. "I'm not going anywhere, anyway. So it must be you that's getting frustrated."

"Yes. I am. Now for God's sake, when can I see you?"

"If you remember, I did say that *I* would call *you* when I was prepared for us to carry on with our 'project'? Now, I don't recall telling you I was ready." There was a long pause, then I heard the clink of ice in a glass. Sean spoke slowly. "I know that you were willing to walk out on me after your last visit. I could see you didn't believe what I'd told you, and wanted to give it all up."

"You're right. I *was* about to call it a day … and I'm still not sure."

There was another long pause before Sean responded. "Well, at least you're being honest. I'll be home tomorrow, you can call round after ten, if you're still interested?"

"I'll be there."

There was an obvious 'atmosphere' when Sean opened the door to me the next morning. I avoided his gaze as he stood resolute in the doorway, then I let out a long sigh and stared into his eyes. "I'm sorry if I upset you, Sean."

He nodded slowly and stepped back, giving me access to the hall. Instead of directing me to the front

131

room in the house, he pointed to the second door along the hall. I went in and he followed me into a large comfortable room furnished with easy chairs, a long settee and picture window that looked out over a non-descript garden.

"Not really into gardening." Sean said as he waved me to the settee. "With a lot of effort and care, I managed to grow - mud. So I gave up." I was only half listening as I looked at the end of a large rectangular paved area where a dilapidated shed stood. He saw me staring at it. "I keep meaning to do something about that, but I'm hoping a strong wind'll solve the problem."

It was small talk, and we both knew it. But it did help to ease the awkwardness that had been present. After a few minutes I relaxed, and so did he.

He sat at an angle to me, on one of the easy chairs, and I occupied another. At first he was stiff and formal, then he slowly sank into the upholstery and I did the same. I took out my recorder and held it out with a questioning expression. He nodded.

"Yes, turn it on. I'm ready." He eyed me carefully then gave me his serious look. "Before we start may I suggest you keep an open mind at least till I have finished and then decide if its truth or fiction. Think about it, if *you* found it hard to believe that I'd gone back to nineteen sixty four - how the hell do you think I felt that night?" It felt like a rhetorical question so I decided to let Sean go on.

Betty, as you can imagine was staring at me with

an uneasy look in her eye, and I was doing my level best to come to grips with reality. I decided it was time to tell her everything, and hope she'd believe me. I hesitated. I guessed she'd think I was really unhinged - probably did already after the confrontation on the doorstep.

Everything that was 'strange' was only strange to me. To her it was normal - apart from my behaviour.

"What is going on, Mister Clarke? I mean, were we at the wrong house?"

I took a chance. "No, Betty, it's the right house - but it's the wrong year."

She stiffened and moved away from me in her seat. "What do you mean?"

I didn't know how to make sense of it to her when I couldn't make sense of it myself. "Do you trust me?" I looked at her with as calm an expression as I could manage.

She nodded shyly.

I tried to maintain my expression. "I wouldn't harm you. You do believe that?"

"I wouldn't be here if I didn't."

"All right. I'll try to explain." I took a deep breath. "Something strange is happening to me, and I can't really understand it."

"You mean, like amnesia?"

"Yes, something like that. I need to think it through. It'll take some time, but I promise I won't upset you."

"I know." She gave me a faint smile as I started the engine.

"Since I can't get in my own home, and we can't spend

all night in the car. I think it would be a good idea if I took us to a hotel. Separate rooms" I added quickly.

"Mister Clarke ..." Betty spoke in a quiet voice as we turned onto Broadway and headed back into Manchester. "Could we stay in the same room, but with separate beds? I don't want to be alone in a strange hotel at Christmas."

I'd been so engrossed with my trouble that I'd forgotten Betty had problems of her own. I grinned at her. "Of course. You won't be alone tonight."

We were both quiet as I drove down Oldham road towards the city centre. Betty seemed to understand that I needed to think - and think I bloody well did.

A million things ran through my head, and none of them made any sense. I've always been a sort of fatalist, and I could only assume that there was a reason behind everything that had happened to me. But why should Christmas eve nineteen sixty four be of any significance?

I mentally went back, trying to pinpoint the moment when all the 'oddities' started to happen. The only incident that I could recall was the weird chilling sensation I'd got when I drove the car away from the garage at New Cross. After that, the fog came, and everything had changed. I'd been 'taken' back in time. But why? For what purpose? Was there something I supposed to do?

We'd almost reached New Cross again when the thought struck me. I remembered the nightmare I'd had on the plane, and I suddenly realised the significance of the date. Christmas Eve nineteen sixty four was the night Peter and Thomas Boswell took a child, Sharon Beckett onto the Moors above Manchester to kill her.

Oh God, I thought. It's tonight. They're going to kill her tonight, and I've got to get onto the Moors to save that little girl. That's why I'm here.

First I had to contend with an immediate problem. Namely, I didn't have any money, and the credit cards in my pocket - to quote the police sergeant - weren't even in date. Most hotels wanted a deposit or a 'credit card swiping' before … Then, a sudden thought hit me. This was nineteen sixty four, and things were different, less severe.

I decided to try a 'better class' of hotel where, if I was lucky, there would be less trouble getting a room. The suit I was wearing was non-crease, and though I'd been wearing my shirt and tie for almost twenty hours, they were still quite presentable. Betty's coat was a little dull, but her dress and her general appearance was enough for her not to seem out of place.

I decided on the Portland Hotel, so I continued down Oldham Road then took a left along Piccadilly before turning right at the lights at the top of Portland Street. There were a few cars parked beside the hotel and I was easily able to find a decent space. Betty looked up at the façade and gave me a nervous smile.

"I've never been to anywhere as grand as this."

"Don't let it worry you. It's just a glorified 'boarding house' when all's said and done." I got out of the car and went to the rear. Betty stood on the pavement and watched as I took out one of my suitcases and a small holdall. She frowned at me when, after locking up the car, I carried the luggage to her. "It'd look a bit odd if we just arrived without any luggage."

"Oh, yeah. They might think we'd come for something naughty." She smiled at me as I handed her the holdall.

The receptionist was a jaded man of about my age. His uniform, however, was smart and his manner was attentive as I asked for a room.

"How long are you likely to be with us, sir?" His glanced strayed to Betty who was standing close to me.

"We thought we might stay over the holiday period, but we haven't decided yet."

"And how will you be paying, sir?"

I took out my cheque book, mentally crossing my fingers as I smiled calmly at him. He glanced at the cheque book and returned my smile.

"That will be fine, sir. You can pay on your departure." I returned the book to my pocket with a faint sigh of relief.

"Room one one four, on the first floor. I'll call for a porter."

"Thanks, but we can manage." I took the key from him and started to walk away. I saw the quick wink he gave me and the suggestive glance he gave Betty. Oblivious of his stare, she was gazing around with a look of delight on her face.

"I hope you have a pleasant stay with us." The receptionist grinned.

I did a quick tour while Betty flung off her coat and began to bounce on one of the beds. The room was

136

reasonably large with cream-painted walls. It was fitted out with two single beds, an adequate dressing table a small table holding a telephone. On one wall there was a small mahogany wardrobe and in the corner beyond it stood a chair covered with some pink fabric. In the adjoining bathroom there was a decent sink, a small medicine cabinet and a toilet.

I unzipped the holdall that Betty had flung on the second bed. She ignored me, seemingly enjoying the experience of being wrapped in a soft warm duvet that she'd curled around her shoulders as she sat watching me. I took out a small bottle and slipped it into my pocket without her seeing.

"I don't know about you, but the sandwich at the police station wasn't enough. I'm going to order a snack and a drink. Would you like something?"

"Can I have a Babycham, and a ham sandwich?"

"It'd be better if you had a soft drink."

Betty pouted. "All right. I'll have an orange."

I took up the phone and called reception who put me through to the kitchen where I placed an order for some sandwiches and drinks. I looked at my watch and saw that it was almost nine thirty. Time was getting short.

The snacks and drinks arrived after about ten minutes, and I suggested that Betty wash her hands before we ate. It was a dirty trick, but I had to make sure she didn't see me. I took the small bottle from my pocket and unscrewed the cap. The tablets were tiny but, from experience, I knew they were fast and effective. Paddy Flynn had given them to me when I'd complained that I

137

found it impossible to sleep during the early part of the cruise.

I dropped a couple into the glass of orange, and swirled it around, squashing the tablets against the glass until I was satisfied they had dissolved. I placed the drink back on the tray only a moment before Betty returned from the bathroom.

The tablets worked far more quickly than I expected. After drinking less than half the orange, Betty started to show signs of tiredness. Her eyes glazed and her eyelids drooped, and a silly grin played on her face. She collapsed slowly as she sat on her bed, folding over and sinking onto the duvet.

I took the glass from her hand and went to the bathroom where I washed it thoroughly. Then I carefully laid Betty out on the duvet and wrapped it around her. I went to the door and looked back at her. I couldn't help but stare at her youthful face, her complexion was flawless but it was marred by a number of deep 'worry-creases' extending across her forehead. I hoped she would enjoy a deep and peaceful sleep as I gingerly opened the door and walked out into the corridor.

I was already aware of the schedule taken by the Boswell brothers. According to the account by Jeff Sommers in his book, which I had read more than once I prayed that it was accurate as it was all I had to go on. The brothers had stayed in the *Ship Inn in* Wythenshawe, drinking until closing time before beginning their dreadful deed.

I glanced at my watch and saw that it was

almost ten as I drove up Princess Parkway. I shivered as again I felt an unexplained cold wind that seemed to swirl around the inside of the car ... I glanced in the rear-view mirror but the car was empty, even though I had the weird sensation that I was not alone.

Again relying on Summers' version of events, I parked outside the Ship Inn to wait. Within a quarter of an hour the brothers appeared in the doorway. I watched them go over to a blue Ford Anglia and I followed them at a distance as they drove away.

I don't know how I lost them, but I did. Maybe I was distracted by another cold blast that filled the car not long after I left The Ship, or maybe I was getting tired. The end result was that I was cruising the streets of Wythenshawe trying to find the Boswell's house on Witton Street. Time was moving on, and I knew that if I couldn't catch them at their home, I'd have to meet them on the Moors.

I gave up trying to find their house, and turned back towards The Ship, then headed for Princess Parkway. I drove slowly, hoping to catch a glimpse of their blue Anglia as I headed northwards. I didn't.

After passing through Oldham and heading out north-eastwards towards the Moors, I slowed down and pulled into a lay-by. I left the engine running as I tried to recall the location that Sommers had described in his book. Taken from the direct confession of the brothers, it pinpointed the site where the murder would have taking place - if I failed to prevent it.

Then I remembered the dream I'd had on the plane. I could see the road over the Moor and I pondered for some time before I managed to recall the exact spot where Sommers stated the brothers had chosen to park. I turned onto the road and put my foot down.

I parked the car and turned out the lights. The night was dark, but a thin moon cast a pale light over the moorland. Dark clouds were scudding past and casting deep fleeting shadows over the landscape as I stepped onto the road.

I headed diagonally away from the car and the road, until I saw the approaching headlights dipping and rising as they followed the course of the road. I strode forward purposefully, heading for a low crest, beyond which I knew there was a deep ditch.

I saw their car stop, and as in the dream, I saw three figures get out. I was making my way to the crest of the rise when two of the figures came towards me. I waited until I heard the sickening sound of a spade breaking the turf, then I stepped forward and upward to stand on the edge of the small gully.

Below me, Tom Boswell had almost finished the shallow grave. Sharon, the small girl was lying shivering on the ground her hands and feet bound. Boswell might have had a gun, he most certainly did have a knife. I didn't think of any possible harm to myself as I became filled with an electrifying red-mist of anger.

"Boswell!" I almost screamed at the man. "Leave the child alone! Leave her be! I command you to take Sharon home now and I will be watching until she is

140

free. DO IT NOW!" I shouted.

Boswell looked terrified. I suppose I must have presented a disturbing picture appearing suddenly out of the night and bellowing at him like a biblical maniac. I'm quite tall, around six one, and standing on top of the gully I must have looked like a giant to him. The wind had risen and was tugging at my coat and thrusting my hair out from my head, making me appear even more startling coming from out of nowhere. I must have scared the life out of him.

Boswell dropped the spade then scrabbled on the ground to pick it up. He stuck it into the soft soil then bent down to unfasten the girl's bonds. Tucking the shovel under one arm, he grabbed the girl's arm and hauled her to her feet. He didn't look back as he scurried back to the car, dragging young Sharon behind him.

I saw the brothers arguing briefly as Tom repeatedly pointed in my direction. Then all three figures disappeared into the Anglia and the engine started. The tyres squealed as the car did a panic U-turn and accelerated down the road.

I walked back to my car, trusting that everything would be all right, and hoping that the brothers would release young Sharon safely. I hoped with all my heart that she would eventually get home, and grow up with no memory of this terrible night. A night where I felt my part in this nightmare had been played.

As I climbed into the car I began to wonder how it was possible that those two demons were able to get that young girl to go with them. Of course I know now that Sharon was the daughter of Sheila Beckett, Tom

Boswell's girlfriend and unfortunately even demons at times can seem like ordinary people.

The two men had been constant visitors to Sheila's flat, and the young Sharon had obviously regarded them as her mother's friends and would have trusted them. Sheila was an alcoholic, and on that night she was indulging her addiction and Sharon was at home alone. The Boswells had lightly drugged the girl before carrying her off.

When they got back from the Moors the Boswells had taken Sharon home where Sheila was slumped in a chair in a drunken coma. They sent the girl to bed, telling her she just had a bad dream and then they left.

The following morning, Sharon told her mother what had happened, and Sheila hadn't believed the girl's story and gave her a good hiding for telling lies, and for being out late at night. It was many years before the terrible truth was to come to light, mainly due to Jeff Sommers book "Brothers in harm"

I started the car and began to drive back towards Oldham. As I stared into the darkness, a sudden thought came to me. I realised that, having already saved one child, I might be able to rescue another. I knew that Janet Anderson was killed on the night of the twenty ninth of December. Perhaps it would be better if I went to the police and told them. Told them what? That I'd come back from nineteen ninety four to unmask the Manchester Murderers?

The more I thought of it as I drove southwards from the moor, the more I realised that I had little chance of convincing the police. I couldn't even show them a current driving licence. I'd need to give the matter some serious thought.

I arrived back in Portland Street sometime after two o'clock in the morning. The streets were quiet and the pavements deserted as I made my way into the hotel. The night porter was reading a novel as he sat behind the reception desk, and he raised his head to stare at me. I satisfied his curiosity when I took the room key from my pocket and gave it a jaunty twirl around my finger as I headed for the stairs. He ignored me, and went back to his novel.

Betty was fast asleep when I crept into the room. She was still lying on top of the duvet which I'd wrapped around her, and she didn't stir as I turned on the bedside lamp. I looked down at her, and felt a surge of gentle concern for the girl. Now she was in a deep sleep her face was calm and peaceful. The lines had gone from her forehead and she radiated an aura of contentment.

I couldn't help myself. I leaned over her and gently kissed her cheek then smoothed a stray hair from her brow. I decided that tomorrow, I would try to sort out her problems. I glanced at my watch then realised it was Christmas day. I silently wished her a happy Christmas then I went to the bathroom.

Like Betty, I lay on top of the duvet on the other bed, after I'd turned out the bedside lamp. I was tired, a leaden tiredness that dragged at my limbs and made them seem alien and unresponsive. In the faint light, I turned my head and looked at Betty's supine form. I wished I could have slept the innocent sleep she was enjoying, but I couldn't.

My eyes burned, as if they were filled with sand, my arms and legs ached for sleep, but sleep just wouldn't come. I peered at my watch and saw that it was nearly a quarter past three. I gave a mental groan. I was exhausted and I needed to sleep; but the more I worried about it the less sleepy I felt.

I climbed off the bed and went quietly to the bathroom where I filled a tumbler and drank a half glass of water. When I returned to bed I lay down and stared at the faint shadow of the window pane, cast on the wall to my right. I made patterns, I counted sheep, I even tried something Marianne had mentioned years ago.

I lay quite still, and I concentrated on my toes, willing them to relax. Then I focused on my ankles … then my calves, and so on. By the time I got to my stomach I came to the conclusion that it wasn't going to work. I was even more tired than before, but I just wasn't sleepy. Then I started to recall every song I'd ever sung and tried to remember each hall and club that I'd played.

My watch told me it was almost four o'clock, and I saw that it was getting light, or at least that's what I thought. I gave a shiver and for an instant the hairs stood up on the back of my neck. Then I shrugged and realised that the light must be coming from the corridor outside. I raised my head to look at the gap between the door and the carpet. There was no appreciable gap, and there was no light.

I rubbed my eyes and closed them, waiting until the hairs on my neck had laid down, then I opened my eyes. There *was* a light. It was faint, almost non-existent, but the area between the end of my bed and the door was not as dark as before. It appeared as if a very faint mist was hanging in the air beyond the end of my bed.

The hairs on my neck rose again as the mist started to gather together, coalescing into a tiny sharp point of brilliance. That was when I felt the chill. My whole body shivered and the air around me felt like ice, as the tiny pinpoint began to grow. I forced myself to look across to where Betty lay. She was still sleeping, oblivious to the 'thing' that was growing less than a couple of feet from her.

My mouth became dry and I could hear my heart pumping madly in my chest as I watched the light grow stronger and larger. It became a nebulous shape, narrow at the base and elongating until it was almost four feet high. All the time this was happening the cold became more intense until I could see my breath steaming before my face.

I don't know how long I sat on the bed, huddled inside the duvet watching in awed terror as the mist slowly took on a recognisable shape. But when I was finally able to discern the features of the apparition that stood before me, my mouth fell open.

All traces of fear faded, leaving me with a sense of wonder. I was staring at a small boy who stood smiling at me. I recognised him instantly. It was the boy whose picture I'd seen at the police station. Brian Thompson. I took a deep breath and spoke.

145

"What do you want, Brian?"

He looked back at me with the saddest eyes I'd ever seen. He still smiled at me as he replied, "Thank you. Thank you for saving Sharon." He blinked, "I didn't like dying, and she wouldn't have liked it either. Please pray for me." He drifted slowly away towards the door, diminishing as he went until he was no more than a minute speck of light which flickered then went out.

"No! Wait! Don't ... go." I called out. I closed my eyes and shook my head in disbelief. I waited for several seconds before I tentatively opened them again. The room was totally dark, so dark that I couldn't see a thing. I groped to my side, found the bedside lamp and turned it on. What I saw then gave me a shock as physical as being punched in the face.

There was a TV set standing where the small chair had been. The wardrobe was larger and a completely different coloured wood and the walls were covered with patterned wallpaper. I couldn't contain myself. I spun round quickly, calling out to Betty. "Oh my God, Betty. Would you look at ..." The words choked in my throat when I found myself staring at an empty bed.

I stood up and went to the second bed. It was neat and clean, and unused.

It didn't take me long to realise that I was no longer in nineteen sixty four, and not much longer to appreciate that I was in a predicament. I had not checked in at the hotel, and I was here 'illegally'. My only instinct was to get the hell out of there as quickly as I could.

My first idea was to grab my luggage and climb

146

down the fire-escape, but I dismissed it as being impractical and downright silly. I pondered for a few minutes then I came up with the idea of calling a porter, having him take my luggage down to the car, then following him a few minutes later. I rejected that idea too. I could imagine the porter with my luggage wouldn't attract the attention of the head night porter on duty in reception, but I would surely be noticed if I traipsed out only shortly afterwards?

When the solution came to me I analysed it for flaws, and came to the conclusion it was my best bet. I left the room and went up to the third floor to check the room numbers, and to note that at least a couple of rooms had a pair of men's and a pair of women's shoes put out to be cleaned. I picked one of the room numbers at random then went back to my own room to collect my luggage.

The head porter was sitting behind the reception desk when I came down the stairs into the foyer. He was reading, but he looked up at me before I'd got halfway across the foyer. I smiled calmly and nodded to him.

"I wonder if you would mind getting someone to help my wife down with the rest of our luggage. It's quite heavy and I'd rather not carry it myself."

"Er ... Certainly sir. What room are you in?"

"Three oh six. Third floor. There is a bit of a rush - we're taking an early flight to Paris and we have to be at the airport before seven thirty." I put down my bags and went to the desk. Taking out my wallet I removed a ten pound note and handed it to him. "For your trouble."

"Oh, thank you very much sir."

"Merry Christmas to you." I called out to him as I picked up my luggage and headed for the door.

"And to you, sir. I'll have the rest of your luggage brought down as soon as possible."

"Thank you." I called cheerily.

It was still dark when I got to the pavement, and I didn't hurry. But I certainly didn't loiter once I was out of the hotel. I stowed my suitcase and holdall in the back of the Mini-Traveller and got into the driving seat. The interior was well-worn and dirty but, to me right then, it could have been a Rolls Royce. The engine started at once, and within a minute I'd driven down Portland Street, turned into Chinatown, looped around to York Street and was at Piccadilly square heading for home. Having negotiated New Cross and heading north up Oldham road, I glanced to my left as I passed the garage where I'd collected the Traveller. I smiled to myself a few minutes later when I saw the crumbling façade of the Playhouse on my left.

The road was quite empty and I saw only a few other cars and a couple of vans before I reached Broadway. Bathurst road was deserted, as was Sefton Avenue. I slowed to a halt outside my house and let out a great sigh of relief. My head was starting to throb, and my eyes were smarting and beginning to water.

I unloaded all my luggage and carried it up the path, planting it beside the doorstep before I went to open the door. I fumbled in my pocket and came out with a boiled sweet, a handful of small change, and a small dark button. No key. I lifted my head and stared at the front door. In an instant a picture flashed through

148

my mind, a picture of a thick-set angry man knocking a key from my hand. By now the lines between dreams and reality were becoming blurred, but the fact was I had no key.

All I could think of was getting inside and throwing myself into bed. I was having trouble staying upright, and was swaying about as if I was drunk. I thought everything would be fine after a good night's sleep.

I went back to the front door and retrieved our spare key from inside a cunningly designed stone set at the corner of the lawn. We'd bought the stone so we could leave the key outside in case the kids ever lost theirs. Up 'til then I was the only person to have used it.

It took me less than ten minutes to get all my stuff into the house, where I dumped it all in the room at the front. I staggered upstairs and into the bedroom, scattered most of my clothes on the floor, then dived beneath the duvet. I was asleep within five minutes.

*   *   *

SEVEN

I woke up at around five o'clock on Boxing Day morning, having slept for a good eighteen hours. I didn't feel refreshed. On the contrary, I felt awful. My head was really throbbing and I felt queasy. To cap it all I'd just had the most bizarre dream I could remember...

It began simply enough. I was on the *Pacific Princess* and I was dancing, or trying to dance. Marianne was my partner and she was complaining that I kept kicking her and standing on her toes. After one particular 'bad move' she stopped and glared at me. She warned me that if I did it again, she'd leave me and never take me back again. Less than five steps later, I really crunched her foot.

Within seconds I was driving a young girl onto the Moors and she was telling me about her step-father and his brother who spent their spare time killing children. The girl seemed familiar, but I couldn't place her.

Then I was performing at the Portland hotel, standing on a small stage in front of a crowd of party-goers. Halfway through one of my numbers, a young girl climbed onto the stage beside me and started tugging at my arm. She pulled at my arm until she could whisper in my ear. Unfortunately the microphone picked up everything she said, and the whole crowd started cheering and yelling obscene comments as they heard her tell me she was 'Betty' - whoever that was, and she wanted to spend the night with me in one of the rooms upstairs.

I was then driving a Rolls Royce through the centre of Manchester with Michele and Jason in the rear seat. They were leaning out of the window and shouting at the people walking along the pavement. I remember feeling embarrassed when I heard them saying I'd been deserted by their mother, and that I'd responded by stealing an old car and breaking into one of the larger hotels in the centre of town. Michele in particular, kept calling out for someone to get the police and have me arrested. I came to a halt and turned round in the seat, ready to give Michele a good telling-off. It wasn't Michele and Jason who were sitting behind me, but Nurse O'Malley, from Belfast. She shook her head at me and made a tutting sound.

"My goodness! You have been a very naughty boy, haven't you?"

"Hold on Sean can we stop there!" I called out, and I must have made him jump as he looked at me with a startled expression.

"What's the matter, Andy?"

"You've already explained how you managed to remember a lot of *incidents* clearly - but those dreams ..." I shook my head. "I know some people are supposed to have almost photographic memories as far as dreams are concerned - but to recall them with so much detail after that length of time takes some believing, especially as they are such a jumble."

Sean smiled and shook his head slowly. He fixed his gaze on me and I saw a mild sadness in his eyes. "I thought we'd finished with all that and you would let me finish my story before you started a steward's enquiry?"

I hunched my shoulders. "I'm only saying what others would say."

"But you aren't *others*. I thought we understood each other?"

"For Christ's sake, Sean, I'm a journalist, I've got to show some objectivity. I can't help being sceptical. It's my nature."

Sean pursed his lips and regarded me silently for several seconds before he spoke again. "All right. I'll tell you how I'm able to remember those dreams. *Firstly*, they scared the hell out of me. When something like that happens it leaves such a deep impression that you can't forget - even if you wanted to. *Secondly*, I've been through those dreams a hundred times since ninety four, both consciously, and when I'm asleep. *Thirdly*, I was asked to write them down."

"What?!"

"When you suggested writing the whole thing down, it wasn't the first time I'd received that advice. But only about those dreams it was part of my therapy."

"You never said anything to me at the time I suggested it."

"I didn't know you well enough then." Sean gave me a patronising smile. "Anyway, you'd have heard about it eventually, if you'd been patient. Now, is it all right if I carry on hoping you've got the point that my dreams where a complete jumble of real people in mixed up situations- or do you have any other questions?"

I felt chided. "Sorry. Carry on."

"Thank you." Sean settled back in his chair and avoided my gaze as he started again.

It was five o'clock on Boxing Day morning, black as Hades outside, and I felt like death warmed up. I stumbled out of bed and after finishing in the bathroom I dressed and went downstairs. My head felt as if I had a hundred line-dancers inside trying to stamp out my brain, and I thought that if I had a meal and a hot drink, they'd go away.

The hot drink was fine; I was good at boiling a kettle - but the meal was a different matter. I'd spent all of my adult life eating meals that were prepared for me. Apart from making an occasional sandwich, I had never cooked a thing. So, my first instinct was to make a sandwich which proved difficult when I opened the bread-bin to discover - like Old Mother Hubbard - that it was empty.

I sat down to eat, rather proud of myself as I surveyed the feast before me - a plate of beans and sausages (from a tin, and heated in the microwave), a slice of stale almond cake, and a cup of coffee. Hardly Keith Floyd.

Still the meal did appease my hunger, even if it didn't do a thing for my headache. If anything, it was worse than when I got up. I'm not a person who takes drugs - not unless it's absolutely necessary, but I did resort to the medicine cabinet where I found a packet of Aspirin. Two hours later I did start to feel a little better and I decided to unpack my luggage.

My guitars and my tuxedo were no problem, but I did start to have a mild panic when I realised that I would be forced to wash my 'day-clothes', and all my underwear. I did think of leaving them until Marianne got back, but I guessed it would not help our fragile relationship if I greeted her with a pile of dirty washing.

I felt quite pleased with myself after I'd loaded the washing machine and succeeded in starting it. Thinking to myself, 'what's the big deal about operating a washing machine?'

I retired to the lounge and treated myself to a drink - to toast my newly acquired 'home-skills'. I slumped into an easy chair, and I relaxed. Pretty soon I was feeling not too bad, and well satisfied with myself.

The return of my headache coincided with the moment I opened the washing machine and took out a medium-sized soggy pink mountain of clothes. . The rest of the pile - shirts, socks, and underwear had come out in varying degrees of colour, shade, and shape. Some were larger than I remembered, and some were definitely smaller. Some were almost unrecognisable as the items I'd loaded.

Undeterred, I transferred the pile to the tumble dryer and punched a few buttons on the front. Satisfied once the machine began to rumble, I went to the fridge where I found some ice, wrapped it in a handkerchief. I tottered into the lounge holding the ice-pack to my head then I flopped into the easy chair.

By half-past ten I decided that something wasn't right. I felt more than just queasy, I felt diabolical. It was

155

as if I'd been riding a bucking bronco on the deck of a trawler in the middle of a North Sea gale. I thought it would be a good idea to call the doctor. Perhaps I should have taken the American woman's advice and had someone examine my head at the airport as concussion might explain the disorientation I was experiencing.

The regular doctor wasn't working, (I'd forgotten what day it was) but a pre-recorded voice gave me the number of a locum to be contacted 'in the event of an emergency'. I dialled the number and after a short wait, spoke to a woman. She grilled me about my condition, and after checking that I wasn't just drunk, said I could drive to somewhere in Blackley. I argued that, in my present condition I could hardly negotiate our garden path let alone drive to the address she'd given me. She agreed that the doctor would come to me, and that he would be about a half hour.

I slumped into the chair and held the ice-pack to my head, as my 'breakfast' kept threatening to disgorge itself over my shoes.

Twenty five minutes later, the doctor did arrive. He was an Asian, and dressed in an immaculate suit. He was polite and attentive as I described my symptoms; and after he examined me, paying particular attention to my eyes and the lump on my forehead, he declared as I suspected that I probably had a mild concussion.

He advised me that I should go to hospital, and telephoned Crumpsall hospital, or North Manchester as its now called, while I looked on. Then he said he didn't think he could organize an ambulance, and it would be unwise for me to attempt to drive.

I contacted our local taxi company and was told that a car would call for me within the next half hour. It was late, but I didn't care as I climbed into the cab.

The driver must have been annoyed with me, for calling him out, or he had a vendetta against passengers in general. He found every pot-hole and every piece of uneven road between Sefton Avenue and the hospital. I repaid him in kind by giving him a five pence tip.

 "Hope you're going in there to die!" he shouted as he drove off.

The doctor at Crumpsall confirmed what the locum had suspected. I was diagnosed as having concussion, and I was admitted to a ward before two o'clock. I stayed there for just over twenty hours, and had another nightmare dream similar to the one I'd had on Christmas night. I woke up shouting, disturbing the other patients and attracting the attention of the night nurse.

The following morning, I had a visit from a clinical psychologist. We had a long talk, during which she asked me to describe my bad dreams and she gave me a list of reasons for them. Linking my rocky relationship with Marianne and the disastrous departure from the Cruise ship were enough to trigger some bizarre 'incidents'. As for my trip back to nineteen sixty four, she could only guess that, since I'd been very ill in Belfast, I'd associated all my current problems with my past illness. She also said that perhaps the plot from a book I might have read could also intermingle with real events thus creating more mental confusion and I had to

157

admit her theory made sense. Finally she suggested that I write down what I remembered each time I woke up after the nightmares.

"Satisfied *now*, Andy?"

I ignored the remark and let him carry on.

I stayed at Crumpsall something like twenty hours. I got back home a little after eleven o'clock on the twenty seventh, feeling like the man who missed Christmas.

Marianne and the kids would be back in just less than a fortnight. God! I'd have to look after myself for twelve whole days. The prospect was a sobering one, so I bolstered my confidence with a couple of drinks before I started to organize myself. It was while I was in the process of mentally working out some kind of domestic routine, that I remembered what I'd been doing before I went to Crumpsall.

The washing was dry, and that's about all that could be said for it. I felt a deepening despair as I examined the articles I dragged out of the dryer. I held out a pair of once-comfortable underpants and mused that the only thing they would fit now would be one of Michele's old Teddy-bears. I wondered if Bobby the bear would appreciate having a pair of purple-pink shorts.

I did eventually get myself into some sort of a routine, both with the housework, and with the dreams. I managed to boil an egg, grill bacon properly, and cook one or two simple meals. I even taught myself to iron, though not very well. With the paucity of provisions I was forced to go shopping, which was a bit of a hilarious adventure, and a tale in itself.

I took the mini-traveller back to the garage at

New-Cross a couple of days into the New Year, and was delighted to find that my own car was ready. I thanked Charlie, and promised to let him know when I was next doing a 'show' locally.

The dreams came less and less frequently, and the night before Marianne and the kids were due to come back, I slept soundly, like a baby. I was now convinced that all the weird things that had happened to me were brought on by the concussion an explanation which makes a lot more sense than time travel. So I hadn't 'gone back' to nineteen sixty four, and I certainly hadn't taken a young girl to the Portland hotel. Real as it seemed, it was all just a dream like the others I'd been having, and now I was cured I felt ready to tackle anything. 'Be positive', I thought.

I had no idea what time Marianne and the kids would be home, but I thought that, as a surprise, I would make some sort of meal for them. I didn't choose anything too difficult, but I peeled some potatoes and had the chips ready to cook and eggs in a bowl beside the cooker. I'd boiled the water ready for the poached eggs, and I'd prepared the tea, needing only to put boiling water into the teapot, and then pour it into the cups. The dining table looked good with a clean table-cloth that I'd washed and ironed; and I'd laid out heat-proof mats and all the cutlery in readiness. I really did feel pleased with myself.

I ate some egg and chips alone, at half-past one. I cleared the table and washed the plate and cutlery then flung the remainder of the uncooked chips in the bin. I retired to the lounge where I poured myself a large Brandy and sipped it slowly as I sat in an easy chair and brooded. Then I thought, 'typical of me, no one asked me to prepare dinner and why would they even think that I would? So why am I getting annoyed?'

When I'd risen that morning, I'd been filled with a kind of anxious excitement. Not sure if excitement is the right word maybe trepidation would be more applicable. I was looking forward to seeing Marianne and the kids again, but I was also dreading the meeting. I wanted to ... No, I didn't know what I wanted... Well, yes I did. I wanted things to be as they were before I'd heard about the work in America, but not exactly. I wanted things to be as I thought they were before she'd told me she was going away to Switzerland with the kids. ...Even that wasn't precisely what I wanted.

I knew I'd been a dreamer. I suppose I still had a romantic hope that, once Marianne came home, and could see that, to an extent, I was becoming domesticated, she would realise that I'd changed. As the Michael McDonald song goes, 'What a fool believes'.

I'd finished the Brandy, so I refilled my glass and sat down again. Some of the despondency began to fade as I drank the Brandy, and by the time I'd finished my fifth, I wasn't upset. I was angry!

Marianne knew I would be at home. The least she could have done was to have telephoned to let me know what time they'd be coming. That was just like her - concerned only for herself and never giving a single thought to how I felt. Well if that was how she wanted it, all right. I'd show her that two could play at that game.

I got up and wobbled a bit as I went to the hallway to get my coat, ready to take the cowards way out and go to the pub. I wasn't drunk, but I was a little unsteady on my feet. I went to the coat-rack and fumbled in my coat pocket for the house keys, dropped them, and staggered as I bent down to retrieve them. I lost my balance and sort of rolled onto the floor. I was in the process of getting up when the front door opened…

My anger had gone. It's difficult to be annoyed when you're discovered crawling aimlessly around on the floor. Trying to maintain some remnants of my dignity, I'd kept quiet while Marianne and the kids pretended there was nothing wrong as they walked past me, Marianne going into the lounge, and the kids disappearing upstairs.

The atmosphere was so thick you couldn't have cut it with a finely honed razor. I sat in the easy chair and Marianne half-faced me from a position at the far end of the settee. She said Michele and Jason had gone upstairs so we 'could talk'. So far neither of us had said a word.

Finally Marianne focused her gaze on me. I couldn't read her expression, but the look in her eyes didn't give me much confidence.

"We can't go on like this, Sean. And you've made it pretty clear that you don't give a monkey's for me, or the children."

"What makes you say that?" My anger was starting to rise again.

"Are you joking, or has your memory suddenly deserted you? How do you think we felt when we

161

walked through the door and found you sprawling on the floor like some legless old wino?"

"I fell, and I was trying to get up. That's all."

"You were, and still are, pie-eyed."

"What do you expect? I'd got everything ready for a family lunch, and you don't show up 'til almost tea-time. All right, I did have a couple of drinks, but I was upset. You could have let me know what time you were coming…"

"I did."

".. Instead of just turning up like that.." I blinked slowly, and then stared at her. She was looking at me with one of her 'cool' confident expressions. I shook my head. "I may have missed something, but I don't recall you telephoning me at all today."

"That's right." Marianne replied calmly. "I left a message on the answer-phone last night. Check it if you don't believe me."

"Oh." I hadn't even thought of listening to the answer-phone. Deflated, I hunched my shoulders. "Sorry."

She gave me a conciliatory half-smile without losing the coolness in her expression. It was then that I remembered something odd. I frowned at her.

"I didn't notice you bringing any luggage - are you getting it later, or something?"

"We left it all at Philip's."

That one short sentence left me feeling as if I'd just been hit by a Jumbo-Jet. It said more in a second than I could assimilate. I just stared at her while I went through all the implications. Not one of them was palatable. Marianne sat quietly and watched me go

162

through my mental analysis of what she'd told me. Her face remained quite passive, while mine must have gone through a dozen different expressions. After some moments, I couldn't help letting out a heavy sigh.

"When you said you were going away for Christmas, I was afraid you'd found somebody else; but I didn't think it was quite this … serious."

For the first time, Marianne showed a vague hint of sympathy. Her voice too was gentle. "I can see you're upset. We can talk about it later, if you want?"

"Would it make any difference? I mean, you're going to leave me, aren't you? No matter what I say."

She didn't answer, but blinked quickly then looked away for a second before facing me. "What you say won't make a difference to what I'm going to do. But it will make a difference to how we get on afterwards. We could have a stand-up flaming row, and I'd storm out and never speak to you again, except through a lawyer. Or we could try to act like civilised people, and work out what we're going to do."

It sounded so simple, the way she put it; so logical and 'correct'. If I disagreed, I thought, she would accuse me of being unfeeling and unreasonable. Yet, here she was, telling me that the last ten years was going to be wiped out in the bat of an eyelid. Even though I had, sort of, expected this conversation, it had come too soon for me. I wasn't prepared, and as Marianne had said, I was still a little 'unfocused' because of the drink. The one time in my life when I needed my wits about me and I blew it big time.

I didn't want to say anything I'd regret later, so I

163

thought carefully before I spoke. "Marianne, I don't want you to leave - but I can see that you've made up your mind." I looked straight at her. "Would it make any difference if I told you that I've already started to change?"

Her lips were closed tightly, and she inhaled noisily through her nose before she let out a heavy sigh. "I know you. I know what you're like." She shook her head. "It just won't work."

"I've already taught myself to cook. I'll admit, it isn't *cordon bleu*, but it's getting better. I can even wash, and iron without making too much of a mess." God, I was starting to sound pathetic. "You should have seen the things I took out of the dryer the day I got back from hospital."

"You've been to hospital?" Marianne did show some concern. "What was the matter?"

"Oh. I had a mild concussion - banged my head on the luggage compartment when I was flying back from America. Nothing to worry about. I'm fine now." I looked at her steadily, I'm even drinking less … though I'll admit, I have had a few this afternoon. But that was because-"

"I know, Sean." She almost smiled at me. Then her smile faded. "You were right when you said I'd made up my mind to leave you. It wasn't a spur-of-the-moment decision, and I brooded over it for a long time. I spent more than a few sleepless nights worrying about it." She exhaled and looked at me with a sad smile. "I'd more or less come to a decision before you left to go to America." She gave another deep sigh as she stared at

164

me. "There isn't anything you can say or do, that will make me change my mind."

I gave her a glum grimace. "Then there doesn't seem to be much point in our talking, since you've already …"

"It isn't as simple as that. We don't just have to think about ourselves. We have to consider Michele and Jason. They haven't had a full-time father for as long as they can remember, and I think it's about time they did."

I tried to get my brain around the implications of what she had just said.

"Hold on! Don't you think it should be up to them to make a decision?"

"They've already decided. They're upstairs packing some of their clothes right now."

I was totally stunned. I could accept that Marianne had reached a point where she wanted someone else - but what could have made Michele and Jason feel the same way? I instinctively thought that Marianne had been 'working on them' during their holiday; then I dismissed the idea. Whatever else she might do, I would never believe that she would have tried to influence them. That left me with only one conclusion. They, like Marianne, didn't want to stay with me.

I gave a low sigh, and turned to her. I could see that Marianne wasn't gloating. In fact, she did look quite sorry, in a strange kind of way.

"Like I said earlier," Marianne said after a long silence, "I did call you to tell you that we were just going to drop in while the children collected some of their things."

165

"How are you going to carry them? I mean, will you want a taxi, or something?"

"No. Philip's waiting for us. He brought us here, and he's parked around the corner, on Bathurst road."

A sudden and harshly sarcastic thought came to me, and I nearly suggested she call him in so we could have a 'going away party'. I held my tongue. I knew at that moment, if I'd have come within fifty yards of the man, I'd have taken a swing at him. But I also knew that if I had said what I thought, the situation would have gone really sour on me. Maybe a few years ago I would definitely have stormed outside and started punching at the man; but now I was less volatile. Don't get me wrong, I was still angry, but I had the sense to realise that fighting with *Philip*, God I even hated saying his name, would have given Marianne even further ammunition to use against me. So I spoke as calmly as I could.

"Will there be room in his car for all the kids' things?"

"Plenty. It's a big car, with a lot of space."

"I would have thought they might, at least, have wanted to speak to me about going with you."

"I did try to get them to do that, but they both said they couldn't see the point, since you hardly ever spoke to them anyway."

My spirits sank even lower, but I was determined not to start feeling sorry for myself. I remembered what Paddy Flynn had said to me in Los Angeles; I had brought about the situation and I had to accept the consequences. Paying the piper can be a bitter hard thing to do.

I heard sounds coming from upstairs, voices and the occasional thump of something heavy being dropped on the floor. In the past, whenever that had happened, I'd shouted up to them to keep quiet; now I was hanging on to each sound, knowing it might be the last time I would ... I checked myself. I was starting to get morbid.

"Right." I forced a smile. "What do you have planned out?"

Marianne shrugged. "I haven't looked much further than today. I thought I might leave things for a couple of weeks, then ..."

"No. I think we should sort it out right now."

She gave another shrug. "All right, if that's the way you want it. Philip has said that we won't need you for anything. He's quite well-off and he's prepared to look after Michele and Jason without any contribution from you."

"Hey! Just a minute. They're my kids for God's sake, and I want to have something to say about their future. I'm not going to hand them over like some out-of-date groceries."

"You *have* changed." I detected a note of mild sarcasm. "The last time I spoke to you about the new school curriculum, you hardly listened to me, and said it was hardly important and I should deal with it."

I couldn't remember the incident, but I could well believe that was what I'd said. It started to dawn on me that I hadn't really taken a genuine interest in any of the aspects of my kids' life. I'd played with them, and horsed around, OK, but now I accepted that I did

167

dismiss them when I had 'so called important matters' to deal with.

It was like taking a very slow icy-cold shower. Normally, when I've had a few drinks, I become so amiable that I could love the devil. Right then I couldn't even love myself.

They say you never miss what you've never had, but at that moment, I missed my kids so much it brought tears to my eyes. I could picture a bleak future without them, and I didn't like what I could foresee.

Marianne must have felt some empathy with the misery I was feeling. She too had a few tears in her eyes as I spoke to her.

"I really have messed things up all round, haven't I?"

She could have been patronising, and said that it wasn't all my fault, but she didn't. She just stayed silent and let me wallow for a short time. When she did speak, her voice was soft.

"Sean, the children still have a lot of love for you … and if you give them half a chance, you'll see it for yourself. Why don't you treat this as a positive step, and try to gain something out of it."

It was easy for her to say. She wasn't the one who was going to be left with what? What was I left with? I had to accept that I had lost the love of Marianne but surely my relationship with Jason and Michelle was not beyond repair.

*   *   *

EIGHT

Sean was once again re-living the experience, and it was some time before he shook off the sombre mood that had taken him over. He avoided my gaze but I could see the process he was undergoing as he fought to dispel the shadows of the past.

When he turned to me, his expression was bright and there was a twinkle in his eyes.

"You know, life has a few hard lessons to hand out. How you deal with them is a measure of 'the inner man'." That time was a concentrated course of lessons, and it had shaken me to the core.

An artist is made up of a barrelful of confidence, an irresistible compulsion to 'take Centre stage' on any occasion, and sometimes, a wee bit of talent. When they left me that afternoon my whole persona was being called into question. Everything about me, all my traits and characteristics, had combined to engineer the situation that broke up my marriage, and I wasn't well prepared to deal with it. I didn't know what to do."

"So… How did you handle it?"

"At first, I didn't. There were quite a few tears when they were leaving the house, and Michele in particular really let herself go. I never realised what an emotional person she was until then. I shed a tear or two myself when they finally stepped out onto the path."

"And what did you do then?"

Sean gave a vague shrug. "I don't remember exactly. I

do know that I had a couple more drinks and went to bed early."

"And how long did the 'binge' last?"

Sean looked up, angrily. He opened his mouth to repudiate what I'd implied, but then he just gave a shrug. "A couple of days, I suppose." He laughed without humour. "I had sort of lost track of time." He frowned as he stared at me. "I suppose it was obvious that I'd hit the bottle after what had happened, standard procedure I would have thought for someone feeling sorry for himself."

"It would seem to be in character … at that time in your life." I added quickly.

Sean grinned. "Nicely done Andy, no sympathy expected." He continued to grin. "You're right though. I was a mess, and I hadn't a clue what to do. That was, until the bottles ran dry." His eyes took on a faraway glaze as he went on. "I remember getting up one morning and going to the bathroom. I looked in the mirror and this unrecognizable savage was staring back at me. It gave me a hell of a fright, in more ways than one. That was the start of my 'recovery'."

"They say the first step is always the hardest."

"Do they really? You know, you're full of tritisms - if that's a proper word. Who the hell are this anonymous 'they'?" He almost snarled at me.

After a moment he grinned. "Don't panic, Andy, I'm just having a little joke at your expense." He cocked his head on one side and stared into space. "It's funny, but ninety percent of humour depends on some poor sucker getting dropped into the shit, one way or

170

another. I suppose the rest of us think it's funny because it wasn't us who landed in it. The proof is Bernard Manning, God help you if he picked on you."

I didn't respond, since I could see he wasn't really talking to me. I just sat and waited, trying to remain as 'neutral' as I could. Sean swivelled his head until he faced me. "One thing I'll say for you, Andy - you know when to keep your mouth shut."

I nodded an acknowledgement, and then paused before I spoke. "You were about to tell me how you managed to get over the break-up?"

Sean pulled a face. "We're getting back to the invisible 'they'. They say that time is a great healer." He smiled to himself. "I suppose that's as true as any of these 'sayings'. What 'they' don't tell you, is how bloody long a time it takes before things do start to get easier." He gave a slight shrug. "I guess the length of time is proportional to the size of the hurt. In my case I was lower than I'd ever been in my life - and that includes the time when I was a boy dying in a Belfast hospital."

I hadn't turned off my recorder, and I was debating if I should. I decided that what he was telling me was still part of the story, so I let the machine run. I eased myself so I could rest an elbow on the arm of the chair I was in as Sean went on.

"After twenty-four hours of 'sobriety', I started getting melancholy just being in the house. Everywhere I looked reminded me of Marianne and the kids, and it was getting worse. It got so I couldn't even turn on a tap without thinking of some incident involving one of them. I decided that I couldn't stay in the house, or I really would go out of my head. I contacted one of the local travel agents and got myself booked on an off-season trip to Spain.

We'd gone to Spain a few times, and I picked a place that I knew wouldn't be too overcrowded with the 'winter bargain' people." He looked at me. "Do you know Benalmedena?"

"No. I've never heard of it."

"It's on the southern coast of Spain, not too far from Fuengerola, but far enough to be 'quiet' even in the height of the season. I picked up a hire car at Malaga airport, and drove to the resort at a leisurely pace. We'd been to the hotel before, and since it was almost directly off the coast road, I had no trouble finding it. The only problem was getting to the hotel car park.

'La Roca' is situated on a very narrow, very steep street that leads up from the coast road, and I arrived there just as some dirty great lorry was delivering something or other to a shop opposite. But I decided to adopt the Spanish attitude, 'manyana', if it was good enough for them, so I let it be good enough for me. I left my car parked behind the lorry, and walked the few yards up the hill to the hotel."

Sean glanced at me as he got up. "I think it's time for a drink. D'you fancy one?"

I nodded then smiled my thanks as he handed me a good measure of Hennessey. We both settled down with our drinks before Sean carried on with his tale. I remember thinking, 'at this rate we will both end up in The Betty Ford Clinic'.

Well, at first, the change in scenery did nothing to help the foot-dragging slough I was in. There were a good number of guests at the Roca, most of them pensioners who'd come over to 'winter' in the sun. One or two tried to open conversations with me, but I wasn't capable of responding. I suppose I got a reputation for being big-headed, deaf, or downright rude. At that time, I just didn't care.

Let's face it, I was just a plain miserable sod, and I wore my distress like a gold lame suit. I was still the performer, and I guess I revelled in the role even though I didn't acknowledge I was doing it at the time.

There was one positive aspect. I wasn't drinking as much. All right, I still did have a drink - at those prices who could resist? But I never took so much that I wasn't aware of what was going on.

I'd been there a couple of days and, as I said, kept myself to myself. By then I didn't have to discourage the other guests. They must have had a bush telegraph since nobody approached me after the first day. It suited me, but it didn't help my problem...

It was mid-afternoon on the third day. I'd gone out to the pool area and was sitting in the shade of a palm tree staring at this bronze statue of a girl holding up a dolphin. I wasn't really looking at it, just staring with a vacant mind.

"It's part of a local legend." A soft educated voice broke my self-imposed isolation. I turned my head to find the speaker, a grey-haired, pleasant-faced, old lady, standing beside me. She was dressed in a rather

173

dated, and not very new, dress; and had a battered straw hat on her head. Her eyes were grey, and had a deep sensitivity about them.

For the first time since I arrived, I hadn't felt annoyed by someone trying to break through my wall of self-pity. I didn't object when she lowered herself onto a chair beside me, and I felt some genuine interest when she qualified her initial statement.

"You've heard of 'The little mermaid'?"

"Hans Christian Anderson."

She nodded. "Yes. But there's a belief that he stole the tale or was influenced by a local legend about a young girl who was drowning not far from here. She was miraculously saved by a dolphin, and was reputed to have spent half her life in the sea after her rescue. You'll notice the symbol on a great many local artefacts."

"I'm sorry but I'm not really into legends."

"You have the look of a man who's 'not really into' anything at the moment."

"Is it that obvious?"

She gave a chiding sort of laugh. "You know it is, mister …?"

"Clarke, Sean Clarke."

She extended her hand. "I'm Constance Farrar."

I took her hand, and noticed that even though her skin was wrinkled and marked with a couple of small liver spots, her grasp was quite firm and warm. "There," she smiled at me, "that wasn't too much of an effort, was it?"

I frowned, disturbed by her manner. She seemed oblivious to my coolness as she carried on.

"I assume you've had some recent upset in your life, and have come here 'on retreat'?"

"As a matter of fact, I have." I couldn't help but sound surprised. "How did you know? Hold on, you're not a Clairvoyant are you?"

She laughed a short tinkling sort of laugh. "Oh my God, heaven forbid. Mister Clarke, one doesn't have to be a fortune teller to appreciate your situation. You've been here three days, and you've hardly spoken to a soul, and made it clear that you don't wish to indulge in conversation ... You are here on your own, but you don't have the air of a solitary man. "

It wasn't a question, not even in a devious way. I'd only just met the lady, but I got the impression that she was genuine. She wasn't trying to pry into my affairs to satisfy some sick quirk of character. She seemed genuinely interested in me and my plight. It was then that I realised that *I* was interested enough to want to know something about her.

"Are you here with a group - or are you on your own?"

"Like you, I'm 'flying solo'." She paused before she went on, "my husband died a while back, and I came here to drag myself out of the doldrums."

"Oh, I am sorry."

She shook her head. "Don't be. Arthur and I had a great many good years together. I must confess I was devastated when he died, but we'd always said that life must go on." Her smile was tinged with sadness. "I always thought it would be I who 'went first' - since I was older than he."

"May I ask how are you coping - with the grief?"

175

She shrugged. "We have little choice. Either we give up, and allow ourselves to fall into an ever deepening pit of despondency, or we look life straight in the face and say … 'All right, I'm hurting, but there's still a great deal of living to be done'. When a widow - God I hate that word - books herself for example on a cruise she is supposed to say 'It's what he would have wanted'. Well if I book a cruise it will be because it's what *I* want." She looked at me and I felt ashamed of my self-pity as I stared into her eyes.

She sighed then got to her feet. "Mister Clarke, I don't know what has happened to you and, unless you feel compelled to tell me, I don't want to know. But I would hope that you come to terms with your life, and 'spit in its eye'. You're still a young man, and there's a wonderfully entertaining world out there."

She gave me another smile then turned and made her way past the pool to the hotel building. I watched her slight, almost frail, figure and marvelled that there was more strength in her tiny frame than I could have imagined.

I met Constance at dinner that evening. We'd gone to the self-service counter at the same time, and without noticing had gently bumped elbows. I turned to apologise, then grinned when I saw who it was. We shared a table, and I felt confident enough to tell her my tale.

She listened quietly and said nothing for some time after I'd finished. Then she looked me straight in the eye.

"What are your priorities?"

"I ... er, what do you mean?"

"Apart from getting over the break-up of your marriage - what are you looking for in the future?"

"I don't know."

"Mister Clarke, we all need a goal. Without a target we're like an unfletched arrow. We wander about aimlessly, causing pain to ourselves and more importantly others. You said you were an entertainer - are you a good one?"

The bluntness of her question startled me. I floundered for a second then started to say I was brilliant but what came out was. "I'd like to think so."

"Splendid!" Constance beamed at me. "The greatest asset to becoming a happy human being is to have self-knowledge. If you aren't aware of yourself, how can you ever find what you're looking for?"

"I'd never thought of it."

"Not many people do, Mister Clarke."

"I still haven't a clue what I want from life."

"Well let's start with your children. What did you say they were called?"

"Jason and Michelle" I replied.

"Do they like you?"

"Of course, they love me."

"That's not what I said; I asked do they like you. There is a difference. As you are their father they will always love you but it is the things you do with them and the time you give them that will make them like you. Remember you are starting a new life and they can be a big part of that life."

We then ate for some time in companionable silence. When we'd finished the meal I suggested we went to the bar. Constance hesitated. "It's almost forty years since a man asked me to have a drink with him." She chuckled. "I'll agree, as long as you don't get the impression I'm the sort of person who'd let any young man come along and 'pick me up'."

I got the drinks and we took them outside. The evening air was cool but not unpleasant. There was a faint breeze, and Constance suggested we sat in a sheltered spot beneath a clear plastic awning.

I raised my glass. "To you, Constance. You've helped me more than I can ever say."

She gave an embarrassed smile as she sipped her drink. She held the glass in both hands, placing it on the table. "It's helped me, too. I can tell that you're a good person, and worth the effort. But you have got to make an effort as well." She looked around before her gaze fell on me again. "Have you been here before?"

"Yes, a number of times. Marianne and I said it was one of the most relaxing holidays we'd ever had."

"Then let it work for you again. I assume you and your family did 'the tourist thing' while you were here?"

"Yes, we did."

"Then go to those places again, and instead of feeling sad when you remember how it was when you were a family, try to feel the happiness you enjoyed. When you can do that, you will have started on the road to ... who

178

knows what? But you will be able to face the present, and the future with a much more positive attitude. Remember to face the future you must first come to terms with the past. You will always be part of those memories so don't shut them out."

I celebrated my 'New Year' by doing what Constance had suggested. Officially nineteen ninety five was already two weeks old, but it was the time of my new beginning. I went back to all the places I'd visited with Marianne and the kids, and I tried to glean some pleasure from revisiting them. I recalled how Jason had stood at the edge of a high rocky ridge that ran close to the beach. He wobbled precariously and Marianne rushed to save him. She discovered there was a concrete ledge only a few feet below the edge.

I drove up a tortuously winding, terrifyingly steep, mountain road to the tiny village of Mijas. Perched on the edge of the Cordillera it was typical of the picturesque inland villages of the region. Some few miles inland from the coast, it stood over a thousand feet above sea-level and, from several vantage points at the upper end of a municipal garden, it afforded dozens of panoramic views of the lower slopes of the mountains sliding away to the coastline.

Mijas wasn't much more 'developed' than I remembered, and the bull-ring was just as it had been, and I did recall telling the kids what someone had already told me. It was the only square 'ring' in the whole of Spain, and had been used as the setting for a scene in the film *Caravan to Vacares*. Just like kids, they'd been suitably un-impressed, and I recalled watching Michele as she had danced in front of the gates and waved her arms artistically, pretending she was a matador. Down the slope from the bull-ring the plaza was exactly as before, and the bar where we'd eaten was still serving the same simple but excellent food.

I went back to Benelmadena and wandered around the marina admiring the expensive boats moored there. Then I walked to the end of the jetty and stared out to sea as we'd done the last time we were there. I ate ice-cream, and tapas, tortillas and tartes. It became such that almost everything I did started to evoke a whole series of wonderfully cheerful memories. It was a kind of gentle therapy, and towards the end of my stay I had started to feel a little bit more at peace with myself.

I chanced to be in the foyer of the hotel the day Constance was leaving. I'd gone down to make sure I could drop my hire car off at the airport the following day. Having been assured that there'd be no problem with the car, I turned from the desk and saw her sitting on one of the seats beside which was a pair of battered and obviously well-used old suitcases. I joined her and we chatted until her taxi arrived to take her to Malaga airport. As the driver collected her luggage and she rose to follow him, I impulsively kissed her cheek. She blushed.

"I hope everyone saw that." She smiled mischievously.
"Then I could leave with the reputation of being 'a scarlet woman' or a procurer of toy boys." The reception echoed with her laugh.

180

I arrived home at about eleven o'clock on the morning of the nineteenth of January. The weather was dull and overcast, quite miserable, with a sharp wind gusting down the Avenue and flinging cold rain into my face. I paid off the taxi and carried my luggage into the house and found a few envelopes on the mat behind the door.

I gathered the mail and after leaving my suitcase and holdall in the front room, I went into the kitchen to make myself a coffee. I discarded the mail while I filled the kettle, but I did check the answer phone.

Marianne had called me a number of times, leaving a request that I get in touch with her. Each call became more anxious than the previous one, and her voice was quite animated on the last message.

I made the coffee and took a sip before I reached for the phone. It gave me a start when it began to ring just as I touched it.

"Marianne?"

"Who? No, it's me, Ronnie London, your favourite agent. I heard about your little mishap in the States, and I don't want you to worry about a thing. I doubt if they'll bring charges ... and I won't press you for all of my commission ... just yet."

"Ronnie-"

"We should look on it as an experience. Right, are you listening? I have some great news. I got you a four month booking ... guess where?"

"Ronnie, I couldn't care less-"

"All right, I'll tell you ... I got you a fabulous booking in Zimbabwe. What do you think of that, Sean?"

181

"Ronnie. Hang up. I want to make an important call right now."

"Didn't you hear what I just said?"

"Yes, I heard, and I have to make a call."

"Fine. You make your call, and I'll fix things up for your trip to Africa."

"No! Hang on, Ronnie. I didn't say I was going."

"Yes, but I know you. You'll take it with bells on."

"Not this time. I've had some personal problems and-"

"Personal problems? Who do you think you are - George Michael or something? In your position, you can't afford to have 'personal problems'."

"This time, I can. Sorry, Ronnie. I'm hanging up now."

"You hang up on me, and you won't get any work 'till hell freezes over."

"I'll take my chance on that. See you Ronnie." I put the receiver down firmly and treated myself to another sip of coffee before I picked it up again.

Marianne had left the number where I could contact her, and I dialled it. A man answered. His voice was 'cultured' and had an accent I couldn't place. I guessed it was Philip, and he confirmed my suspicion when I asked if I might speak with Marianne.

"Sorry, she's taken Michele and Jason into Manchester to get them some new school uniforms. I'll get her to call you when she gets back. You're not going anywhere today, I take it?"

"No. I'll be at home all day." I started to lower the receiver.

"She's been worried about you." I heard him say as I took the receiver from my ear.

"What?"

"When you didn't answer her first two calls, she had me drive her round to your house. Then she had me contact all the local hospitals. Have you been ill?"

"Er … No, I just took a short break."

"And you're well?"

"Yes, I am."

"Good, I'm glad to hear it. I'll tell Marie when she comes home."

"Thanks." I put down the receiver and frowned at nothing in particular. I wanted to be angry with the man, but I couldn't. He seemed a pleasant enough person, but he did annoy me when he called Marianne 'Marie'. She never let me call her anything but her 'proper' name.

During my stay in Spain, one thing that had played on my mind was how I would react when I spoke to Philip. Now it had happened I was puzzled.

Somewhere inside, I wanted to hate the man for what he'd done to me; but the 'new' me realized that it wasn't completely his fault. I simmered for a few seconds then accepted that he didn't seem to be such a bad choice - when I thought of the type of man Marianne could have ended up with.

I finished my coffee then went to take my case and holdall upstairs. I unpacked and separated the clothes into hanging-up and washing. I hung the hanging-ups then started to divide the washing into piles, doing my best to ensure that each pile contained 'compatible' clothes. I felt a faint twinge of pride when I'd finished. It might not seem much, no world-shattering accomplishment, but to me it was as big as a Neil Armstrong step. I had already finished one load of washing and had split it into air-dry and machine dry, and was putting a second load into the washing machine when I heard a knock at the front door. I recognised the fresnelled shape of Marianne through the frosted glass of the door, and I felt a sudden lump in my stomach. I was surprised to find that my hand was shaking as I opened the door.

She looked different. I'm not talking about the new clothes she was wearing, but her manner, her attitude, and the expression on her face as she smiled at me from the door-step. I stared at her, and she smiled at me. Then, with a slight twist of her mouth she cocked her head on one side.

"Can I come in?"

"Oh, yes. Sorry." My mouth was dry and I still couldn't stop myself from trembling as I allowed her to pass me. I followed her into the kitchen and stood a few feet from her as she glanced at the washing machine.

"You *have* changed."

"So have you." My tongue felt about the size of a wrestler's forearm in my mouth, while Marianne seemed totally relaxed.

"You don't mind me calling like this? Unannounced, I mean."

"No." I forced a weak smile. "Sorry, won't you sit down?" It was difficult, and I couldn't help thinking it was as if I was talking to a sort of stranger. I suppose it

184

was. After all, I thought I knew her and she proved me totally wrong. I was on edge and being overly polite, but she seemed quite normal, and was dictating the mood.

She sat at a small glass table and I sat facing her. I clenched my hands to stop them trembling and tried to calm myself.

"Philip said you've been away."

"Yes, that's right. I felt like I needed some time away from things."

Marianne nodded. "Did it help?"

I shrugged. "I suppose so."

"I don't really know how to put this without seeming a bit ruthless. I know that what I'm about to say will hurt, but I have to say it."

"You want a divorce."

She seemed a little shaken for the first time since she came in. She took a deep breath and swallowed hard before she nodded. "Yes." Her voice wasn't as controlled as before, and her eyes had misted. I could see her steeling herself, and I was pleased - not that she was upset, but because she'd finally shown some feeling. It got to me and I was forced to clear my throat before I spoke.

"It's a bit soon, don't you think?"

"For you, maybe. It isn't all that soon for me. I don't want the children to … No, it isn't about the children, at least not completely. When you left for America, it was the end for us, or if I am honest even before that I'd got to a state where I knew I just couldn't take any more, it just helped me make an inevitable decision. I could see that you were shocked and hurt, but I couldn't help it. I had to get away." She forced a tremulous smile and let out a soft sigh. "Oh God, I had this all planned. I knew exactly what I was going to say, but …" She shook her head and closed her eyes.

Part of me wanted to make it difficult for her. I wanted some sort of revenge for the way she'd destroyed my life.

But the new me realised that she hadn't destroyed my life, she'd only tried to save her own. Instead of responding harshly, I waited, and then shrugged. "I had one or two things I wanted to say to you, too." I tried to grin. "But I can't, for the life of me, remember what they were. Would you like a coffee?"

"No, thank you."

"All right, then would you like a divorce?"

I didn't expect her to cry but she did and as she was leaving I said "Marianne. It wasn't all bad, was it?"

"No Sean, it wasn't."

It took a couple of further meetings before we were finally able to talk without letting our emotions run riot. Once we were able to look at the situation rationally, or as rationally as we could, at the time, I realised I knew nothing at all about divorce.

I'd known plenty of fellow entertainers who'd gone through it, but I'd never discovered exactly what a divorce entailed. I found out that it wasn't as straightforward as I thought. In my ignorance, I expected that, once we had agreed that we should divorce, that would be it. Some solicitor would 'sort things out', and we'd be divorced.

Eventually, it was agreed that I should divorce Marianne, on the grounds of her adultery and desertion. It wasn't an ideal solution to my way of thinking, but it was the most expedient. The only alternative, was to claim 'irreconcilable differences', and I found out that it could have taken a few years.

By that time I'd become resigned to losing Marianne, and I really didn't want to stand in her way. In response to my agreeing to sue Marianne for divorce, she and Philip said they'd offer no objections to my having complete and unlimited access to Michele and Jason. They also agreed that I should have sole ownership of the house on Sefton Avenue, and they would not demand any maintenance for the kids. I had them agree that, rather than completely 'neglect' Jason and Michele, I should be allowed to contribute financially towards their upkeep.

While waiting for the court case things did get a little better. I got some local bookings and I felt some confidence coming back when I was on stage. It was different, though. Even when I got a couple of standing ovations, I didn't let it go to my head. By the time I'd got home I was under no illusions about my future. I knew I was never going to be a super-star, and I was going to treat 'the stage' as nothing more than a job.

I was starting to sleep more soundly, and the weird dreams were coming less and less frequently. Each morning I woke up feeling a little more refreshed and ready to face whatever that day might bring. All round, things were beginning to pick up.

The most important thing that happened during that

187

time was getting to know my kids. I thought of Constance and her four important words, "Do they like you?" I'd had parent-dreams of what I thought they were like, but the reality was astounding.

As I said earlier, I discovered that Michele was quite emotional - not in a 'girly' sort of way, but more like an adult. Jason, on the outside, was 'all boy'. He was loud and physical, but he too had another side.

They were obviously wary of me when I had them to myself for the first time. It really was a first time for all of us. Not in all their years had there been an occasion when they'd been completely alone with me. In the past Marianne had always been within calling distance, and now for the first time the buck was really stopping with me. Still I suppose we all felt the pressure, new ground that sort of thing.

I'd listened to the advice Marianne offered, and planned to take things easy. I wasn't going to force anything on them, and I would let them dictate the pace of our new relationship.

The first 'outing' was a simple matter. I'd met them at the door when Marianne had dropped them off, and like my first meeting with her after the break-up, I also thought they had changed.

They wore casual clothes, but even so they looked smarter, neater than I ever remembered. Like my first meeting with Marianne, I was nervous, and I could see that they too were not at ease. The truth was, I didn't have a clue how to act with them. In the past, on the few occasions I had been with them, I'd treated them as junior members of my fan club, now it was time to really be ourselves.

We sat in the front room, not saying much until Michele pointed to one of the photographs hanging on the wall.

"Are you going to keep them, dad? I think you should. You and mum look ever so ... happy on them. And there's a lot of really famous people with you." She gave me a shy stare. "I think it's nice to remember times when you've been happy. It helps you to not hurt as much when you're upset. Promise me you'll never throw them away."

She was, I think, ten years old at the time.

We decided to go to Heaton Park. I couldn't think what we might do there, but it was what they wanted, so I didn't argue. The weather was mild. There was a thin watery sun, and a few wispy clouds in the sky, and the wind was hardly more than a zephyr.

Michele and Jason were in the back seat, and for the first few minutes I could see them eyeing me, I grinned at them, through the rear-view mirror. "This is going to be an adventure for me. I haven't been to the park for as long as I can remember."

Once we'd parked the car, the kids jumped out and waited for me. Jason picked up a couple of pebbles from the ground and hurled them at nothing in particular while Michele stayed close to me. I felt her small hand slip into mine and I looked down at her. Her eyes reminded me so much of Marianne's that it threw me for a moment. Then I saw she was frowning.

"What's the matter, love?" I bent down to bring my face closer to hers.

"Mum says that we're going to stay with Philip all the time."

"Don't you like him?"

"Yes, he's nice. But I don't want you to go away and never see us again."

I put my arm round her and hugged her slight frame to me. "Don't worry, Michele. I'm not going away. "

"You did before, and left us for a long long time."

"I know, and I'm sorry. Didn't mum tell you that was because of my work?"

"Yes, but I missed you. Philip works, but he comes home every night."

"That's because he doesn't do the same sort of work as I do. But I promise you that, even if I do have to go away sometimes, I'll always come back, and I'll always want to see you."

"Is that a 'hope-to-die' promise?"

"Yes, hope-to-die." I released her and took hold of her hand. It was a strange feeling, really pleasant, when she squeezed my hand.

"Dad?"

"What?"

"Is it true that you haven't been here for a long time?"

"Yes it is. Why?"

She smiled at me. "There's lots of lovely places I can show you."

"Then, let's go!"

We caught up with Jason, who was hiding in some bushes by the side of the path, and jumped out to surprise us. He came to my side and looked up at me.

"Philip's got three cars, dad."

"Is that a fact?"

"Yes. He's got a big Bentley, a sort of van, with windows, and a little car - like yours."

"That's - nice for him."

"Will you buy me a kite, dad?"

"If you want one … but not today, eh?"

"OK."

I did buy kites for them both, and the next time I saw them, we had some fun assembling them. As you might have gathered by now, I am no great handyman, and the kids thought it was hilarious as they watched me trying to put the pieces of the kites together. Jason in particular ended up rolling around on the floor and making such a noise that I thought he might upset the neighbours. It was he who suggested it might be a good idea to read the instructions - so I did. This caused even more hilarity, since the kites were made in China, and the instructions were printed in something less than English. The writer must either have been a ten-year-old, or someone related to the owner of the company who thought they could speak the language.

By the time I'd finished reading the instructions, we were all quite helplessly bellowing with laughter. The whole thing didn't last more than a few minutes but, right then, I was as close to the kids, closer in fact, than I'd ever been in my life.

Admitting failure, I handed the job to the kids, and it took them a couple of minutes to complete what had had me struggling for over half-an-hour. I don't remember if we ever flew the kites, but the day we put them together was one memory that will stay with me forever.

It took longer than I'd expected, but the divorce case finally reared its ugly head. It was as simple as it could be, but it was still messy. I'll never forget the feeling of awe as I stood in court facing a judge. It was as unpleasant an experience as I'd ever undergone, and I never want to go through anything like that again, EVER.

NINE

Sean gave me an easy smile. He sighed as he stretched his arms then rotated his shoulders.

"Do you know Andy, It's surprising how just sitting and talking can make you feel stiff."

"Do you want to call a halt, Sean?" I looked at my watch and saw that it was well past three o'clock. He seemed surprised when I told him what time it was.

"Good God, I thought my stomach was getting annoyed. I'm going to have a bite now, before I go to pick up some arrangements I've had written."

"OK then, let's call it a day."

"Fine. I'll expect you the same time tomorrow?"

"Suits me."

Sean saw me to the door and gave me a friendly nod as I set off down the path. Like him, I was hungry, and I drove to McDonald's where I picked up a burger, some fries and a coke. I found a space on a superstore car park, and ate.

My mobile rang as I was wiping my hands on an inadequate paper napkin. It was Amanda.

"Hi, Andy. How are you?"

"I'm fine, and you?"

"I'm puzzled. I've not seen you around for a while, and I wondered if you'd moved to another planet?"

"No. I've been busy working."

"On what?" When I didn't answer, her tone became a little sharp. "Don't tell me you're still visiting that singer chap?"

"As a matter of fact …"

"Have you become one of the 'other side'?"

"No. I'm still heterosexual or maybe Sean's just not my type!"

"Then why haven't you called me?"

"Don't tell me you've just been sitting around in your flat, knitting while you waited for me to telephone."

"Well, no I haven't. But I might have - for all you knew. In fact I could have been dead!"

"That's a laugh, the last time I saw you was when you asked me to drop you off at a night club so you could be with your friends."

"Really, what a memory you've got. Anyway how d'you fancy a night at- Tell you what. Since you've neglected me for so long - why don't you take me out for a nice meal?"

"I've only just finished eating."

"Shit!"

The mobile went dead and I grinned as I slipped it back into my pocket. Amanda was good fun, but she could be a bit of a pain when her money ran out and she was looking for a meal-ticket. I made a mental note to call her soon as I had a feeling that we could make some sort of a go at it. Let's face it she was beautiful. Long blond hair, great legs in fact great everything. Maybe we could have some fun together before she meets Mister Right which certainly wasn't me.

I was about to start the engine when my conscience kicked in. I remembered how, during our student days, and even afterwards when we were out in the big bad world, Amanda had treated me to meals when I'd been out work. I took out my mobile and returned her call.

"It's Andy. Are you still hungry?"

"What do you think - that I just ate a seven course gourmet meal in the last ninety seconds? Of course I'm hungry."

"Fine. I'll pick you up, say half six, and we'll eat out."

"Where?"

"Does it matter?

Amanda gave a deep sigh. "I have to know what to wear, you pleb. Cocktail or sweater?"

"Sweater, I think."

"Right, I'll see you around six thirty." I pocketed my mobile and drove onto Oldham road. Depending upon her mood, Amanda could provide me with a welcome diversion from all the heart-pouring I'd been listening to for what seemed like half a lifetime.

Amanda was ready when I called for her, and she seemed to have a mischievous air about her as she climbed into the car. She was dressed, as I'd suggested, in sweater and jeans, beneath a stylish coat, but she looked like what she would look like whatever way she was dressed. Stunning. There was something about her that seemed different but I couldn't think what. I puzzled over it as we drove out to Rochdale, where I'd booked us in at a fine carvery.

We talked casually, small-talk, but I got the impression that she was holding something back. I didn't question her directly until we were eating. I'd expected her to 'hit the grub' like a starving urchin, but she ate daintily and sedately; and she still had that impish gleam in her eyes. I couldn't wait 'til we finished.

"You're a lot more perky that I expected."

"Mm." She nodded at me. I waited until she swallowed the food in her mouth, expecting her to say something, but she didn't.

"Amanda. What's the matter with you?"

"Matter?" She stared at me, her fork poised over a thick slice of turkey. "Nothing's the matter. I'm just pleased to see you."

"How long have we known each other?"

She shrugged. "Seven, eight years."

"Yes, and don't you think that, by now, I've got to know you reasonably well?"

"I suppose you have - and you always were a sharp devil." Her face lit up and she beamed at me. "I wasn't going to tell you right away, but you might as well hear it now. I've got a new job."

"A good one?"

"Fantastic. I've been taken on by a sort of entrepreneur as her private secretary. I'll be getting my own car next week."

"What's the salary like?"

"Beyond your wildest dreams, mine too."

"Amanda, I'm really pleased for you."

"You were the first person I thought to tell … and I can tell you I was pretty pissed when you fobbed me off." She gave me a warm smile. "I'm glad you called me back."

"So am I." I picked up my glass. "Here's to you, and your new career."

196

We ate for a few moments then Amanda frowned at me. "How's your bank balance these days?"

"Oh, so-so."

"Has this 'entertainer' paid you anything yet?"

"I'm not working for him. I'm gathering notes."

"What for? I mean, what do you intend to do when you've got all your 'notes'?"

"I don't know Amanda, I honestly don't know."

We continued the conversation during the meal, at a pub afterwards, and during the drive home. Amanda's main argument was that, in the past, I'd been more than mercenary, but now I seemed to have lost all sense. She even told me she thought I was a little mad to have done so much work for nothing.

We were still talking when she invited me into her flat, and we continued talking even when she enticed me into her bed, not that I needed much enticing as Amanda can be extremely sexy when she feels like it, and when she feels like it, you feel like you've won The Lottery. I'm not saying sex was matter of fact or cold in any way, far from it. It's just that to say "I love you" seemed surplus to requirements. We didn't talk much for a long while as we lay in each other's arms, but later, about two in the morning, she woke me.

"Andrew, I've been thinking, there must be something special about this singer for you to take so much trouble with him. Could you try to explain what it is?"

"Amanda," I sort of mumbled through the duvet, "leave it until morning."

"No. You've got me intrigued, and I won't sleep until you tell me what is so special about this man."

I dragged myself into a sitting position and couldn't help leering cheerfully at her nakedness. God, she has a great body. From her expression I understood that she really did want me to explain why Sean's story was so important to me. So I reluctantly started to tell her some of the incidents he'd related to me....

When I'd finished I gave her a weary smile before I lay my head back on the pillow. It was there less than a minute before Amanda spoke.

"It's quite a story."

"Yes, isn't it? Now let's try to get some sleep..."

Fully awake, and showing the keener side of her inquisitive nature, Amanda wasn't going to let it drop. I gave a protesting sigh, and sat up. She frowned at me.

"If I told you I'd 'gone back in time' - you'd laugh at me. What's so different about this Clarke character?"

"He hasn't said he's gone back in time. He said he'd *dreamed* that he was back in nineteen sixty four. For God's sake!"

Her expression told me she wasn't convinced, but she didn't take the matter further. Instead, she leaned over and gave me the sort of kiss that would melt stainless steel, and I ... I responded.

I was bleary-eyed and only half-conscious when I turned up at Sean's home the following morning. I could have called to postpone the meeting, but I felt that, now I seemed to have won his complete confidence, I didn't want to do anything to destroy the fragile link I'd been able to fabricate.

Sean shook his head as he looked at me from the hallway.

"You look like you had a night-and-a-half last night. What were you doing, drowning sorrows, or celebrating?" He stepped back and ushered me into the hallway.

"Celebrating. A friend of mine has just got a new job."

"That's nice. We'll be in the kitchen this morning. I've got a pot full of coffee."

"Thanks, but I've already had a couple."

"Doesn't look as if they've worked. Another will do you no harm." He directed me to the glass-topped kitchen table and went to the work-top to my right where he filled two large mugs with coffee. I must admit that the aroma did have a mildly stimulating effect on my 'low-ebb' brain. I smiled as he brought the mugs over to the table.

"Smells good, Sean."

"It should do. It's 'Blue Mountain' we got the beans from the plantation in Jamaica, and it made my mouth water just grinding them. It's the most expensive coffee in the world and I can't recommend it highly enough. Once you've tasted it, all the others will seem ordinary in comparison. Take a sip."

I did as he urged, and I must confess that the drink was exceptional. The flavour was strong, but sort of mellow, and smooth. I had to admit, he was right, and I told him so. We drank in silence for a few moments, then Sean, put his mug down.

"Are you fit to carry on, or would you like to leave it until another day? I have to warn you though, I have a long-term booking at the end of next week, and I'll be away until the end of the month."

"Then we'd better get on with it." I dragged my recorder out of my pocket and set it on the table. I rewound the tape a little then pressed the play button and we listened. I watched Sean's face as he heard himself describing the divorce, and I noticed that he didn't seem as affected as he'd been yesterday.

The machine gave a faint click and I pressed the record button. Sean sipped his coffee, gave an appreciative sigh then set his mug down and began...

I was on my own for the first time in my life. Even when I'd come from Belfast to Manchester I'd stayed in a boarding house, and was pretty much looked after by the landlady. Now I was starting to develop some self-reliance. I won't say I enjoyed it ... but in a way, I did. I was on a sort of 'voyage of self-discovery'.

Each day I found myself faced with problems. Most of them were what you might call insignificant, but at the time they caused me some distress. In the past I could have passed the problem on - to the landlady, or in later years, to Marianne. In fact I was probably unaware of most of the problems since Marianne had already dealt with them. She'd often collared me when I'd come home from a show, and she'd tell me about her day. But I never remember listening to her - I mean, really listening; and the first few months after she left, I found myself wishing I'd paid a little more attention to her complaints.

But, by effort and more than a little slice of good fortune, I did become adept at resolving most of the everyday hazards I encountered. I think the main reason things got easier was because I started to think about them rather than just ignoring them and hoping they'd go away. There were some things I couldn't deal with, and I asked for advice. Most times, I called Marianne, and to her credit, she listened to my questions and answered them without much 'edge'. Looking back there must have been dozens of opportunities for her to tell me how hopeless I was, but she didn't.

My attitude towards Marianne had changed. I no longer lusted after her, at least that's what I told myself, and I was quite content to regard her as a friend - not a close friend, but a friend nevertheless. Not long after the divorce was made final, she telephoned to tell me that she was getting married to Philip. I was surprised that it provoked nothing stronger than a pang of regret. She said I might go to the wedding reception if I wished, even told me the kids wanted me to go, but I decided against it.

After thinking about it carefully for a couple of days I sent them a card wishing them well. It felt strange I'll admit, but I found that I really did mean it.

That weekend, when Marianne dropped Michele and Jason off at Sefton Avenue, she stayed a little longer than usual. While the kids were in the kitchen, she asked if we could talk. I couldn't imagine what she wanted to talk about, but I agreed.

We went into the lounge and remained standing as we talked. Marianne seemed quite different now, she had an aura of confidence and self-assurance that I'd not noticed before. She was half-smiling when she spoke.

"Thanks for the card. I know it might sound silly, but it really did matter to me that you didn't hold a grudge."

I shrugged. "I know when I'm beaten."

"Sean, it's not a contest, and you weren't beaten."

"All right." I found myself getting irritated. Had we been married, this would have been the prelude to another argument. I smiled to myself when I found that in a perverse way, I was glad we were no longer a couple. "Sorry, I didn't mean to be so sharp."

"You always did 'rise to the bait' too quickly." She checked herself and let out a sigh. "This isn't how I'd planned it. I didn't mean for us to have a post-mortem on what's happened."

"No," I agreed, "It won't do any good anyway. What did you want to talk about?"

"You know Philip and I will be getting married?"

"Yes and you want me to sing at the wedding." I frowned.

"Sean," She paused awkwardly and pulled a face. "I … er, I have a favour to ask."

"Then go ahead, ask away."

"This is going to sound rather, cheeky."

I had no idea what she was talking about and I tried not to look too mystified as I waited for her to continue.

After a prolonged pause, Marianne spoke in a rush, the words coming out in a torrent. "Philip and I will be going away on honeymoon, and we'll be away for a month. Philip has no close family, and Michele and

Jason will be on school holidays while we're away. So I wondered if …" She paused for breath and stared at me with an anxious expression. "I wondered if you'd mind looking after the children while we're away."

"Is that all?" I grinned.

"I mean - they'd have to stay here."

"Yes. No problem. In fact, I think it's a great idea."

Relief flooded over Marianne's face. She beamed at me, her expression radiant. "I'll tell them … thanks, Sean." She hurried out of the room and a moment later I heard the kids voices raised in response to the news.

It was then that the significance of my offer hit me. I'd volunteered to take care of the kids for a whole month, when I'd not been alone with them for more than a few hours at a time for the last ten years. It was a sobering thought, and at the same time intriguing. I went to the doorway and I was only half aware of her when Marianne walked past me along the hallway and out of the front door.

I joined the kids in the kitchen. Michele was standing by the rear worktop, holding a glass of orange juice in her hand while staring out into the back garden. Jason was sitting at the table clasping a glass of Coke. He turned and stared up at me, but Michele continued to look away.

"Great news, dad. We're going to have the whole holidays with you." He was bubbling with excitement.

"Yes, it'll be really fantastic." I answered him but I was looking at my daughter. I went to her and gently put my hands on her shoulders. I could feel her body rigid beneath my touch.

"What's the matter, love?"

Her expression was solemn when she looked at me, and her eyes were large and troubled. She hunched her shoulders. "I don't know, dad. I just feel, sort of … sad."

We spent that day quietly. I had planned on taking them to Heaton Park again, but the weather had other ideas. Within twenty minutes of their arrival, the heavens opened and released a big bucketful of rain.

Jason was easy to please. He went upstairs and found some of his toy cars, and was quite happy, speeding them around a track and crashing them with great gusto. Michele was a different matter. I'd gone into the front room, and she followed me. She was still subdued, and seemed unwilling to leave my side. It wasn't that I wanted her to go, I just wanted to bring her out of the depressed mood she was in; and I thought that being with me was making her worse for some reason. No matter what I suggested, Michele shook her head.

Finally I took her by the hand and led her to the settee. I placed her at one end and sat beside her. She sat perfectly still, staring at the unlit fire. A jumbled mass of questions ran through my mind but I didn't know where to start. I just waited, trying to appear as normal and unconcerned as I was able. I was almost on the point of breaking the uncomfortable silence when I felt her hand creep into mine.

I looked down at her and smiled. She squeezed

my hand and let out a big sigh.

"What are you going to do, dad?"

The question baffled me. When I couldn't find a suitable response apart from "about what?"

Michele went on. "You're going to be on your own, all the time. Who's going to look after you?"

I smiled at her. "I'll be all right. I can look after myself now."

"But, who'll iron your shirts and make sure you have a clean handkerchief when you go out - and who'll answer the phone and tell you when your agent has called with a new booking?"

I put my arm around her and hugged her to me. "Oh, Michele. You don't have to worry about me. I really will be all right …"

"You promise? You aren't just saying it to make me feel better?"

"Cross my heart and hope the devil'll get me."

The rest of the day seemed to speed by. I persuaded Jason to join us, and we played Monopoly and Cluedo. We had a makeshift lunch and they persuaded me to sing for them. I sang a couple of numbers and noticed Michele seemed 'choked' when I finished singing *Leaving on a Jet Plane*. It had always been a favourite of hers, but I realised how sadly appropriate the lyrics must have seemed to her at the time. I quickly changed the mood by singing *Paddy McGinty's goat*, and was rewarded by them joining in. By the time I put my guitar away, the atmosphere was back to normal.

In the shortening weeks leading up to Marianne's wedding I was kept pretty-well occupied. My 'local' agent, once he realised I was once again reliable, and if anything more accomplished than before, started getting me some decent bookings. I was coping well enough at home for me to feel confident about having the kids with me full-time. I even contacted an old baby-sitting family Marianne and I had used in the past.

I knew I'd not be home most evenings, and the Callaghan's had always provided a very reliable source of instant cover. The family was large, and as the children grew older, the 'next-in-line' took on the task. It had proved a good arrangement for all concerned and they seemed eager for the added income to continue.

I saw Michele and Jason at weekends, and no matter what we did, the conversation always seemed to end up at 'The Wedding'. I wasn't interested at first, but it was obvious the kids, Michele in particular, were getting excited about the coming event. I thought it would be churlish of me to disregard what was, to them, a pretty important occasion, so I went along with them, and began to take a mild interest myself. I even joked that it was a pity they missed their Mums first wedding

I heard about the new dresses, the jewellery, the suits and the flowers. I was given a long description of the 'Country House' where the reception was to take place, and a detailed account of the menu. I got totally caught up in their enthusiasm by the time the wedding arrived.

On the eve of the big day, I telephoned Marianne to wish her luck. It was only a small gesture, but I felt good about it …

I'd made sure that I had no booking for the night of the wedding, and I was ready for them when a taxi brought Michele and Jason to my door. What I wasn't prepared for was their appearance. Standing at the door was a very attractive young woman dressed in a gown that could have graced an event at Buckingham Palace, and a young man who looked as if he was off to the casino at Monte Carlo. I couldn't help it, I gaped at them. Were they really my little girl and boy? Then they started giggling at my expression and I grinned too as I picked up the cases they'd brought with them. I was still grinning when I followed them into the house.

They hadn't lost any of their earlier excitement later in the evening as we sat in the lounge. I listened to a jumbled-up account of their day, delivered simultaneously at times which made it somewhat confusing. I heard about the wedding - which Jason described as taking place in a small room at the 'house where they all had the party'. He went into detail when he recalled the food, but he was a little vague about everything that followed.

Michele on the other hand gave a very precise account of almost everything that had happened from the moment she awoke that morning. I was amazed at not only the extent of her memory, but the small details she was able to recall. She described Marianne and Philip's clothes so accurately that I could almost picture them as they stood before the registrar, who was also described in detail. Michele's description was so vivid that I could clearly picture the room, and all the guests at the ceremony.

After a few hours I could see that the kids were starting to flag. Jason began to yawn and Michele's eyes began to look 'distant'. When I suggested they get ready for bed, neither of them complained. I was treated to a couple of hugs, and a brief kiss from Michele before they collected their cases and went upstairs.

I stayed in the lounge and took a small Brandy, savouring it and sipping slowly as I heard the unfamiliar sound of voices coming from upstairs. It was a good feeling.

I wasn't in the habit of getting up not long after dawn on Sundays, but I did the day after the wedding. I had little choice, since I was awakened by the sounds of rattling pans and chattering voices coming from downstairs. I took a quick shower and dressed in my casual track-suit along with a battered pair of trainers, and before I was halfway down the stairs I could smell the sausage, bacon, and coffee.

That was the first revelation. I expected to find Michele standing at the cooker, but no, both the kids were involved in making breakfast. I was impressed, not only with the quality and quantity of the meal, but by the lack of friction generated by the act of cooking it.

Whenever I'd been in the house I always remembered the wild arguments that went on between my kids and, as far as I was concerned, they just could not behave with civility towards each other. That Sunday morning was an eye-opener.

208

After the meal I joined them in clearing the table and washing the dishes. It was only a mundane chore, but it felt good.

We stayed in the kitchen while we discussed what we should do with the day. I had a couple of ideas, but I wanted to give the kids a chance to tell me what they wanted to do. It seemed that they'd already decided. We went to Blackpool.

It would take an hour to relate every detail of that day. We arrived sometime after ten o'clock and stayed until about five. We ate enough to keep an army on the hoof for a month, and we went on every hair-raising ride on the Pleasure Beach. That's an exaggeration. Michele and Jason rode all the rides, I gave up after the first three. We went on the sands, and paddled in the almost warm sea. We spent a small fortune in half a dozen amusement arcades on the Golden Mile, and by the time we got home, the kids were dreamily tired, and I was just tired.

I don't think I'd ever had such a hectic day in my life; and I don't think I ever felt so rewarded for my efforts. The kids offered no argument when, not long after nine o'clock, after they had a warm drink, I suggested it was time for bed. They trooped upstairs to shower and change into their pyjamas. They both looked pink and rosy when they came downstairs briefly, and they both smelled fresh and fragrant as they slipped onto my knee for a goodnight hug.

I didn't stay downstairs too long after they'd gone to bed. I had a slow drink, and then cleared up the few plates from the light supper we'd had. I crept up the stairs and gently opened the door of Jason's room. He was already fast asleep, as was Michele next door. I stayed for a moment at the door of each room, staring at them with so much … love and pride that I felt a lump in my throat.

I lay awake for a while that night, thinking about the day we'd just had. All right, it was only one day, and I couldn't expect every day to run as smoothly, but it was one hell of a good start.

A couple of things played on my mind. Both Michele and Jason had asked me why I hadn't found myself a 'girlfriend'. It had shocked me for a moment and I'd floundered for an answer. My instinctive reaction was to say that it was none of their business - then I realised it *was* their business in a way. Michele had put it rather more delicately than Jason. She told me how happy her mother was, with Philip, and she just wanted me to find someone to be happy with. She added that it would be smashing if they could have two families!

Something else that had cropped up was gardening. I never realised that both of them liked gardens and flowers, and all that sort of thing. Since there was never a proper garden at Sefton Avenue, I assumed that the kids weren't interested. Wrong.

I started thinking about our day in Blackpool to when we left the Pleasure Beach, and took the tram along the promenade towards the Golden Mile, but we'd stayed on the tram until it passed the north pier. I had intended taking them up the coast to Fleetwood, but as we passed the brightly painted amusement arcades, they

210

both started begging to go there. So we got off the tram at Gynn square and started to walk back. Rather than cross the road, we stayed on the sea side of the promenade and as we walked we passed numerous displays of flowers and shrubs. I was astounded by their knowledge. They seemed to know the name of almost every plant we saw.

When I complimented them on their knowledge, they started to tell me about the gardens at Philip's house. As I might have mentioned, gardening was anathema to me but, for their benefit, I did try to show some interest. I nodded and smiled when they told me about the well-tended lawns, and the banks of shrubs, and beds of flowers, the names of which were totally foreign to me.

It rained hard the following day, and we played indoors. Monopoly had always been a favourite of theirs and they duly robbed me of every property and pound that I had. We played a couple of times then I protested that I was fed up of being fleeced, and suggested we watched television for a while.

There was some early afternoon 'chat-show' on, and not long after we sat down to watch it, Jason pointed to the young female presenter.

"Do you fancy her, dad? I mean, she is a cracker, isn't she?"

"Well, she's ... all right, I suppose. Why don't we just watch the programme?"

Jason lapsed into silence, but Michele took up

211

the theme. "If you did get a girlfriend, dad - would it be anybody who looked like her?"

"I haven't really thought about it."

The truth was, I hadn't.

The middle of the week marked the start of my engagements. I had a booking to perform at a club in Chorley and I wanted to make sure I wasn't late. I called the Callaghan's and expected their middle daughter to arrive for a stint of baby-sitting. Instead it was her younger sister who turned up. Elaine was fifteen and, like the rest of the family, a sensible enough kid. Before I could ask her, she volunteered the information that her elder sister had 'got herself a boyfriend' and wouldn't be coming round again. When I started to explain what I expected, she cut me short.

"It's all right, Mister Clarke. Bernice had told me everything I should do, and she reminded me to ask for the phone number of the club where you're working - so I can call if there's any real trouble. She also told me that you said you don't like mobile phones as they only encourage people to talk too much rubbish and you hate computers as they make lazy people even lazier and she told m-"

"Yes yes I think she told you all you need to know, and maybe a bit more."

I left the number with Elaine, and loaded up my car. I called out to the kids as I was leaving, and they called back. Just as I closed the door I heard one of them saying. "... Shall we play Monopoly?"

*   *   *

TEN

I gave a low laugh as I saw the expression on Sean's face. He frowned at first then started laughing with me. He let out a sigh.

"I never realised how much fun it could be, just being with them. Don't get me wrong, it wasn't all buns and Brandy. There were times when they had me so uptight you could have played me with a violin bow; but all in all, it was great being with them." He stared at me. "I assume you don't have any kids?"

"No." I hunched my shoulders. "I'm not sure I want them - I'm not really a 'kid person'."

"That's because you don't have any. Believe you me, when they do come along and, like I found out when Marianne left me, you make the effort…"

"I don't know if I ever want to 'make the effort', Sean. You've just told me they take up your time, and they complicate things."

"'Course they do. They're individuals and have their own personalities, like everyone." He looked at me with an intense expression for some time before he spoke again. "You don't strike me as being a selfish sod, and I've already figured out that you can be quite understanding when you forget you're a journalist."

"That still wouldn't qualify me to be a natural father, and anyway, you yourself didn't discover them until your wife left now you're sounding like father of the year."

213

"Alright I get your point, but there's no such animal - or more correctly, most men *are* 'natural fathers', they're just not natural parents. We all chase after women, with a few exceptions, and we all - deep down - have the same instinct ... and it isn't to bring up a family. We have to work hard at it to learn to do that properly."

"Yes I agree...but what if you're not prepared to learn to be a parent? Once you commit yourself, it's too late."

"It's never too late. Look at me! I was like you, only I was married at the time." He studied me for a while. "Do you have a girlfriend?"

"Sort of. Amanda - the girl I brought to your concert in Preston."

"Ah, the one who dragged you out before I could meet her. Are you serious about her?"

"It isn't like that. We're friends, good friends she drifts in and out of my life."

Sean shrugged. "Don't misunderstand me, I'm not trying to coax you into anything ... It's just that life has been so much fuller, more rewarding since I got to know my kids. I sort of wanted to share it with you."

"In a way, you are sharing it with me. I can see how it affected you, and I'm glad for you. But I'm not envious of you, yet. Now can we get on with the story?"

Sean gave a shrug. "Sorry if I seemed to be trying to 'convert' you. I didn't mean to preach. God knows with my track record as a father as you were more than quick to mention I wouldn't have the right. It's just that I'd like you to share in the good feelings..."

"Maybe some time later when I'm your age." I smiled at him. "In the meantime, Sean, can we please get on with the story?"

"You know Andy you can be cruel at times. Right." He paused and seemed to drift into a mild reverie. He 'returned' after a few moments.

"You know, that first time when I had them to myself was the most frightening and exciting time of my life. I was forced to think about other people before myself, and I didn't find it easy. I assumed they'd want to do the things I wanted, and for most of the time, they probably didn't. But, after the first week we developed an understanding and things ran pretty smoothly. One thing that did trouble me, until I learned how to sidestep, was their eagerness to see me hitched again. As I've said, even when we were watching TV they'd pick out some young attractive woman and ask if I fancied her. I was paired off with more women in a week than I'd known in the whole of my life." He grinned at me. "The funny thing is that the more they went on about it, the more appealing the idea became. I wasn't used to being on my own, and the prospect of having someone new with me did present a tempting picture."

Sean gave a short laugh and shook his head. "I remember it got so bad that one night, as I was just about falling off to sleep, I started going through a mental list of 'potential girlfriends'. There were a few, but no one special. Then for some strange reason I started to think about the girl I'd met in the police station, and mused that she, if a bit older, she would have been almost perfect. I really liked her in more ways than one, and I felt sure that if I met her again ..." Sean smiled when he saw my expression. "Yes," he nodded.

215

That's what I thought. Am I losing it or what? I'm falling for a girl who only exists in my concussive dream.

... and once the realization came to me, I had a good laugh at myself." He was still smiling as he went on.

It was about halfway through their stay when I decided we'd all benefit from a holiday. I wanted to get away from the house for more than just a day, and I really wanted to be pampered. All right, the kids had shared with all the chores, but I thought it would be nice if we could go to a hotel and let other people do the cooking and the washing up.

I put it to the kids and they leapt at the idea. That was when we had our first really major disagreement. Michele and Jason had been pretty amicable towards each other, but when I asked them where they thought we should go, they came up with wildly conflicting suggestions.

Jason wanted us to go back to Blackpool, but Michele made it plain that, although she'd enjoyed the day we'd spent there, she wouldn't want to stay for a week. Personally I wasn't worried where we went, so I stayed out of the argument and acted as a neutral referee. When it became clear that they had quite differing ideas of what a holiday should be, I suggested they compromise and pick somewhere that appealed to them and where they could both indulge themselves in whatever they wanted.

It took quite some time and I was getting a bit annoyed by the time they did finally come to a kind of agreement. It was their idea that we 'toured' and visited a new place each day. This would ensure that each got at least one good day out of two … me, I got the dubious distinction of being the treasurer and chauffer.

They'd selected Cornwall as a final destination, and they spent the rest of that day trying to sort out an itinerary. I'd warned them that I wasn't going to consider staying at five star hotels, nor would I think of living in a tent. I kept out of it as much as I could, and to their credit they came up with what I thought was a reasonable travel plan. My only condition was that we should break the journey both going down and coming back. They disagreed and argued that my suggestion would take two days out of their holiday. I warned them that the drive from Manchester to Cornwall was a long one, but my warning had no effect.

Jason and Michele slept for most of the drive southwards. We'd left home quite early, around four o'clock in the morning, and although they'd had little sleep, they were kept awake for the first couple of hours by the excitement of the trip. Before we'd reached Stafford on the M6, they were both fast asleep, and they stayed like that until we reached Exeter.

At that time - I don't know if it's still in force now - there was a county-wide by-law that made it an offence to sleep in a car in a lay-by or car-park. I was driving on auto-pilot by the time we reached Bude, and I drove onto the beach in the misty light of pre-dawn. I let the kids out, with strict orders that they were to stay within sight of the car while I had a quick nap. The sun was up when I was awakened by the feeling of hands tugging at me and the sound of frantic voices calling in my ear.

We left the beach just as the tide came to cover the patch of sand where I'd been parked.

I had a marvellous time during that week, and I was so relaxed I was almost comatose the whole time. As far as I can tell, both the kids enjoyed themselves too. We stayed in pubs or boarding houses and we visited a dozen or more places in the county.

We found a delightfully secluded little bay on the southern coast. Approached by a narrow tree-lined track, Lamorna Cove was a sense-shock when it appeared. One moment we were driving beneath an arched canopy of trees forming a dark green 'tunnel', and the next we were staring at a circular 'amphitheatre' of rock which sloped down to a gently shelving sandy beach. We swam in the clear warm water, and we lazed in the sand afterwards ... well, I lazed and the kids explored the rock pools.

At Land's End, we walked to the tip of Britain and looked out over the grey-green Atlantic. Jason was intrigued by the mile-post indicating distances to far-away cities, and I had to drag him away.

Michele had shown her horticultural side, and had ignored the post and spent her time examining the shrubs and grasses battling to survive in the bleak sandy soil. She'd shown the same interest in plants wherever we'd gone, and she'd known the names of most of them. When we'd spent some time in a particularly fine garden not far from Padstow, she'd taken me to task and pointed out that the garden at Sefton Avenue was, in her words, a complete mess. It wasn't the first time she'd

218

mentioned it, but I'd managed to by-pass the question. This time I couldn't. She faced me squarely and waited until she extracted a promise from me.

All right, I was on holiday and Manchester was a million miles away. What harm was there in agreeing to 'sort out' the front garden once we got home? With luck Michele would have forgotten about it by the time our holiday was over.

We spent some time in Tintagel, where Jason had said he wanted to see King Arthur's castle. He seemed a little disappointed firstly with 'The Vale of Avalon' which was little more than a cobble-strewn track leading down to the shore, and secondly by the castle itself. He'd obviously expected a castle much as he'd seen on TV and films, so when he came across the grass-covered rocky piece of land jutting out to sea he couldn't help but show his feelings. He did recover somewhat when, not long after we got down to the castle, a tremendous blast of water jetted out of a blow-hole showering dozens of people standing close-by.

Jason adamantly insisted that we went to stand by the hole, and we reluctantly went. I can't say that I enjoyed the experience of hearing the terrific rumble of the sea forcing its way through the narrow inlet then surging up the vertical hole in the rock… and I definitely did not enjoy the experience of being drenched by the hosing spray that emerged.

Boscastle was the last place we visited. I parked on the approach to the long narrow harbour which was almost dry when we arrived. I'd been warned by some locals that the sight of the tide coming it was spectacular, and I'd managed to persuade Michele and Jason that it would be exciting to watch.

While we waited for the tide, we called in at a tiny 'Witch Museum' where I spent most of the time trying to stop the kids from laughing at the displays. When we emerged, the tide had started to come in and the harbour was filling with swirling water. The kids took interest when a particularly large wave rushed into the narrow channel and surged almost halfway up the stone-lined approach. Both Michele and Jason squealed with delight as the waves got larger as they were funnelled into the gorge, and they yelled out when the largest waves battered at the short angled stone breakwater and flung spray tens of feet into the air. I think we were all stimulated by the experience of sheer power that we'd witnessed that day.

We'd gorged ourselves on cream teas at almost every place we visited, savouring the delightful Cornish cream mixed with various sorts of jam. We ate al-fresco, devouring Cornish pasties which seemed larger than local buses and slavering over fish and chips eaten from paper while sitting on rocks or walls while staring out at the sea.

The memories lingered with us as I started the drive northwards at the end of the holiday. I was startled, and more than just pleased when, while we stopped for a snack at a motorway service area, Michele flung her arms around me and gave me a kiss. I was even more delighted when she told me it'd been the best holiday of her life.

Life was beautiful, and even the bills that were waiting on the mat when we arrived home didn't manage to dispel the feeling. Along with them was a postcard from Marianne, addressed to all of us, and we read it together later that evening after we'd organised the washing. As I read her words, I realised that she no longer meant anything to me. She wasn't a stranger, but she wasn't part of my life any more, and I wasn't bothered. The Cornish holiday had done more than just bring me closer to my kids; it had completely expunged her from my emotions.

Next morning I checked the answer phone and found that my local agent had got me a booking at a club in Heptonstall for that night. I told the kids and they understood that I had to spend some time rehearsing. I don't know how they occupied themselves, but they were quiet enough, and the house wasn't 'retextured' when we had our tea together at five o'clock.

Elaine Callaghan arrived in good time, and I set off for the drive into Yorkshire. I was still thinking about Cornwall and the great time I'd had, and the journey passed quickly.

The club was situated at the end of a newish looking estate and was set inside a low fence. Beyond the fence forming the car park was nothing but the rolling Yorkshire Moors, and I paused for a moment just to stand and stare at the scenery. I hadn't done that in a long time.

The dressing room, for want of a better word was little bigger than a broom cupboard adjoining the

221

low wide stage. I'd expected to be the only performer, so I was a bit surprised when 'Lola Latino' swept in as I was changing. Lola's real name was Barbara Bretherton, and she came from Liverpool. We'd been on the same bill a few times, and weren't strangers.

She gave me a peculiar look, and I understood why when she spoke.

"Hello, Sean. I heard that you and your wife have split up." From the look in her eyes you'd have thought she'd won the lottery. She dropped her case on the floor and sauntered over to me. I took hold of her wrists as she tried to drape her arms around my neck.

It wasn't that she was ugly, in fact she was quite attractive. She had long shimmering dark hair and deep-set dark expressive eyes. She was tall and slender, and even though I held her wrists she managed to force her slim body against my naked chest. Her breath sighed the words as she spoke.

"I've always had a thing for you, Sean. I expect you didn't notice?"

I had noticed, and I'd been wary, since I'd heard a good many tales about 'weird Lola' and her funny bedroom games. Before I could stop her, she'd leaned forward and kissed me. I shook my head.

"It's true what you heard - but I've got myself a new girl now."

She stepped back and pouted. "That was quick. Mind you I always thought you were a fast worker. What's she called?"

"Michele. She's from Cheadle."

"Michele from Cheadle, sounds posh. Where'd you

meet her?"

"Not that's it's any of your business Lola but if you
must know, we met in Cornwall." I saw the expression
on her face and guessed that what I'd said wasn't
enough to put her off. I spoke quickly. "She's at home,
waiting for me."

"Oh …" Her pout became more pronounced as she
turned away.

I hadn't arrived home until after two o'clock, but the
kids still woke me just after nine the following morning.
I felt tousled on the inside as I joined them for breakfast
and I wasn't really listening to what they said. I nodded
where I though it appropriate, and I scowled when it
seemed right. So I was puzzled when, after we'd cleared
the table and done the dishes, they went out to the back
garden and disappeared into the old shed.

I gaped at them when they emerged carrying an
assortment of spades, hoes and forks. I was standing at
the kitchen door, as I called to them.

"Are you clearing out the rubbish?"

"No." It was Michele who answered. "I persuaded
Jason to help me. You can join in too, if you want."

"Sure. I'll help." I tried to sound eager, but I'd no idea
what she was talking about. "What should I do?"

"Carry these to the front, dad. They're heavy." She held
out a spade and a rusty fork.

"Right … er what're you going to do there?"

"You promised I could do something with the garden,
remember? Mum would never let us touch it, said it was

your job to sort it out. She let us do the back but it's the front is what people see first, and it's not very nice, dad."

She was being diplomatic. The front garden resembled a cross between a building site and a disused railway siding. The lawn, that's what I called it, was covered with thigh-high weeds which hid liberally distributed rubbish, while the surrounding strip, which I laughingly referred to as 'the border' was little more than a narrow trench filled with an accumulation of assorted detritus.

I carried the implements through the house and out to the front garden where I dumped them on the path. The kids joined me, and we had a quick conference.

It was decided that, since I was the strongest, I would start by cutting down the forest of weeds on the lawn, while Michele and Jason emptied the border. I had a frightening picture of the path being swamped by a garbage heap of rubbish, so I suggested we find something in which to collect the stuff we were going to discard.

We lined the path with a dozen cardboard boxes and half a dozen bin-liners, and then we set to work. I steadily chopped away at the lawn and I listened to the kids' chattering as they attacked the borders. By half-past-eleven I was ready for a break. I'd cleared two thirds of the lawn and I was horrified at what I'd revealed. I know there had been grass there at some time in the past, but it was non-existent now. I mentally groaned at the thought of what lay ahead, but I tried to keep a cheerfully confident grin on my face until I got in the house.

The kids joined me about twenty minutes after I'd retreated into the kitchen. I was drinking a beautifully cool glass of Shandy, and they asked for some. We sat, sweaty and glowing as we poured the cool sparkling drinks down our throats.

Michele finished her drink first and smiled at me. "Dad. We found some things in the corner, close to next-door's hedge." She put a hand in her pocket and pulled out a dirt-covered object. "I think it's a brooch … could I wash it, and save it?"

"It's …" I was about to say 'disgusting' but I didn't. I shrugged. "See if it will wash clean." I watched her as she went to the sink and doused the object in warm soapy water.

"There!" Michele beamed when she turned round to show us the results. "It's as good as new."

I wouldn't have agreed with her, but the brooch did look reasonable. She brought it to me and I could see that it was made in the shape of a butterfly and was now quite shiny. The pale amethyst stones set in its wings had still retained some sparkle.

"Yes," I said, "it's … quite nice."

"I think it could be valuable." Jason wiped a dribble of Shandy from his chin. "I reckon we should have a special box where we can put all the treasure we find."

I was about to dismiss his suggestion when I realised it could be a good way of entertaining them. "Yes, I think you should."

By mid-afternoon the lawn was down to its naked and

startling reality, and I was down to the last dregs of my energy. The kids were still crouching at the edge of the lawn, scrabbling in the mucky border and muttering cheerfully. I left them to it.

I'd showered and changed by the time they came in, and the first thing I did was have them clean up. They'd brought in a battered cardboard box, and I had them leave it on some paper in the hall.

Scrubbed clean and glowing with excitement, Michele and Jason brought the box into the kitchen and started to wash the items they found. It obviously gave them a lot of pleasure and it seemed churlish to chide them for the mess they were making.

"Look, dad." Michele held up a tiny pink figure. "I was only tiny when I lost this doll."

"And I found some money!" Jason held up a few coins. "Can I keep them?"

"Sure … it's treasure trove." I smiled. I watched them bending over the sink, cleaning their 'finds' and I was reminded of my own childhood. It was a happy feeling.

"Dad…" Michele had turned to me and was frowning. "I can't get this clean … could you help me?"

I got up and went to the sink. Ignoring the dark muddy slop, I looked at the object she was clutching. It was covered with a thick green growth but there was no mistaking what it was. It was a key. I held out my hand and she dropped the verdigris-encrusted lump of metal onto my palm. I felt something like a shock, and for an instant I again had a vision of a short thick-set, red-faced man standing in the doorway as he slapped at my hand. I saw the key as it went spinning into the dark corner of the garden on that Christmas Eve in my dream.

That night when the kids were in bed, I took an old toothbrush from the bathroom and found a half used tin of metal polish in the kitchen. It took quite some time, but I was able to clean the old key up until it looked as new. I fished my front-door key out of my pocket and compared it to the one I'd just cleaned. I felt a leaden lump in my stomach as I saw that the two keys for all intents and purposes looked identical.

I went down the hall and opened the front door then stepped outside. A cold shiver ran up my spine as I held the key and guided it towards the lock.

*　　　　　*　　　　　*

ELEVEN

Sean looked at me with a chillingly distant expression in his eyes. I waited for him to carry on. He didn't, and I couldn't contain myself.

"Well … what happened?"

"What?" Sean gave a slight shudder and took a deep breath. His eyes were misted when he looked at me. "You'll never believe what was going through my mind that night. I told myself I was being stupid even thinking what I was thinking … and yet I couldn't help myself. I had to see if the key fitted."

"And …?"

He smiled slowly. "I've often been accused of having an over-dramatic sense of occasion."

"I can understand why. Now will you please tell me what happened?"

"I chickened out. I put the key in my pocket, came back into the house, and went to bed."

"For God's sake why?"

"What would you have done? Like I said, I didn't want to be stupid about it, but I was scared of the implications. What do you think I would have felt if it had fitted the lock? I just wasn't prepared to find out."

"So… Did you try it the next day?"

"Not on your life. I did my best to forget it. I even thought of flinging the key into the dustbin and putting an end to it. Don't you see? I'd managed to adjust myself, and disregard all that had happened, or might

229

have happened, in the past. I'd become a 'new person', happy with my life, my kids, and the fact that I was single again. I didn't want anything to spoil it all."

"Then, what *did* you do?"

"Nothing. I just got on with my life as if the key didn't exist. I pushed it to the back of my mind during the rest of the kids' holiday. We finished the front garden and turned it into something half-respectable, and I promised Michele I'd keep it in order."

Sean gave a low sigh. "Marianne called me when they got back from the honeymoon, and she came with Philip to collect the kids and the first thing she said was "I see at last you've sorted out the front garden". It was funny, but when I met her at the door, I didn't feel a thing, except to notice that she was well-tanned and obviously happy. I spoke to Philip while Marianne was organising the kids, and he told me about the places they had visited. I wasn't really keen on hearing about their itinerary, but he made it sound interesting. I know it's awful but as hard as I tried I couldn't help but like the man.

When the kids appeared they hugged him, and that's when I did feel uncomfortable. The feeling didn't last long, and by the time they came to hug me, I was glad... glad that they both liked their new step-dad, and glad that from then on I'd still have a part to play in their lives."

"And you just forgot about the key?"

"I tried." Sean gave a wry smile. "I could see all the problems it would create and I wasn't prepared to face them. But the more I pushed it to the back of my mind,

230

the more it kept springing back at me.

I lasted three whole days. The nights were the worst; I lay in bed scared of going to sleep, because when I did I kept having some God-awful dreams like the ones I had after my trip to America. In those three days I reckon I had just about six hours sleep in total."

"But in the end tell me you gave in?"

"I had to. It was either that, or running completely off the rails. I could see I was getting more and more paranoid about it, so I had no choice ..." He became distant again as he carried on. "It was Wednesday morning. I'd hardly slept, and I hadn't eaten. The key was still in my pocket and it felt a bit like the 'ring' in Tolkien's book. I couldn't think about anything else ... I knew that we'd fitted new locks throughout the house after a burglary scare in the district. That was just before I went on my American trip, in ninety four. So, if the key did fit and then I thought, 'hold on maybe I'm looking at this all wrong. The key won't fit and I've been driving myself mad for no reason'." He let out a long expressive sigh, and I felt some of his tension. He glanced at me with solemn eyes. "I went outside and fished it out of my pocket then slipped it into the lock.

It fit perfectly."

"What are you trying to tell me, Sean?"

Sean frowned. "What do you think?"

I couldn't help but give a little laugh. "You're not trying to say that you honestly think I'm going to believe that you actually went back in time?"

Sean's face coloured and his voice became sharp. "And why shouldn't you believe me? Don't you

231

think I'd played the devil's advocate often enough myself? Don't you think I haven't gone through all the arguments over and over? I'd convinced myself it was all a dream, because that was the logical explanation for the situation. But finding that key changed it all. Don't you see that? I told you I'd got to a state where I was starting to be content again - so why would I want to destroy it all?"

I reacted instinctively. "Because it would make a bloody good story." I knew I was goading him but I wanted to see how he reacted.

Sean leapt from his chair and came towards me, his face like thunder. He stood over me and I could see he was trembling with anger. He leaned forward. "Look! I'm not a scientist. I'm just an ordinary person trying to make sense out of a very un-ordinary event. The kids had found coins and other stuff that they'd lost during the whole of their lifetime. That key had been there much longer than the things they found. I told you it was thick with verdigris."

I hunched my shoulders, a move which seemed to aggravate him even more. He stood over me for several tense seconds then he seemed to deflate. He let out a long expressive sigh. "All right Andy, if that's how you want to treat it, I reckon you should go … and if you can't come back with an open mind, then don't bother coming back at all!"

When I got outside I began to go over what Sean had said, and how I'd received it. I felt, deep inside, that he really did believe what he'd told me, but my naturally phlegmatic nature prevented me from accepting it at face value.

"FOR FUCKS SAKE PEOPLE CAN'T GO BACK IN TIME. FACT! "

Now I had a real problem … I was certain he was quite serious when he'd said that I should accept his word, or forget the whole thing. I needed to talk to an outsider…

I called Amanda as soon as I got home. Without giving away too much detail, I told her I needed to speak with her.

Amanda came round and we had a meal in my flat while I debated the best way to tell her what Sean had told me. She was diplomatic enough to wait until I'd decided the time was right.

I'd already told her much of his tale, and I just repeated what he'd told me that afternoon. Amanda listened without a flicker of emotion, and when I'd finished she shrugged. "So you believed him?"

"What, time travel? Of course not. Although having said that, Sean can make the impossible sound plausible. I'm pretty positive he believed it."

"It's what you believe that matters. That's why you have to make sure it isn't a complete hoax and it goes without saying you just can't accept things at face value. So, have you checked the earlier parts of his story?"

"I did confirm that the details he said he'd seen in the newspaper were genuine. But I haven't looked into the facts concerning the brothers and the 'Manchester Murders'."

233

"Why not?"

"Because, my bewitching lovely, he only just told me this afternoon, until then he thought it was a dream. I've been with him each day, and when I wasn't there, I was putting the rest of his story on my computer … I just didn't have the time to research everything he'd told me." I pulled a face at her. "I'm not even halfway through it."

"So … are you just going to leave it at that?"

"No, of course I'm not. But I can't see how I can do the research until after he's finished. And if I don't turn up, he's going to think it's all over, that's if he doesn't think that already … and I do want to hear the rest of it."

"So - you're going back?"

"I have to go. I just can't drop it."

Amanda shrugged. She looked thoughtfully at a point a few inches above my left shoulder for a few seconds then she nodded. "I could do the research for you … if you like? I don't have to start my new job until a week next Monday, so I have a bit of free time."

"You'd be doing me a tremendous favour if you could check up on all those facts for me."

"Right," she said, "give me all the details. You know … the brothers' names, the name of the young girl, your 'singer' said he rescued … and anything else you think might be a help to me. "She gave me a coquettish smile. "It'll cost you a decent dinner - a cocktail dress dinner."

"It's a deal; you pick the restaurant and I'll wear my best cocktail dress."

234

Sean gave me a questioning look as he opened the door to me the following morning. Neither of us spoke as he led me into the front room, I declined his offer of a Brandy and Sean took his customary chair while I faced him from the settee. He savoured the aroma of his spirit then sipped. Putting his glass down, he stared at me.

"This is the 'real crunch', isn't it? Everything I've told you so far was just a story, but now it's taken on a new significance."

"Yes."

"And you've turned up, so I assume you want me to carry on? Or are you here to tell me that you've had enough? If that's the case, thanks for being civil, and not just phoning me."

I took out my recorder and placed it on the arm of the settee. "You've held my interest so far, and I don't like to leave jobs half-finished."

Sean relaxed. He picked up his glass and saluted me. I just nodded and sat back.

He blinked slowly and drew a sharp breath. "You know, it took less than a heartbeat for me to realise the significance of fitting the key into the lock, but it took hours for me to come to a decision as to what to do about it." Sean then sank into his seat and I made myself comfortable as he began.

Yes, the episode concerning the Key was the catalyst that instigated my search to prove what really happened to me on last Christmas Eve but it was just the start.

The first thing I did was to drive down into Manchester. I parked off Shude Hill and walked to the Portland hotel. I went to the reception desk and smiled at the petite red-head behind the desk.

"Hello. I wonder if you can help me."

"Certainly, sir. What can I do for you?"

"I would like to ask you a favour. Is it possible for you to check your records to see if a certain person stayed here on the night of Christmas eve nineteen sixty four?"

She gave me a doubtful smile then frowned. "We're completely computerised now, and I don't think our records go back that far. If you could wait, I'll find out for you."

"Thank you." I went to one of the easy chairs dotted around the foyer and sat down. I must have waited a quarter of an hour before she returned and, as I went to the desk, I could see from her expression that she didn't have anything for me. She confirmed my suspicions.

"I'm sorry, sir, but I was right. Our records only go back a few years, and we have no way of looking back any further than that. I spoke to our manager, and he couldn't suggest how you might find out if a person was here. I'm sorry."

"Thank you for trying. It was an off-chance anyway." I said as I turned away and headed for the street.

Once outside I started to make my way back to the car, and as I walked I tried to decide what course I could take. Now I'd started on 'the quest' I wasn't going to let it go ... But what should I do next?

By the time I reached the car park, I'd come to a decision. Another focal point of my dream recollection was the events that took place at the police station on Willet Street. So I headed out of the city centre and drove along Rochdale road figuring out what I was

236

going to say when I got there.

I'd been disappointed when I could get no confirmation of my stay at the Portland, and I was even more disappointed when I arrived at Willet Street. The police station was no longer there!

I'd passed a relatively new police station at Collyhurst as I was driving north on Rochdale road, so I turned round and headed back towards the city centre. I decided to use the same ruse as I was about to use at Willet street. I would pretend I was asking about someone else, and casually drop the word 'research' - which seemed to generate far more response than a straightforward question.

I went up to the main desk and was greeted by a young sergeant.

"Good morning sir, what can I do for you?"

"I'm doing some research on a family who lived locally, and I wondered if you could confirm some details about one of them who was taken to Willet Street Police station. It was a few years ago …"

"It must have been. Willet Street hasn't been used for ages. Now, if you could give me a name, I might be able to check the records from the old place."

"I gave him my name, then told him that the 'man in question' was taken there on the twenty fourth of December nineteen sixty four."

"1964, you'll be lucky, do you know what the charge was?"

"I'm almost certain it was a drink-driving offence - but I don't think any formal charge was brought against him. I believe he was just examined by a doctor who said the man was not drunk."

"Oh," the sergeant hunched his shoulders. "If there was no charge, then there won't be any record. I'm sorry sir."

Another dead end was all I needed. I was in a depressed and frustrated mood when I emerged from the station. All my enthusiasm had faded and I couldn't see how I could go any further with my investigation. Another idea came to me as I passed newsagents on the way back home.

When I'd taken the girl Betty to my house on Sefton Avenue in nineteen sixty four, the owner had given me a newspaper. I know I'd read it while sitting in the car with Betty, and, as far as I could remember, I'd tossed it on the back seat before I drove down to the Portland Hotel.

New hope sprang up as I turned back towards the city. It was only a while since I'd been forced to borrow the mini-traveller, there was a good chance that either Charlie, or Tony would remember seeing a new version of a very old newspaper in the car when I'd taken it back.

Tony was in the cabin when I got to New Cross, and he gave me grin of recognition as I walked across the forecourt. He stepped out to meet me.

"Hello, Mister Clarke. Got problems with your car again?"

"No, nothing like that. The car's been fine since you fixed it up for me. I wanted to talk to you about the mini-traveller you loaned me."

"Right … Want to buy it?"

"No … I wonder … did you clean it out after I dropped

238

it off?"

He frowned at me. "I didn't ... If it was cleaned, it'd have been Charlie who did it. Is there some problem?"

"No. Is Charlie about?"

"Yes, he's in the workshop. I'll get him." He sauntered over to the workshop door and disappeared inside. Moments later he reappeared with Charlie by his side. Charlie gave me a wide grin as he came up to me.

"Mister Clarke, nice to see you. Tony said you're asking about the 'traveller' ... said you might have left something inside?"

"Well, not exactly. I was just wondering if you found anything unusual in it after I'd brought it back."

Charlie frowned thoughtfully for a moment then shook his head. "Can't say that I did. It was pretty clean when ... just a minute! You're not talking about that newspaper on the back seat, are you?"

I tried to remain calm. "Yes. That's what I was after. Did you notice anything ... odd about it? And did you keep it?"

"To be honest, I just picked it up and threw it into the waste-bin." He must have seen my expression. "Is it important?"

"The bin's been emptied, I suppose?" I said partly in jest, partly in hope.

"Yes. We have it cleaned out every week by the Council. Was there something special in that paper?"

"Yes ... but if it's gone ... It doesn't matter, it was just an article I meant to read."

"I'm sorry, Mister Clarke. If I'd known, I'd have put it on one side for you."

239

"That's all right. You weren't to know."

Charlie gave an embarrassed shrug. "Have you got any local performances lined up?"

"Not this week, but I'm in Rochdale next Tuesday. I'll send you a couple of tickets if you want?"

"Oh, that'd be great … Sorry I couldn't help you with the other matter."

"Forget it. I'll post the tickets to you here, should I?"

"Yes." Charlie reached into the top pocket of his overalls and pulled out a grubby card. "It'll be a nice surprise for the wife. See you next week."

"Yes." I took the card and slipped it into my pocket as I walked back to the car.

I was in a sorry sort of mood when I got home, and I had a couple of stiff drinks before I checked the answer phone.

I cheered up a little when I listened to a message from my agent. He'd managed to get me an audition for a small part in a TV play based on some of the 'troubles' in Northern Ireland. He'd already found me some walk-on parts, and now it seemed I was being considered for some real 'acting'. I contacted him and found out that the audition was to take place at the Granada studios the following day. It helped to keep my mind otherwise occupied, and I found I was quite excited when I thought about the prospect of getting bigger acting parts.

I turned up at the studio in good time. I didn't want to

be there too early - that would show my inexperience and anxiety, nor did I want to arrive at the last minute which would have left me a nervous wreck.

The uniformed security man at the desk told me the auditions were being held in one of the smaller studios and he checked a list fastened to a clip-board then made a telephone call. A trim young girl appeared a few minutes later and gave me a warm smile. She escorted me down to the production level where she steered me to a small 'green room' where a couple of other men were already installed and reading a couple of pages of script.

I didn't recognise either of them, and we barely glanced at each other as the young assistant handed me a copy of the two page script and told me there'd be a call within the next hour. We waited.

I and the man sitting directly opposite were the first to be called. It was a bit of relief to get out of the room which had taken on the atmosphere of a condemned cell - which made me think we were all novices. It sort of gave me some confidence to think I wasn't competing with 'established' pros, and I was quite relaxed when I and my companion were led onto a small set.

The director outlined the setting for us, and gave us his impressions of the characters we were to play. The test itself was nothing elaborate. I stood beside my companion from the green-room, and we were asked to run through the script while following the simple directions as the camera tracked us.

I have to admit, once the scene started, I was

pretty nervous. I was still a bit tense after I'd finished. When I was told to go home and wait for a call from my agent it seemed like a bit of a let-down.

While Sean had been talking I'd kept a neutral expression on my face. I'd glanced down at the small recorder to check that it was running and had plenty of recording time left. When he started to talk about his experience at the TV studio I began to wonder if he'd gotten off track.

Interesting though it might be, I wasn't really concerned with his TV career. I came to hear about the 'past-time' experience, and I was prepared to stop him if he didn't get back to the proper story.

He obviously noticed the change in my expression and he stopped talking. He looked at me with a hint of a challenge, and I was tempted to voice my uneasiness at the way his story had started to move away from its original course. He cocked his head to one side and grinned.

"I can see what you're thinking, Andy." He shook his head. "I haven't lost my marbles, and I'm not starting to ramble. I'm still telling you a part of the same story. All right?"

"All right, Sean … but I can't see how what you've just told me has anything to do with your going back in time."

"That's because you want me to just give you the simple facts in an A-B-C order, and it wasn't like that. If you want, I can just give you a brief sketch of …."

"No, Sean. That isn't what I want."

"Good … just as long as you know that I'm not flannelling, and everything I'm telling you has a reason for being told." I nodded, and he smiled at me. "I daresay I might have gone on a bit about the audition and all that, but I was trying to get the message over that it did take my mind off my 'problem' … You'll see that the TV thing was more important than it appeared."

"OK, Sean, sorry. You just carry on."

"This is not a James Herbert novel, my story is about a supernatural event against the backdrop of natural ordinary people's lives. Any more questions Andy?"

"I'll let you know."

He grinned. "I'm sure you will. Anyway, I'll cut to the chase. I got the part and a few weeks later I spent a couple of days doing my scene in the studio…."

On the final day of shooting my scene, the director finally called it a 'take' and a wrap just before lunch so I went to the dressing room and got changed. I was on my way out when one of the actors, who had a sizeable part, asked if I'd like to join him and a few others for a drink… Is the Pope Catholic?

They took me to *The Old School*, a bar only a few hundred yards away from the studio. I recognised a couple of the crowd who were already drinking and I acknowledged them as I joined my new companions. Someone made a quick check then called out in a real

'stage-voice', "Four pints of Guinness, Annie."
Over the hubbub of background noise, a man's voice called back. "Annie's taking the rest of the week off."

There was something about the accent that caught my attention. I turned round to see if I could see the barman, but he was hidden by the press of bodies clustered around the bar counter. I indulged in some passing conversation with my new friends at the table, then I looked up as the barman brought our drinks. Both he and I gaped as we saw each other, but it was I who called out first. "Fuck me, as I live and breathe, Paddy Flynn. What the hell are you doing here?"

"Of all the gin joints in the entire world you have to walk into mine."

"Paddy Flynn, that is the worst impression of Humphry Bogart I have ever heard, you sound more like Frank Carson."

"What do you expect? You're the entertainer. Anyway, we'll talk later when it gets a wee bit quieter."

Much later that afternoon, after the bar was almost cleared, I was able to talk to Paddy. He told me he had quit the ship not long after I left. He said that conditions, already bad for the staffing crew, became far worse, and he'd had an almighty argument with the cruise Hotel Manager, and walked off the ship.

He'd come to Manchester because, as I remember him telling me, he had a married sister here and some friends living in the area. He was staying with his sister until he was able to find a flat. The job at The Old School, he added, was on a 'needs' basis. He didn't work there regularly, but filled in when the permanent

244

staff were away. We both would have liked to carry on with the conversation but another crowd from Granada surged in. We exchanged addresses and phone numbers, and agreed to meet up again as soon as we were able.

I got a call from him a couple of days later asking me to meet him at his sister's.

Paddy's sister, Bridget, lived in a council house on Brunswick Street not far from the University and Manchester Royal Infirmary. The house was neat and clean, and Bridget was a lively once-attractive woman. I could see the reason for her worry-lines when I met her husband. The less said about George the better.

There was only one room downstairs, apart from a small kitchen, and George made it clear he wasn't going to leave us free to talk. Paddy and I got out and found the nearest pub.

Paddy wouldn't accept my offer to let him stay at my house until he found somewhere to live.

"No. I can see you're getting yourself together now, and you don't need another bloke getting under your feet. Thanks all the same, but I've got a few places to look at this week, so I'll probably be fixed up soon."

"If it doesn't happen, you know you can call me."

"Thanks." He drained his glass and held it up. "Are you having another with me?"

He got us a couple more pints and we drank in silence for a few moments. Putting his glass down, he grinned.

"You'll be pleased to hear that your 'friend' Shawnie has left the Senator. He's under pressure, fighting to retain his hold on the State, and I suppose she reckons he's going to go down. Guess where she's gone?"

"I'm only interested if its bad news. Where?"

"Las Vegas. Rumour has it that she's got herself tied in with one of the heads of a large syndicate that runs a parcel of casinos." He stared at me. "You really are looking a lot better than when we last met. The way you looked when you dragged yourself out of that bar in 'Frisco got me worried for you. So... how has everything worked out?"

I spent the next few minutes telling him about the divorce, and my new-found relationship with my kids. He nodded occasionally but remained silent while I was speaking. When I finished he raised his glass.

"Here's to you - the *new* you. I hope things stay on an even keel for you from now on. The last thing you need right now, are new problems." He frowned at me. "Are there new problems, is there something you haven't mentioned?"

I hunched my shoulders and felt a bit uncomfortable under his friendly but inquisitive gaze. "It's a bit of a weird tale, Paddy."

"After spending the last week cooped up with my brother in law from hell George, I'm ready for something out of the ordinary."

I hesitated. I liked Paddy, and I didn't want to say anything that might put a strain on our friendship. He obviously saw my reluctance, and gave me an encouraging smile. "Unless you're about to tell me that you've been abducted by aliens, I'm ready for anything."

"You weren't too far from the mark actually." I held his gaze and his smile faded. He became quite grave.

"It's troubling you. I can see that." He paused. "You had the confidence in me to pour out your troubles on the *Pacific Princess* …Nothing has changed, Sean. I'm still a bloody good listener."

"Yes, but this is … bizarre."

"Right, it's bizarre, that's OK I can do bizarre but you can't leave me hanging in mid-air, now, can you?" He stared at me. "If you're worried that I'll blab about what you tell me …?"

"No. No, it's not that I don't trust your discretion. It's just that I don't want you to think that I have completely lost it."

"Sean, tell me! You've whetted my appetite now, and I'll pester you 'til Armageddon if you don't." He grinned. "I can promise you, I'm a devil of a pesterer when I get going."

I studied him for a while, remembering how understanding he'd been when I'd really needed someone. Even so, I was still doubtful about his ability to truly understand what I had to say. I thought about it for a moment then realised that if Paddy couldn't sympathise with my predicament, nobody could.

I told him about the accident on the flight, and my subsequent concussion leading to what I believed was a series of nightmares. He sat quietly, hardly moving; and his expression remained constant as I progressed to the part of my tale that needed the most delicate telling. He

247

was quite still as he listened. I could see in his eyes that questions were rising, but he maintained his calm unruffled interest until I reached the point where I'd fitted the 'old' key into the lock. He couldn't contain himself.

"Holy Mother of God!"

*   *   *

TWELVE

To his credit, and my relief, Paddy showed no sign of doubting the truth of what I'd just told him. I could see he was having trouble with the facts themselves, but he made no mention of this when he spoke.

He asked me if I'd taken any steps to verify my story, and I recounted my failure to corroborate one single fact. He offered his sympathy, but more important, he offered his help.

"I have a fair bit of free time ... So, if you're agreeable, I could do a bit of 'digging around' for you. In fact when it comes to digging I'm yer man."

"But where would you start. I've exhausted all my options and got nowhere."

He tapped the side of his nose, then winked at me. "I told you I have a few friends around here. Some of them have been 'a bit naughty' in the past, but I daresay they could help me find somebody who remembers your Willet Street police station in the sixties. I'm assuming that, since that's where you went after the hotel, that's where you'd like me to concentrate?"

I shrugged. "I don't know. It did seem the most logical place to begin tracing the people I met that night."

"All right, that's where I'll start."

"Would you mind if I came with you?"

"Ah ... I think it would be better if you left it to me. Some of the people I'm having a mind to visit wouldn't take to strangers easily. They are nick named 'The Quality Street Gang' and they are nice lads really, or so their mothers say." still they might not volunteer any information at all if you were with me. No offence Sean, but leave this to Paddy Flynn?"

I shook my head then drained my glass. "Now it's my turn. Will you have another?" I carried our empty glasses to the bar and got a couple of replacements. Paddy was staring into thin air when I got to the table. He looked up and smiled. "I've already thought of three old mates who might be some help. I'll try to see them tomorrow. Should I telephone if I come up with anything?"

"Yes. I have a concert tomorrow night, but I'll be in until about half-past-four. There's no rush."

"Liar." Paddy grinned at me as he raised his glass.

Paddy was certainly right in assuming that I was eager for any news that might substantiate my story, and I waited impatiently for his call the following day. It didn't come.

Since the next day was Saturday I played host to Michele and Jason. The weather was beautiful, bright blue cloudless skies and a hot sun beaming down on us. I asked for suggestions where we should go, and Jason said he would like to ride on a canal boat.

I hadn't a clue where we might find a canal with passenger boats, but Jason gave me a superior look and said that Philip had been talking about some place near Blackburn where canal trips were a speciality. I was about to call Philip when Michele told me Marianne and Philip had gone out for the day.

I dug out an old map and the three of us pored over it until Jason jabbed a triumphant finger on Colne. We went to Colne.

We did ride on a canal boat, but Michele and I were not over-impressed. Michele pretended to be interested, but I could see she was being polite. I had my mind on other matters. Even so, it wasn't a bad day. We called at a McDonald's on the way home and the kids stuffed themselves with burgers and fries.

We were all quite tired when we got back to my house, and we just lazed around in the back garden, sitting on some old plastic chairs Jason had uncovered in the shed. I had a couple of Beers and the kids drank Coke while I played some oldies on my acoustic guitar.

I got a special hug from Jason when Marianne called to collect them, but Michele was quiet. She hesitated on the doorstep.

"You … you aren't getting fed up with us are you, dad?"

"Whatever made you say that?" I hugged her to me.

"You've been different today - like you weren't all with us. If you know what I mean?"

"I'm sorry love. I have some things on my mind, and I shouldn't have let them interfere with our day."

"You're not in trouble, or anything, are you?"

"No, nothing like that. There's not a thing to worry about, I promise." I was glad to see she was beaming as she walked down the path to Marianne's car.

251

The following morning, after breakfast I busied myself with the housework, I loaded the washing machine and took a duster to the lounge and the front room. Michele and Jason had told me they were going on a drive to the Lake District with Philip and Marianne, so I knew I'd have to amuse myself by doing some house cleaning, which I did, using the feather duster whilst doing an impression of Ken Dodd.

I wasn't in a 'watching TV' mood, and the weather outside seemed to be turning dull and windy. I was never an enthusiastic enjoyer of the great outdoors, and I didn't want to puddle about in the garden, so I got a few old long-players and stacked them up at the side of the hi-fi.

I fixed myself a good measure of Brandy and lay down on the settee, sipping it while the voice of Roy Orbison filled the room. He was more than halfway through *Only the Lonely* when the telephone rang.

Paddy sounded guarded as he spoke. "I don't want to raise your hopes, Sean, but I think I might have a lead on somebody who worked at Willet Street in the sixties."

"How did-"

"Don't ask me. Have you got a pen and paper?" He waited until I'd found a scrap of paper and a pen, then he dictated a name and address. "I won't be able to go with you. I have to go to the old school again. But give me a call. No … better idea - I don't like taking calls at my sister's place - George gets annoyed - You know, the stupid Pratt he is, he never says a word to me, but Bridget gets it in the neck. One of these days …. Ah well, that's my problem. It'd be better if I gave you a call.

How about later tonight …if that's all right with you?"

"That's fine, Paddy. Leave it 'til after midnight and I should be back."

"Then you can let me know how you got on. Speak to you later."

I didn't recognise the name Paddy had given to me, but I was familiar with the address. In fact, the area was quite close to the new police station at Collyhurst. I telephoned the man and although doubtful, he did agree to see me later that morning.

Fred Hawkins was pipe-cleaner thin, a sallow-faced man who moved like a stick insect. His muddy-brown eyes were shaded by a mop of lank straw-coloured hair that formed a curtain over his forehead. He gave me a long suspicious stare as he opened the door, and after some moments allowed me into the house.

He led me into a small comfortable room at the front and invited me to sit. Once again I used the magic word 'research', but this time instead of opening a door, it just provoked a question.

"What sort of research?"

"I'm gathering information for a novel, and I'm hoping to include some authentic data about local police stations. Willet Street is one of them."

Fred pondered for a while before he spoke. "So, what sort of information are you after?"

"Oh… General sorts of things."

"You mean like incidents that stand out?"

"Yes, that sort of thing … and I'd like some personal

recollections about a specific time. I've decided to set the novel around Christmas time in nineteen sixty four."

"Oh." Fred's face finally showed some animation. "Yes, it was a pretty eventful time. "He gave a deep sigh and shook his head. "But I don't think I'm going to be much use to you. Not as far as Willet Street is concerned. I did serve there for a few years, but I didn't go there 'till eighty five."

I did my best not to show too much disappointment. "Never mind, just tell me what you can about the time you were there …Oh, one thing that might be a help. Do you recall the name of the desk sergeant?"

"You mean Jack Hargreaves?"

"Was he on the desk in sixty four?"

"Oh yes. He stayed there 'till he retired. Now he would the right man to help you. I never knew anybody like him. He could remember practically everything that ever happened at the station, he was like Leslie Welch."

"Who?" I frowned.

"Leslie Welch - The 'Memory Man' on radio. Jack was a bit of a celebrity, and we all used to call him the walking encyclopedia."

"I don't suppose he is still alive?"

"Yes. He lives on an estate over in Audenshawe."

"Great, you don't happen to have the address? I thought I might pay him a visit after you've told me what you remember." I sensed it would be wise to give the man his moment rather than just run away once I had Hargreaves' address.

Fred frowned for a moment then uncurled his

lanky frame. "I think I do still have it, somewhere." He went to an old upright bureau and opened a couple of drawers before he found a well-worn hard-backed notebook. He scanned several pages before he jabbed his bony finger against the paper. "I knew I'd got it! Seventeen, Wellmore Avenue, Audenshawe. Sorry, I don't have a telephone number."

"That's all right. Now," I smiled as he put the book away and returned to his seat, "You were going to tell me about your time at Willet Street…?

I stayed with Fred for well over an hour, and he even smiled at me as I was leaving. I'll admit, a lot of what he told me was interesting, amusing, and sometimes downright frightening; and if I had been writing a novel, it would have given me a wealth of material.

Once I got home it didn't take me long to find the number of a Mister *J. Hargreaves* living on Wellmore Avenue in Audenshawe. I'll admit, my fingers were trembling when I picked up the phone, and my voice was a bit unsteady when I spoke. I told him I was researching the station at Willet Street and asked if he'd be prepared to talk to me about his experiences there. He didn't hesitate for a second, and he invited me over at once.

I found Wellmore Avenue without difficulty. It was an orderly street of ageing semi-detached houses fronted by small well-tended gardens. I parked in front of number seventeen and admired the immaculate lawn and the regimented borders as I walked up the path to the door.

I hadn't felt as nervous since I made my first live performance at 'The Talk of the Town' in Belfast. I could feel a faint tremor in my stomach, and my hand was quivering as I reached for the doorbell. A muted version of 'Westminster Chimes' sounded beyond the door, and I noticed a curtain flick in the house next door.

Jack Hargreaves smiled when he opened the door to me. I must have gaped at him for a full second, since he didn't look very much different than he had when he'd been standing behind the desk at Willet Street all those years ago. All right, his hair was a little thinner, and he had a few more wrinkles around his eyes, but the eyes themselves were still crisp and clear and intelligent behind a pair of steel-rimmed glasses. 'At last,' I thought, 'the first tangible thing.'

"Would you like to come in, son?" His voice was deep and powerful, as I'd remembered. He led me along a flowery hallway and into the front room.

The room was small, and made to seem even smaller by the amount of furniture and the muted flowery wallpaper, broken only by a band of darker paper which covered the chimney breast. A low table stood beneath the window, and on it was a collection of at least a dozen framed photographs. A leather settee stood against the wall by the door, and a pair of matching easy chairs flanked a long mahogany cabinet on the wall facing an old fashioned tiled fireplace in which stood a modern gas fire.

A heavy mahogany table dominated the centre of the room, and its surface was covered with what

256

seemed to be hand-made white Doilies and a collection of coasters. A tall Grandmother clock stood in an alcove beside the fireplace and its soft ticking gave the room a restful placid air.

"Would you like a mug of tea?" Jack asked as I paused in the doorway. "We always used to have fiddly little cups when Alice was alive, but I've gone back to proper mugs now. You get a much better drink out of a mug."

"Thank you, I quite agree. I'd love some."

"Come on then," Jack turned and ambled down the hallway, "I don't want to leave you on your own ... and we can talk while I'm making the tea."

The kitchen, like the front room, was old but well maintained. It wasn't too big, and Jack's bulk seemed to dominate the space as he filled a kettle and placed it on the hob of a gas cooker. Through the leaded windows above a white ceramic sink, I could see a small immaculate garden. Jack saw me staring and he smiled. "That was Alice's pride and joy, her garden. I've tried to keep it how I think she'd like it, but I'm not the gardener she was. She had more than just 'green fingers' ... I used to say she had green arms too." Jack moved to a glass panelled wall-mounted cupboard and opened the door. "You'll have a biscuit, or two with your tea? Alice always told me off for not 'looking after' our visitors. We used to have dozens of people calling in on us...Most of 'em were her friends, and now I don't hardly get many callers." He took out a metal biscuit tin decorated with a collection of gaudy fruit. Taking a large plate from a shelf in the cupboard he loaded it with a handsome collection of biscuits. "I don't know what sort you like, so we'll have a good selection, eh?"

I hunched my shoulders and smiled. "Yes, why not."

Jack took out a couple of mugs and poured a little milk into them. "I don't like anaemic tea. Never could stand it - like flaming dishwater." He glanced at me then added the same small amount to the second cup. "You don't look like a Nancy so I'd guess you like a good cup of builder's brew." He spooned two heaped spoonfuls of sugar into each, and then he paused and turned to me. "You do want sugar?"
I nodded. "Yes, thanks."

He stared at me with friendly curiosity. "So, you're writing a book, then?"

I felt a little guilty as I nodded. "I'm only in the very early stages of my research right now, and I'm gathering as much information as I can."

"Good idea, son. Too many of these 'new writers' set off like rockets without getting their facts sorted out before they begin. Most of the things on telly nowadays are half-baked and don't make sense. They're so bad that I've stopped watching most of them ... a five-year-old could figure out 'who dunnit' long before the stupid detectives."

"So, what do you do with yourself? "I asked as someone once told me to never start of by asking what you really want to know.

"Not much. When the weather's fine I get out into the garden - always something to do out there. When it's bad, I read a lot ... You'll have to send me a copy of your book when it's finished - or I could read it for you before you send it off … check it for mistakes and that sort of thing?" His eyes twinkled as he stared at me.

"It'll be a long time before I get to that stage."

"There's no rush … I can wait." He turned to the cooker as the kettle began to boil, and for the next few minutes he was occupied with the tea. He let the tea brew in the teapot and he faced me after he'd put the kettle on a cold hob.

"What sort of book will it be - fact or fiction - or a mixture of both?"

"I haven't decided yet. I thought perhaps a sort of fiction based on fact."

"Safest sort … If you start quoting too many truths, somebody might take offence and come to 'sort you out'. I've seen that happen a few times - when somebody got the wrong end of the stick." He lifted the lid of the teapot, nodded then started to fill the mugs with the strong brew. He handed me one of the mugs and I offered to carry the plate of biscuits, but he declined. "You go on, I'll bring them. "

I went back along the hallway and into the front room where I waited for him. Jack made a tutting sound when he arrived. "Don't stand there on ceremony, get yourself sat down.

I chose the settee and he joined me, placing the plate of biscuits between us. "Help yourself - but don't take all the Arrowroot. I'm a bit partial to them myself."

I judiciously avoided them and took a custard cream.

Jack grabbed a couple of his favourites and jammed one in his mouth. He munched for a while then smiled. "I never used to like these … It was Alice who got me on to them. Now they're my favourite."

"Were you married for long?"

"Fifty two years. I was only a sprog when I met her, but I knew as soon as I clapped eyes on her that she was the only one for me." He shook his head and gave a wry smile. "She wasn't that keen on me … More cautious and careful. Never did anything without thinking about it first … But she did finally come round … We went to Llandudno for the honeymoon, and it rained all week … I can still remember the room we were in … It had bloody awful paper on the walls, and the bed creaked something shocking." He laughed. "I bet we kept the landlady up for a few nights."

"Were you in the police force at the time?"

"Oh yes. I never wanted to do anything else. It was a bit of a problem in the early days, what with me having to do odd shifts and that, but Alice never complained." His eyes became unfocussed and a smile played on his lips. "She was a real gem." He gave a start and looked at me. "I'm sure you didn't come here to listen to me babbling on about my wife."

"Don't worry about it, Jack. I think it's marvellous that two people could stay together, happily for so long."

"It wasn't all plain sailing, but we did seem to be able to 'pull together' whenever things got rough … Are you married?"

"Divorced."

"Any children?"

"Two, a girl and a boy."

Jack's smile faded a little. "It's a damned shame when

families split up. There's always somebody who suffers. Are you all right?"

"I got over it."

"Aye, that's the only thing you can do. You made sure the children were all right?"

"Yes, they've come to terms with the situation, and they seem quite happy now."

"That's good. I have three, and they've all moved out of the area. I hear from them now and then, and get pictures of my grandchildren ... But it isn't the same as having them here with me. Take my advice ... enjoy every minute you spend with your children - you never know when they'll be gone."

There was a long thoughtful silence. We drank our tea and ate our biscuits until Jack let out a long sigh. "I'm sorry about that. I didn't mean to sound so melancholy. I'm getting bloody moody in my old age."

"Have you been on your own for long?"

"Four years. I'm just about getting used to it or as used to it as I ever will." He took a deep breath then smiled at me. "Right then ... What do you want to know?"

I didn't want to seem too eager to talk about that weird Christmas eve in nineteen sixty four, so I just shrugged my shoulders and smiled at him. "I think you should just reminisce - tell me some of the really interesting things you can remember about your time at Willet street. "

Jack smiled back at me. "You'd better have brought your sleeping bag, son. You really could write a book about what I've seen." His smile faded and he stared at me. "It'd help if I knew the sort of thing you're

261

looking for. It's nice to talk with you, I don't get many visitors these days, but I don't want you to say I've been wasting your time when we've finished."

"All right, Jack. I had an idea to write about the unusual things that have happened, not the run-of-the-mill events. I'm looking for things that would make a reader sit up and wonder, or smile, or get angry. I want you to tell me about some of the controversial things that must have happened. But, I wouldn't want you to tell me anything that might get you into trouble with the Authorities. I've heard they can be pretty nasty if they think somebody's 'told too many tales out of school'."

"Too true, they can. I remember once, not long after I'd joined the force... a sergeant - I won't tell you his name, or where he was stationed, found out that one of the senior officers was taking back-handers from a local villain. I'm not just talking about a few quid here and there; I mean real money, hundreds of pounds at a time. In those days a hundred quid was almost three months' wages. Anyway, the sergeant couldn't decide what to do, so he goes to see the officer and fronts him out about it ... Next thing you know the sergeant is transferred somewhere down south ... we never saw him again."

"But, surely the officer was guilty of ...?"

"Things were a lot different in those days, son. The force wasn't just a body of men dedicated to keeping the peace. It was like ... you're not a Mason."

"No, I'm not."

"I wasn't asking you. I know you're not. Well the force then was even stricter than the Masons. You 'looked out for you brothers' and they took care of you. It's a bit different now - everybody is looking out for themselves."

"So. Nothing happened to the officer?"

"Not exactly. He retired less than twelve months later, with a 'golden handshake' and a bloody good pension." Jack gave me a wry smile. "I know I said it was different now, but I'm not about to tell you about all the internal hanky-panky that went on."

"I'm not here to dig the dirt, Jack. Like I said, I just want to hear some unusual stories."

"Don't forget you tea, son… and have another biscuit." Jack held out the plate and I took a couple of biscuits. "Right then, where should I start? …" He rubbed his chin and stared into space for a moment then he nodded. "I know ..." He closed his mouth sharply, and frowned at me. "Aren't you going to write it down, or something?"

Luckily I'd had the foresight to bring a notepad with me, so I took it out. "Whenever you're ready, Jack."

For the next hour and a half, Jack regaled me with tales from his past. I heard things that made me shudder, others that had me laughing so much I almost cried. He mentioned things that saddened me, and some that sickened me. I was amazed at the depth and clarity of his memory. He seemed able to recall incidents from forty years ago, and tell them as if they'd only happened yesterday.

He ended with a tale, about a mild-mannered gentle man who became a wild animal when he'd had a

263

drink. …

"... He was stark naked and throwing coping stones all over the place - just picking them up and tossing them about as if they were cardboard boxes. It took ten of us to get him in the 'Mariah' and even then he was trying to punch holes in the side of the van. Next day, when he was sober, he apologised to each of us individually." Jack shook his head. "Poor devil was only fifty two when he died." He gave a long sigh then looked at me. "I'm about ready for some dinner, son."

"Oh, I'm sorry. I didn't realise we'd been talking for so long."

Jack laughed. "Get it right ... If you let me, I could talk for England. Now then, would you like some pork pie and a few of last night's boiled potatoes?"

We were in the kitchen, sitting at a small square table. I had almost finished my meal when I saw Jack staring at me with a strange expression. I put down my knife and fork.

"What's the matter, Jack?"

"I might ask you the same question." He fixed me with a steely-eyed stare and I did feel uncomfortable under his gaze. "If you're a writer, then I'm Bobby Charlton's uncle. You didn't really want to hear all those stories ... did you?"

"Well, I ... they were very ... you see ..."

"Why don't you just come out with it, son? Why don't you tell me what you really came to find out? "He gave me a peculiar half smile as he put down his knife and

264

fork. "I thought I recognised you when I opened the door, but it took me a while to realise where I'd seen you before." He frowned and stroked his chin. "It was …. That odd Christmas eve … nineteen sixty … sixty four! And I know it's impossible but I have to believe my own eyes. I'm right, aren't I?"

I swallowed heavily. "You really *do* remember me?"

"Oh yes. I remember you. How could I forget?" His eyes held mine. "Why have you come here?"

"I'm not sure really, I just thought it was all a dream until something happened to make me think otherwise. Now I'm trying to make some sense of it all and with your help maybe I can."

"You know, seeing you has brought it all back. I remember when you'd left the station." He smiled at me then got to his feet. "Stay there for a minute."

"What?"

"I have something for you. It's upstairs - I won't be a minute."

True to his word he was soon back in the kitchen. He stood beside me holding a grubby folded piece of paper. "You forgot this." He held the paper out to me.

I opened it and stared for some time before I looked at him. He hunched his shoulders. "I was writing out this official reminder - for you to produce your insurance and driving licence - but I never got the chance to give it to you. You were so keen to get that young girl out of the station that you left your blood sample and the note for your doctor on the desk." Jack gave a shrug. "I trusted you."

Jack sat down again, and stared at me with a faintly puzzled smile on his face. "I put the reminder in my pocket, then I had a look at that sandwich wrapper you gave me to put in the waste basket. It fair threw me when I saw the little label printed on it... It said the sandwiches should be eaten before January the second nineteen ninety five ... I thought it might have been a misprint at the time - giving you the benefit of the doubt so to speak." Jack looked thoughtful for some time then he nodded. "All right. I'm going to have another brew ... d'you want one?"

"Please." I watched him carry his plate to the sink, and I took mine to him.

Jack suggested I went back to the front room while he made the tea. I saw no point in arguing, so I went. I sat on the settee again and glanced around the room while I waited. The only sounds were the soft comforting tick of the clock in the corner and the distant murmur of children's voices coming from outside.

"Here you go." Jack was smiling as he held out the mug of tea. I took it and sipped it quietly, waiting for him to speak. After a few moments he turned to me.

"You're not looking any different from what you did then. I know it sounds a bit far-fetched, but you hardly look a day older." He waited as if to see how I reacted and when I said nothing he smiled. "You know, for a long time, the rest of the blokes at the station thought I was a bit doolally. I told them about you, and your Mickey-Mouse driving licence, and they all said I was imagining things. It seemed funny when they brought out those computerised licences, and I knew I'd already

266

seen one." He looked squarely at me. "I bet you could tell *me* a story - if you had a mind?"

"Yes, Jack, I could. Would you like to hear it?"

"I don't have anything better to occupy me … Go ahead, I'm listening."

Jack did listen. He sat quietly frowning while I recounted my experiences after leaving the police station on that peculiar night thirty years ago, for him, and only a few months ago for me. I could see the amazed expression on his face when I came to the part where I'd 'rescued' little Sharon Becket from the clutches of those terrible brothers. When I'd finished my story there was a prolonged silence until Jack gave a sigh.

"Every station in Manchester was talking about the Manchester murders. We all got to hear details, second-hand, and none of us could ever figure out why the Boswells took that little girl up to the Moors then brought her home again. We all knew she'd been interviewed by some of the top female officers, but we heard they couldn't get any sense out of her … All she said she remembered about the incident was that a 'great big giant' suddenly appeared while Tom Boswell was digging. The giant told Boswell to go away and not harm the girl, and Boswell got frightened and did as the 'giant' had told him. We didn't put much store by her tale when we heard of it, and we all thought the little lass was making it up. Seems like we were all wrong after all."

"Do you know what happened to Sharon Beckett?"

Jack shrugged. "I don't think much did happen to her, as far as I can remember. Well, I did hear that when she was a lot older she got married to some well-off businessman and moved to somewhere near Oldham. I don't know the man's name ... but you might try the newspapers. As far as I can tell, it would be around nineteen seventy six when she got married."

"And what about Betty, Betty Walker. Do you know what happened to her?"

"Betty Walker ..." Jack's face creased in a deep frown. "I don't think she was one of the Boswell's victims. No, she wasn't. Now I remember, she was the young girl who tried to sneak into the picture house without paying. We were trying to get her address when you were brought into the station. I remember she was a pretty young lass. She left with you, like I said - while I was writing out your reminder."

"Yes, that's the one."

Jack stared at me and I could feel my pulse begin to quicken. He smiled. "She'll be about your age now. She was seventeen, or eighteen at the time."

"Seventeen. She'd run away from her step-father ...?"

"Oh yes..." Jack gave a knowing nod and his expression changed. He became rather solemn. "Bit of a tragic case that. You know she was found at the Portland Hotel on Christmas morning"

"Yes, I'd imagined something like that."

"Since we'd already had her at the station, she was brought back here ... She gave us a weird tale about this man - you - who took her to one of the rooms ... didn't do anything funny, just let her go to sleep ... and

268

vanished before she got up."

"Honestly Jack there wasn't a thing I could do about it. Did you charge her?"

"No. The Portland was a bit tolerant, and since it was Christmas, the manager decided not to press charges. But we did have to send for her mother and step-father. Like the night before, she wasn't going to give us her address - not until I told her it was either that or spending some time in one of our cells... The parents came to collect her and they took her away about three o'clock Christmas afternoon. Since you seemed a decent sort, I couldn't imagine you leaving her in the lurch. She'd given us an address in New Moston where you'd taken her ... So in my spare time I went up there and had a word with the fellow that lived there, Stanley... Stanley Fisher, that's it. Stanley Fisher. He told me some lunatic had called on Christmas Eve claiming to have lived there...He hadn't a clue who you were but his description fitted you to a tee. I tried to 'follow you up' but I didn't get anywhere." He gave me a great beaming smile. "It's nice when something that has worried you for years is finally sorted out."

I smiled back at him. "You were telling me about Betty Walker. Was she all right after her parents collected her?"

"For a while, she was." His expression grew troubled and I felt uneasy as I looked at him.

"What do you mean, Jack?"

He let out a sigh. "Did she happen to tell you anything about her step-father while you were with her?"

269

"Well, she did say that he'd tried to molest her on more than one occasion."

"Yes. If you remember, we discussed it at the station?"

"Aye ... well he tried again, not more than a few months after she went back home. The story was, that this time her mother caught him trying it on, and she stabbed him. I had my doubts and I got a sneaking feeling that the young girl might have done it, and the Mother confessed to shield her. Anyway the trial was a quick one and Mrs. Walker was sent down for life. There was a bit of a scandal about it in the papers, but it soon died down. "Jack shook his head sadly. "We didn't know about it at the time, but the Mother had cancer. She died in prison less than a couple of years later." He shrugged. "Maybe that's why she decided to protect her daughter. Who knows?"

"So ... what happened to Betty?"

"As far as I know, she moved away after the trial. She had some relations up in the north-east, Gateshead I think. I don't know why, but I felt sorry for that girl, one more child let down by the system. I had some mates up there and they kept an eye on her. She stayed with the relatives for a couple of years, and then she emigrated."

"Where did she go?"

"Canada, or Australia maybe, to be honest I'm not quite sure. That would be in about nineteen sixty seven or eight. Haven't heard a thing about her since then." He gave me a questioning stare. "You didn't mean to leave the lass on her own that Christmas Eve, did you?"

"No. She was pretty much at rock bottom right then, and I thought that if I could maybe let her have a couple of days without any stress, she might have been better able to cope with things. It sounds as if she had even more aggravation after I left her."

"Nothing you could have done about that, is there?"

"No, I don't suppose. Still, you always think *if only* ..."

"You'll just have to remind yourself that you did what you could, at the time, and leave it at that."

"Yes, I guess you're right."

"So ... Is there anything else I can tell you?"

"Not that I can think of." I started to wonder if I'd tired him out with all my questions so I started to get up.

Jack frowned. "You're not leaving, are you?"

"It's better if I did."

"Ah well, if you have to go I suppose you must. But let me tell you, I'm really glad you did turn up after all these years."

"Yes. Now you'll be able to tell all those 'so-called' mates of yours who never believed you."

"Don't think so. Who would believe me?" He got up and followed me as I walked to the door then into the hall. He stood in the doorway when I went down the path and called out to me as I reached the gate. "Don't be frightened to call me again if there's anything else you want to know. I don't go out much, and I've enjoyed our little chat."

"Yes, Jack. So have I. And yes, I will call back and this time I won't leave it so long!"

*   *   *

271

THIRTEEN

Sean gave me a soft sad smile when he finished, and I could see that his recollection of the visit to the old policeman had moved him. I waited, not wanting to interrupt his reverie, and after some moments he let out a soft sigh. He raised his eyes and looked at me and I felt myself smiling at him.

"Did you go back to see Jack Hargreaves?"

Sean nodded. "Yes. I went round whenever I had the time, and he was always glad to have a natter. He was a remarkable character. His memory was as sharp as mine - sharper in fact - until the day he died."

"When was that?"

"Nineteen ninety eight ... October the seventeenth." Sean's eyes misted for a moment. "I miss going to see him. He was the 'last of a breed 'in my estimation."

I couldn't find a response so I maintained a friendly silence. After a few moments, Sean got to his feet and I followed his lead. In his mind I could see he was still with the old policeman, and he obviously didn't want a stranger's intrusion. He led me along the hallway to the front door where he paused.

"I'll be working at the television studios for the next few days, so I won't have much time to see you."

"That's all right, Sean. I reckon we're just about finished now."

"Oh? Is that what you think?"

I stopped to consider my initial statement, and

273

his reply to it. I started to realize that we *hadn't* completed the story, and there were still one or two 'loose-ends' to sort out. I noticed he was grinning at me.

"Call yourself an 'investigative journalist'?"

"Sometimes." I grinned back at him. "Should I call you - or will you let me know when you're next available?"

"I'm not sure how long I'll be at the studios, and who knows, I might get some other work from it … Better if I called you when I know I'm going to be free."

"Fine …See you soon, then."

"What kind of plonker are you?" Amanda frowned at me. We'd met up later that evening, and she'd suggested we go for an Italian. After the antipasti, I recounted the day's events, including my parting speech to Sean. Amanda had already had a couple of glasses of Chianti and she was relaxed … which usually meant that she spoke her mind with a vengeance.

"I repeat, what kind of plonker are you?"

"I don't know but I've a feeling you are gonna tell me."

"What on earth were you thinking about when you said you'd finished with him - or were your brains in neutral as usual?"

I shrugged at her, trying not to laugh at her expression which was a combination of disbelief and righteous annoyance. I soon discovered why she seemed a bit annoyed with me.

"There's you, sitting with Sean, drinking his Brandy, no doubt, and hearing the most interesting story since …" She waved her arms in a sort of expressive Italian manner - in honour of our surroundings I suppose - then she glared at me. "And do you know what I was doing while you were indulging yourself?"

"I'm sure you're about to tell me."

"Too right I am. I was at the Evening News offices first, then I went to the town hall and I've been in touch with the vehicle licensing authority ... I don't suppose you can imagine how dinosaurian they can be when they feel 'obstructive'?"

I mouthed a vague response but she wasn't taking particular notice of me at the time. I leaned forward and looked at her intently. "I can feel that you have something important to tell me?"

"I don't know if I want to ... If you're so convinced that you've dotted every T and crossed every I ..."

She glared at me when I barely managed to suppress a laugh. "What's so funny?" Her glare became more intense and I just couldn't contain myself. I could see she wasn't at all impressed by my fit of giggling, and for some minutes communications came to a complete halt.

When I'd finally managed to control myself, and she'd decided not to throw some of the cutlery at me, the mood returned to something resembling sanity. I drank some wine and she waited.

"Have you finished?" Her voice, like her expression, was guarded.

"Yes ... I'm sorry. Now, what was it that you were going to tell me?"

Amanda eyed me for a moment then took a slow deep breath. "Did you ever wonder why Sean said he'd 'felt' something strange when he was driving that

275

old mini-traveller?"

I gave her a vague shrug. "Well, I just … to be honest, I never thought about it. Why - do you have some theory about it?"

"Not a theory. I have some facts. Did Sean give you the registration number?"

"No, I don't think he did, why?"

"Would it surprise you to know that the very car Sean drove when he claimed to have 'gone back in time' was originally owned by a Tom Boswell?"

I shrugged. "You read that in Jeff Sommers' book."

"No." Amanda gave me a triumphant smile. "I read the book from cover to cover, and there's no mention of a specific vehicle in it… all right, he does say that the brothers drove their victims onto the Moors - but he never said what kind of car they used."

I started to become more interested. "Right."

Amanda was still beaming. "Furthermore, would you be surprised to hear that Boswell got rid of the 'traveller' just before Christmas nineteen sixty four?"

"Right after …?"

"Yes. Right after they'd murdered the young boy, Brian Thompson. Did Sean say what kind of car they used to take Sharon Beckett up to the Moors?"

"No, I don't think so."

Amanda went on. "They took another victim up to the Moors before the end of that year." Her smile faded to be replaced with a seriously troubled expression. "Did you check anything about the mini-traveller?"

"I … what do you mean?"

"Its previous owners … anything?"

I shrugged. "No, I didn't."

"I did." She gloated at me. "Tom Boswell sold it to a garage … guess where? New Cross! And who do you think owned the garage?"

I shook my head knowing that once Amanda was in full flow it was unwise to stop her. She leaned forward with an excited expression.

"Vincent Brandolani." She frowned at my lack of response then composed herself before she continued. "Vincent kept the car - never parted with it- for sentimental reasons. He said it had a 'special aura' and he maintained it until he died. Don't you see! The car would have been at the garage on Christmas Eve nineteen sixty four and nineteen ninety four!" She gave me an intense stare. "I for one have no doubt that the 'presence' Sean felt was the spirit of Brain Thompson … and I suspect that the little boy was the catalyst in all these 'events'."

I ignored her emotional enthusiasm. "How did you find out … about the car I mean?"

"You remember Sean telling you about the people at the garage where he 'borrowed' the mini-traveller?"

"Yes … Charlie and …"

"Tony … Tony Brandolani, Vincent's son. It's surprising how much he was willing to tell me while he thought there was a chance of getting into my knickers."

"Jezebel!"

Amanda grinned for a second then became serious. "It looks very much like your tame entertainer isn't trying to fool you."

277

"It's a sobering thought, isn't it? But ..."

"What do you mean, but? Surely you're convinced after all this?"

"I'll admit that on the face of it, it does all look to be pretty convincing. But it could still be coincidence."

Amanda gave an irritated sigh and glared at me. "Andy Priest, you're one of the most aggravating people I've ever come across. You can't or won't accept what's staring you in the face. What will it take to convince you that this story is real?"

I shrugged uncomfortably under her gaze. "I ... You know that I have to be objective about the stories I hear. Can you imagine what any editor would say if I just dumped a story like this on his desk?"

"There's a difference between 'being objective' and being just plain stubborn. You once told me the finest attribute a reporter can have is open-mindedness ... How 'open' is your mind right now?"

"You're letting your emotions take over, Amanda. Try to step back and take a rational view. I know all the facts I've heard so far, do make it seem like Sean is telling the truth."

"Then, how much more convincing do you need?" Amanda let out a long sigh. "I got goosebumps when I realised the implication of what I discovered." She looked at me with steady eyes. "You've verified almost every single fact that the man has given you, yet you still don't believe him. Boy did he pick the wrong Journalist..."

"Look Amanda I just can't believe that Sean ... 'went back in time'. I'd like to believe it, and I'm positive Sean is convinced he went back … but-"

"But because you've never experienced it, you can't bring yourself to accept it as fact?"

"For God's sake Amanda we're talking time travel here fucking H.G. Wells.."

Amanda looked thoughtful for a moment then smiled. "Do you believe that men walked on the moon?"

"That's ridiculous. Of course they did."

"It's not ridiculous. There are a lot of intelligent people who are convinced they didn't … and can put forward logical and very credible theories that it was all a great big con trick …"

"But there's evidence … You can see the pictures of …"

"Don't tell me you don't know how a picture or a video can be doctored?"

"We're getting away from the point."

"Are we? You know the story of Doubting Thomas? Well, you're worse than he was." She let out a very deep sigh. "Because you've never had a particular experience, you can't deny its existence. You have to have some sort of faith … in something. Or are you planning to spend the rest of your life questioning everything that doesn't fit your conventional pattern? You told me that Sean gave you an ultimatum not long ago - when he asked you to accept what he'd told you, or forget the whole thing … You went back to him … Why? Were you lying to him so you could hear the rest of his 'fictional tale'? Because if you were, then you've become a dyed in the wool hypocrite, and I don't think I know you anymore."

I toyed with a spoon, fiddling with it while I stared at her. To a great extent, she was right. I had decided to return to hear the rest of Sean's story ... but I still wasn't absolutely sure why I'd gone back.

What he had told me held implications that defied everything I held dear. I'd spent most of my adult life destroying myths and uncovering charlatans, and Sean had eroded my 'logical barrier' to the extent that I was no longer certain... of him, or myself.

Amanda had been correct when she said that I was able to accept on trust anything that appeared 'reasonable', yet I was still unwilling to believe Sean. I really liked the man, and I could accept that he had no doubts about the truth of his tale ... But ...

"I think it's about time you paid the bill, Andy." Amanda placed her napkin on the table and started to rise. "I'm going to the loo. I'll meet you in the bar."

I drove out of the restaurant car-park in an uneasy silence. We'd said very little as we walked to the car, and I got the feeling that Amanda was annoyed or disappointed.

After I'd driven out of the centre of Manchester, the atmosphere had become a little oppressive, and I had to speak.

"I'm sorry you feel the way you do and I'm sorry I swore at you."

"It's like you've let me down, Andy. If you were so convinced it was all a hoax - why did you ask me to do that research?"

I shrugged. "To be fair Amanda, you volunteered to do research and as grateful as I am and even though I honestly don't think the whole thing's a fabrication I just can't see any reasonable explanation for what he said has happened. It's just too incredible. But ..."

"But what?"

I sighed. "I can't find any other explanation."

"So where does that leave you?"

"Totally fucking confused. While I'm with Sean I can believe everything he's telling me. I'm carried along on his wave of enthusiasm not to mention the Brandy. But when I'm on my own, I start to think about the impossibility of it all."

"Then don't think about it!"

"You're not serious?"

I could sense Amanda staring at me. I heard her take a sharp breath and I waited for some acid comment. It never came and I drove her home in an uneasy silence. When we arrived, she opened the door almost before I'd stopped.

She turned to stare at me as she started to get out of the car. "If you want me to do any more research for you, I will ... but only if you tell me that I won't be wasting my time. Give me a call when you've made up your mind."

She closed the car door and left me staring after her as she walked to the front door of her flat. One thing that was for certain was that I would be sleeping on my own tonight.

Speaking of sleep, I got very little during that night. My

whole equilibrium had been upset by Amanda's critical comments about my attitude. I lay awake trying to analyse exactly how I felt about Sean, and his story.

I didn't exactly come to any firm conclusions, but I did at least discover that, as Amanda had said, I was a doubting Thomas. It seemed natural to me, to question everything, to take nothing at face value. God I've seen many a good reporter left with egg on his face for printing a story that turned out to be a hoax... and since I had been like that for the greater part of my life, I could not see how I could be any different.

I was disturbed by the lack of what I would regard as concrete evidence that might support Sean's tale. All right, I myself had read records of old newspapers which could have been seen as corroborating his story ... but that's all they were! Too many times I'd been lulled into a false sense of trust by people who, like Sean, had supplied me with perfectly documented evidence...and my experience of 'stage people' was that they were all too willing to talk about their encounters with ghosts and the para-normal ... A prime example was Reg Presley of the Troggs and his 'Amazing Crop Circles'.

I hadn't lied when I'd told Amanda that I liked Sean and wanted to believe him, but ... there was always that minute seed of doubt. I came to the conclusion that I would never change. I couldn't. There was no way I would accept unproven 'facts' no matter who delivered them.

Everything Sean had told me was substantiated only by some written record. There was not one single

282

living person who I could meet face-to-face and have them confirm what he had said. And without that eye-to-eye physical contact, I knew that I would never be completely convinced.

I accepted that the story was interesting and compelling even ... but that's all it was to me ... a good fictional story.

This presented me with a couple of problems. I still wanted Amanda to help with the research, and I didn't want to lose her friendship. I could see difficulties arising if I couldn't persuade her that I wasn't just stringing Sean along.

Sean was the second problem. The longer the situation went on, it became more likely that I would reveal my true scepticism. It had already endangered my relationship with him, and I couldn't see him tolerating any further doubts on my part.

I really did want to believe him.

The telephone rang as I was in my miniature kitchen preparing breakfast - if you could call a couple of stale ham sandwiches and a mug of microwaved coffee breakfast. I carried the plate and mug into the living room placed them on the coffee table then picked up the phone.

"Andy?" Amanda sounded 'careful' as if she thought I might snap at her.

"Yes?" I tried to sound human but only succeeded in giving out a guttural grunt. I reached for the coffee and took a sip, wincing as the hot liquid scorched my tongue.

"Did I upset you last night?"

"Er … let's say you gave me a few things to think about."

"You sound annoyed?"

"No, I'm just tired."

"Did I wake you? I'm sorry … I can ring back if …"

"No … It's all right. I'm in a fuzzy bear state right now." I took another mouthful of coffee and felt it trickling down to my stomach where it started a warm glow. I lowered myself onto the settee and rubbed at my eyes with my free hand. "You didn't hold back last night."

"Was I too hard on you?"

"You said what you thought."

"Ah … I can see that I bruised your ego. How long is it since anyone gave you a 'verbal mirror'?"

I refused to answer. The last time she'd been in that 'objective' frame of mind she'd bared me to the bone and I hadn't spoken to her for a month. I didn't want to reject her this time and I tried to sound unruffled. "What do you have planned for today?"

"Oh, nothing much. I was going to go into town and do some window-shopping, but I honestly don't feel in the mood."

"What do you feel like doing?"

There was a tense pause and I could sense that she was preparing to 'hit me' with something. I fortified myself with another draught of coffee.

"When you asked me to do that research for you, I was only half interested … Now that I've uncovered so much, I want to do some more digging … and I wondered if you'd like to join me … Unless you've

284

something better to do?"

I met her in the small coffee shop inside Debenhams. I was into my second cappuccino when she breezed in and collected a latte from the counter then sat facing me. She grimaced. "I've seen zombies with more life in them. You look terrible."

"You should have seen me an hour ago." I gave her a wan smile.

"So, you really took my little criticisms to heart last night?"

I hunched my shoulders and smiled at her. "Like I told you on the phone - you gave me one or two things to ponder."

Amanda sighed. "I'm sorry, but you really got me incensed."

"It showed."

"So, did it have any effect ... I mean real effect?"

I knew that this was a crucial moment, and I was facing more than a dilemma. I knew that my response could wipe out years of friendship and end what little sex life I had, so I was careful... "Everything you said about me made sense - especially the point about not having an open mind."

I could see her relax. Her face broke into a warm smile and she leaned forward slightly as she sipped her coffee. "I'm glad, Andy. I know I would have hated it, but I was prepared to dump you for good." She took another sip then put her cup down. "Last night you hinted that you spent most of your time uncovering charlatans ... Sean isn't a charlatan. I know it. Instead of trying to disprove everything he's told you, why don't you start to prove him right? You have all the facts, so come up with an acceptable explanation - even if it happens to be a para-normal one ... Don't forget 'there are more things in heaven and earth than are dreamed of in man's philosophy'."

"Isn't it a bit too early for sage quotations?" I grinned at her.

She smiled back at me. For a few moments we drank our coffees in companionable silence then Amanda beamed. "Right, what do you suggest we do?"

I'd sort of half expected something like that, and on the way into town, I'd thought of something that would keep us occupied. "I thought we might try to trace the man who lived in Sean's house in nineteen sixty four."

"Didn't you say that the old policeman mentioned him to Sean?"

"That's right ... Stanley Fisher."

"Right, let's finish our coffee then go and find the man!"

Our first call was at the registry office where a pleasant assistant was able to dig out a copy of the electoral register for nineteen sixty two that being the closest one to the year we wanted. It was a bit laborious but rewarding when we finally discovered there was a Stanley Fisher living at 1, Sefton Avenue, in 'sixty two.

We then requested the next two records of the electoral register survey and discovered that our mister

Fisher was no longer at Sefton Avenue in nineteen seventy. Left with the problem of discovering where he went after moving from Moston, we decided to take a break.

We had a meal at a small Chinese restaurant, and while we were eating Amanda came up with the idea of going to Sefton Avenue. I didn't respond, and she explained that we might gain something by interviewing Sean's neighbours. I wasn't impressed at first, and she saw my patronising expression.

"Why the 'look' Andy?"

"I'm not sure … I mean, if the neighbours know where Fisher went - why hasn't Sean already been to see him?"

"Why should he? As far as Sean is concerned, he saw the man on Christmas Eve in nineteen sixty four, so he doesn't need Fisher to confirm it … Whereas we do."

There was another possible explanation, but I didn't want to upset things now that Amanda was in a good mood. I paid for the meal and we set off for New Moston.

I could feel Amanda's enthusiasm radiating from her, and although I was not directly affected by it, it did help me to dispel some of my misgivings. I drove into Sefton Avenue and took a quick glance at Sean's house as we passed number one.

We picked a house at random and knocked at the door. After a full minute, we decided that there was no-one home and started towards the adjoining semi. Before we'd gone halfway up the path we heard someone calling to us.

"If you're looking for Steven and Briony, they've gone

down to Chichester to visit their cousin."

I turned to see a tall slender, grey-haired woman who was standing on the pavement behind us. Her expression was friendly but guarded. "You *are* looking for the Patterson's, aren't you?"

I glanced at Amanda and she grinned at me before turning to the woman. "We aren't sure." She gave the woman one of her more appealing smiles as we walked back down the path. The woman took a half pace backwards and regarded us with a cool expression.

I let Amanda do the talking.

"We're trying to find out if anyone remembers Stanley Fisher. He used to live at number one." She nodded towards Sean's house. "They couldn't help us." Amanda smiled at the woman. "I wonder if you recall him."

"How long ago did you say he lived here?"

"I think it was sometime in the late sixties … I believe he moved away sometime before nineteen seventy two, but we can't find out where he went."

The woman ignored me and concentrated her attention on Amanda. I stayed in the background and saw that her cool expression had faded and she now seemed to be quite animated.

"Nineteen sixties …Yes, I remember." She gave a grimace. "We all thought they were a little too loud, if you know what I mean. The mother was all right, but the father and the boy weren't exactly good neighbours - playing that horrible 'rock' music and sitting out in the front garden all afternoon … The *front* garden of all places! Can you imagine it?"

Amanda gave the woman a sympathetic smile.

"I can see how dreadful that must have been for you. Now, can you remember the time they moved away?"

"I recall the mother leaving ... that was almost a year before the father and the boy moved out."

"Can you tell me where they went?"

The woman frowned. "There was a woman who stayed with them." Her sneer indicated that she hadn't thought much of the visitor. "And if I remember correctly, when they left the avenue, they went to stay with her." A deep frown creased the woman's forehead and Amanda took a long slow breath in anticipation. She jumped when the woman snapped her fingers.

"I have it! She was a milliner or something, and she had a shop in Stalybridge ... But she didn't live there ... Her house was in ... Ashton, that's it!" She gave Amanda a triumphant beam. The beam faded and she gave Amanda an apologetic smile. "I'm sorry, but I don't know where ... and I don't know if the man and the boy stayed with her for long ... Knowing what they were like, I very much doubt it."

"That's all right." Amanda gave her a sunny smile. "You've been a great help."

We found the offices of the Tameside registry and followed the same procedure we'd used in Manchester. It didn't take us long to dig out an address where Stanley Fisher had been in nineteen seventy two. We then moved forward to a later electoral register and, to our delight, discovered Fisher was still living in Ashton in nineteen ninety two. We could find no record of his

289

name after that … but we did discover a Wilbur Fisher registered at the same address.

It was a simple matter to find Dungate Drive on the A-to-Z, and it took us less than half-an-hour to drive to the house. The Drive was set back from a main road up a shallow winding streets lined with identical pebble-dash semis. Dungate Drive was no different, and number forty six was as inconspicuous as its neighbours.

We went up a macadam path and knocked at a door whose red paint had long submitted to the sunlight and had turned into a dusty shade of pink - except where it had peeled to reveal a dirty brown undercoat.

I thought we were going to be unlucky. We'd knocked a couple of times without response, and were about to turn away when the door opened.

The man who faced us was middle-aged and going prematurely bald. The hair that he had was wiry and, I guessed, had once been dark brown but was now peppered with grey.

He was tall and slender, and his face was drawn and angular. It was his eyes that caught my attention. They were a very pale shade of blue. He frowned at us.
 "What do you want?" His voice was deep, resonant, and cautious.
I spoke first. "Mister Fisher?"
 "Yeah?" His eyes narrowed.
 "We're looking for Mister Stanley Fisher…"
 "Why?"

Amanda took over, smiling sweetly. "We wanted to ask him some questions about the time you lived at Sefton Avenue - in New Moston."

"I know where it is." His response was marginally less brusque than when he'd spoken to me. He stared at Amanda, and she smiled back at him, while I waited anxiously.

It seemed like an age before the man gave a slight shrug and allowed himself the ghost of a grin. "You're going to have trouble speaking to my father. He died nine years ago."

"Oh." Amanda exaggerated the disappointment, and I could see that it had attracted the man's interest. He took out a cigarette packet, opened it and offered it to us. When we refused his offer he took out a cigarette and lit it.

Exhaling a thin stream of blue-grey smoke, the man shook his head. "If he owed you anything, you'll have to …"

"No." Amanda still smiled. "It's nothing like that. We wanted to ask him about something that happened on Christmas Eve in nineteen sixty four."

"What?" The man stared in disbelief. "I haven't a clue what you're talking about... Who would remember anything from that far back?" He sneered, but seeing the disappointment on Amanda's face, his expression softened and became almost sympathetic. "You said, nineteen sixty four?"

"Yes. Someone called that evening … I don't suppose you saw him?"

He frowned and his face contorted in a grimace, then he nodded. "Now you mention it, I do remember that something funny happened one Christmas sometime in the sixties… but I don't know if it was sixty four. To tell you the truth, I'd forgotten all about it."

"So … You saw the man who-"

"Whoa … Hold on. I never said I saw anybody. I remember I was in the front room watching Morecambe and Wise on TV when my dad went to the door. I heard him swearing when he came back inside … but that's all."

"Did he say anything to you about the incident?" Amanda's smile had gone and she just looked hopeful.

The man shook his head. "No. He never mentioned anything." He reacted to Amanda's desolate smile. "Sorry miss, but I can't tell you what I didn't see, but I did hear Dad going to the door and coming back swearing and that's about it. Sorry."

We had a consolation cup of coffee in my flat when we got back from Ashton. Sitting side by side on my settee, there wasn't much to say, and we were both a little despondent. After a long edgy silence, Amanda reached out and placed a hand on my wrist.

"This hasn't changed anything, Andy." It was a tentative reassurance, but I got the impression she was trying to reassure *herself* that the latest failure hadn't been the final 'nail in the coffin'.

I'll admit it had done nothing to stir up any enthusiasm on my part, but I didn't want to lose her support. I put my hand on hers and gave it a gentle squeeze.

"No," I smiled at her, "it hasn't."

"What will you do now?"

I shrugged. "I suppose I'll just have to wait until Sean telephones me."

"Do you think he'd mind if I came with you? Only I sort of want to see him."

I pondered for a moment. "I don't think it'd be a good idea if you just turned up … I think it'd be better if I asked him while I was with him."

She seemed disappointed but accepted my refusal with good grace. She forced a smile. "OK. But make sure you do ask … won't you?"

I gave her a pseudo-suspicious smile. "Is there an ulterior motive?"

"What do you mean?"

"I remember you saying how 'dishy' he was when we went to see him in Preston. You don't fancy him, by any chance?"

I nearly spilled my coffee as I ducked when she flung a cushion at me.

Two days later Sean called me to ask if I was ready to meet with him again, at his home. I know I'd convinced Amanda that I was now ready to accept anything Sean told me, but that was just for Amanda's benefit…I did ask Sean if he'd let me bring her with me this time, but he politely rejected my request. He said he'd no objections to meeting her, but not until he'd finished telling me the story.

Sean was dressed as if he was about to go out jogging,

and I asked him if I'd called at a bad time. He frowned as he was telling me I was punctual, and then when he saw me staring at his clothes, he smiled.

"I'm pretending to be in training for the Manchester half-marathon - in truth I couldn't walk that far, let alone run it." He led me into the kitchen where he had already laid out a couple of mugs ready for the coffee that was perking on the hob.

Once we'd sat down and started the coffee, Sean smiled at me. "Right then, where was I when we last saw each other?"

"You'd finished telling me about your visits with Jack Hargreaves, and you'd mentioned that he'd given you the name of the man who lived here in nineteen sixty four. Did you ever try to follow that up? Did you try to find the man?"

"Oh, you mean Stanley Fisher. As a matter of fact I did…I had a bit of trouble finding out where his new home was - and by the time I found the address it was too late. I spoke with his son, but he said his father had passed away. I couldn't see any point in pursuing the matter, so I just told him I was an old friend and left it at that. With the father gone, I couldn't see how the son could be of any help, since he didn't see me that night." He lowered his brows and stared at me for a long moment. "I suppose this isn't exactly 'news' to you?"

"What makes you say that?"

"Because I imagine you've been to see the Fishers, and found out that the son doesn't remember anything. And if you haven't been to his home, you're not the man I think you are."

I didn't respond, but remained calmly staring at him.

After a careful silence, Sean shrugged. "It was just another wasted journey … but I'd got quite used to it…"

"So… that was that … the end of your investigations?"

"Not so fast …You seem pretty eager for it all to be finished. Do you have something else to do - are you in a hurry, or something?"

"No, not at all. It's just that I can't see how much more there is for you to tell me."

"I got a letter from Paddy Flynn last week. I didn't tell you he moved back to Ireland, did I?"

"No, you never mentioned it."

"He wasn't too happy in Manchester, and went back home in nineteen ninety six. He found a permanent job in a bar, and has been keeping me up-to-date with all the gossip from Belfast."

"Interesting." I tried to sound enthusiastic.

"As a matter of fact, some of the news he sent me was interesting - as you put it. This last letter, for instance."

"What about it?"

"You remember Shawnie - the Senator's wife who left him to shack up with a casino owner?"

"I remember … what about her?"

"Paddy heard from 'a friend of a friend' over in LA, that she's disappeared, vanished completely. Word is that she started playing around behind her boyfriend's back, and when her man got to hear of it he 'disposed' of her. Paddy reckons the odds are that friend Shawnie is now part of a new highway construction, or holding up a new supermarket." Sean gave a long sigh. "I obviously didn't like the woman, but it's a shame that she should end up encased in a concrete slab…. Still, she was heading for it even when I knew her, the woman was pure trouble."

There was a short but poignant silence before Sean turned to me. "Right then, we'll get back to my side of the story. Just sit back, turn on your little recorder, enjoy your coffee, and listen."
Sean's shoulders seemed to droop a little and his eyes held a distant expression as he spoke…

When I failed to speak with Stanley Fisher, I was disappointed and dispirited. I had a few bookings to keep my mind off things, and Ronnie London, my agent had contacted me.

I don't think I've described Ronnie to you, so this might be a good time to do it.
Ronnie London had a pale almost death-like complexion, and he always wore a camel-hair coat, even in summer. He only came out a night, and then only to drink Brandy for England. He had a London Jewish accent because he thought that's how all agents spoke.

Think of Mother Theresa, then imagine someone totally opposite. His role models were Fagin, and Scrooge. In fact, he once told me that he thought there was nothing wrong with 'old Ebenezer' before the ghosts changed him.
Anyway, Ronnie was phoning to say he'd almost got me a prime-time TV session in Canada of all places. Whenever an agent tells you he's almost got you

something, you can bet that it'll never materialise … he's just trying to justify his existence to you. I didn't expect this one to become reality, so I disregarded the prospect of a trip to Canada.

What I did do, however, was to chase Sharon Beckett, you know, the young girl the Boswells took up onto the Moors and released after I'd scared the living daylights out of Thomas. It proved quite difficult. Even though Jack Hargreaves had given me a little background information I had the devil of a job tracing her. After six or seven weeks delving, I did manage to find out that she'd married a well-to-do businessman called Hanson and had moved to a new housing estate in Shaw.

I was in a bit of a dilemma. I didn't want to just turn up at the doorstep and say 'Hello - I'm the guy who saved your life on the Moors over thirty years ago' …I was a bit concerned that she'd over-react … I daresay I would have done in the circumstances… So I drove to the estate and parked a few doors away from her home and just waited until she appeared.

The estate was quiet and had a sort of upper-class air about it. I couldn't help but admire the neat houses with their well-tended front gardens and the expensive cars park in the drives. Her house looked particularly smart with its perfectly cut, smooth lawn, and a border of really colourful plants. I had no idea what they were, but they had fantastic shades of pink and lilac and seemed to stand out even among the other displays.

"Sean!"

"I know I'm doing it again, for Pete's sake allow me some artistic licence."

I wasn't sure about Sean's definition of artistic licence but I decided it was best to just let him carry on.

Anyway, she did eventually come out of the house, and although it'd been 'a long time' since I'd seen her, and she'd obviously grown up, I did recognise her. She was pretty, very well dressed, and her hair was immaculately groomed I thought, as I watched her walk to the garage. Not long afterwards a new black Mercedes reversed out onto the drive.

I followed the Mercedes out of Shaw and into the centre of Rochdale, but when it turned into a car park in front of a row of shops, I didn't follow it. Instead, I drove to the next corner and pulled up where I could watch Sharon as she got out of her car and walked to one of the shops. When she hadn't re-appeared after an hour, I was undecided what to do. I waited another fifteen minutes then I turned round and drove into the car park.

I paused outside the shop when I saw that it was an 'Oxfam' establishment. It puzzled me. Why would someone as obviously well-off as Sharon go shopping at Oxfam? I'd never been to a 'Charity Shop' as I always imagined all the wares inside were dowdy, battered and hardly worth looking at…

I opened the door and stepped inside with all the confidence of an early Christian stepping into the arena in Rome. Fortunately the sales assistants were occupied with customers so I was able to look around without being accosted. Far from being a 'second-hand' style of shop, I discovered that a lot of the goods on display were high quality ... I noticed several named labels and as far as I could tell, the articles were genuine.

I was fingering a flowing soft pink evening dress when a soft, pleasant voice sounded in my ear.

"An excellent garment ... It hasn't been with us long, and if you're interested, I could, perhaps make you an offer. Is it for a special occasion?"

Completely flustered, I turned and caught my breath. The speaker was none other than Sharon. I stared at her, noticing that her eyes were a soft grey-green, and were sparkling with amusement. She smiled. "We don't often get gentlemen looking at our select range of dresses. I can assure you that the item is quite authentic, and hasn't been worn much. In fact, I had it cleaned myself before I brought it in."

"It's your dress?"

"It was indeed."

I looked at the dress then at her. "Yes, I can imagine ... You must have looked pretty stunning in it."
She blushed faintly. "Why, thank you."

I noticed the first sign of a frown begin to crease her forehead, and a hint of anxiety flickered across her eyes. For a moment I couldn't imagine what had suddenly made her so cautious, then it hit me."

I spoke quickly before she could say anything. "I was going to buy my daughter something for a college dance ..."

"What size is she?"

I tried not to look too discomforted by the question. I hadn't a clue, and I didn't want to resort to the corny old 'she must be about your size' response. Fortunately I'd remembered seeing a number ten on the label whilst I was perusing, so I smiled confidently. "She's a fourteen right now ... and she's still growing."

"Oh dear. I'm afraid it wouldn't fit properly ... and with something as elegant as this, you'd have to be quite certain that the size was absolutely right. Might it be possible for you to bring her with you?"

"Not within the next few weeks ... she isn't due home until the end of term." I hunched my shoulders. "It was just an idea, but I think it would be safer if I got her a bracelet, or something."

"Yes," she agreed, "I think it would be best." She gave an awkward little hunch of her shoulders. "I'm afraid we don't have anything that would interest you."

"Pity ... I would have liked to have helped your cause. I don't suppose I could give you a donation, or something?"

"That's very kind of you..."

She turned as one of the other assistants called out. "Mrs. Hanson, how much did you say the Versace rainbow silk dress was?"

Sharon gave me an apologetic smile and went to the other assistant. While she was talking, I tried not to stare at her. There were a few other customers in the shop, and one of them let out a rather loud gasp an instant before I felt a hand on my arm. I turned to find a middle-aged woman beaming at me.

"It is you - isn't it?"

I just frowned at her.

She gave a sort of excited jiggle. "Could you autograph this for me?" She held out a marker pen and a rather old copy of one of my earlier Lps. "I just found it among a collection of old records ... and it must be fate that I saw you standing there." She thrust the sleeved record at me, and I duly obliged her by signing it. She hugged the record to her chest as if it was priceless. It was then that Sharon rejoined me. Before she could speak, the customer turned to her.

 "It isn't every day we have a celebrity in the shop ...
How did you persuade him to come?"

Sharon looked bemused, glancing at the woman then at me. Seeing Sharon's puzzled expression, the customer pointed at me. "That's Sean Clarke ... you know the singer. He does a bit of acting too. I saw him only last week on ... what's it called? On the telly ... you know ... Morse, or was it something Murders ... I forget."

Sharon smiled at the woman, and then frowned at me. The other woman gave an embarrassed shuffle then started to back away as if I was royalty. "Well ... I mustn't keep you. It was ever so nice to meet you Mister Clarke ... All my friends will be green with envy when I tell them that I've actually met you face to face."

I gave Sharon an apologetic shrug. "Sorry about that. She just appeared out of the blue..."

Sharon gave me an understanding smile. "Now she mentioned it, I must admit that when I first saw you I had the strange feeling that I knew you from somewhere. It's me who should apologise - for not recognising you. Of course, I have seen you on television, and I admire your work."

I hunched my shoulders and felt a flush covering my cheeks. "Thank you ... Now, I offered to give something ...?"

"Oh, yes. How much would you like to donate?"

"Would twenty pounds be all right?"

"It would be more than alright and thank you very much."

I left the charity shop with mixed feelings. Of course I never expected Sharon to know me after all those years, and when she did confess to 'having seen me on TV' I wasn't quite sure I believed her. But, as I drove home and thought about what she'd said, I came to the conclusion that her response was that of a kindly person - one who would not knowingly hurt anyone's feelings. Everything about her suggested she was good natured and helpful. I knew a few well-heeled people, and not one of them would donate almost brand-new clothes to help any cause - other than their own bank balance.

I didn't quite leave it at that. I made a few discrete enquiries about Sharon Hanson, and discovered that the work in the charity shop was only the tip of a bounteous iceberg. Not only did she organise the charity shop, and provide much of the goods they sold there, but she also served on a couple of committees dedicated to helping those less fortunate than themselves.

It was reputed that she alone had raised hundreds of thousands of pounds for Eastern European refugee children after the conflict in the former Yugoslavia. Not satisfied with that, she had organised an on-going and regular supply of essential clothing to those children, and had been the prime mover in the refurbishment of a number of small clinics. In addition to all that, she was working on a project to rebuild a hospital somewhere in Kosovo.

It gave me a really weird feeling - almost like the old Chinese proverb about a butterfly flapping its wings and creating a wind-storm on the other side of the earth. When I saved Sharon's life, without knowing it, I started a chain of events that would eventually benefit hundreds of people I'd never met. It made me feel pretty good I can tell you.

I met her a few times after my visit to the shop, and on one occasion she persuaded me to take part in a charity concert, asking me to bring along as many of my 'stage' friends as I was able. The concert raised over a thousand pounds for one of Sharon's charities, and she asked me if I could urge my entertainer friends to consider doing a few more concerts for her.
In total, I think I did about a dozen shows, all of which were well attended. Even more importantly, I know for certain that they raised lots of money for her charities.
She was on her way to organise another of those concerts when she was involved in a tragic accident.

*   *   *

FOURTEEN

Sean looked at me with a profound sadness in his eyes, and I could feel the anguish in the air as I stared at him.

After what seemed like a very prolonged silence, he let out a soft sigh. "Sharon wasn't killed in the crash, but she was pretty badly injured. She was in a coma, and I managed to convince the staff at the hospital that I was a distant cousin. I can't tell you how bad I felt when I saw her lying there with great bandages around her head and a mass of tubes going to drips and bags and goodness knows what else. There was a big monitor sort of thing at the side of the bed, and it kept up a regular bleeping...

I stood beside the bed and took hold of her hand. I held it while I told her that I was 'the giant' from the moors. I swear I felt her fingers close a little around mine for an instant, and the bleeping sound sort of changed for a few seconds … It was as if she'd told me she knew. I leaned over and kissed her on the cheek, then I left."

Sean gave a sad yet angry grimace. "It was so unfair. She wasn't all that old, and she was doing so much good with her life. Not like me. I just …" He gave a disconsolate shrug.

"You bring a little happiness into people's lives too Sean. Maybe not in the same basic way that Sharon helped people, but still enough for them to want to come to watch you."

"Thanks." He gave me a soft smile.

I had to ask… "In the short time you got to know her, did Sharon ever offer the slightest hint that she'd recognised you as being the man who'd rescued her from the Moors when she was a kid?"

"Not really. There were a couple of occasions when I caught her staring at me with a funny puzzled sort of look in her eyes. But she never hinted that she knew me from nineteen sixty four."

Sean gave a slight sigh, and I stared down at my coffee cup for a moment to let him regain his composure. We both looked at each other then I spoke first.

"You said your agent had told you he had a possible booking in Canada for you … did anything come of it?"

"Not for a long time … about three or four months. To be honest, I'd forgotten all about it. I had a regular supply of regional dates, and I got a small part in a one-off TV play. I spent some time with Jason and Michelle and life was becoming steady - no upsets or hitches to worry about." Sean gave a half smile and continued.

I was in the process of making arrangements to take the kids on holiday when Ronnie called me to say that the Canadian booking had been confirmed. At first I thought he was joking. The more I thought about it, the less sense it made.

I'll admit that, thanks to my burgeoning acting

career I was becoming better known in this country, but I was a complete nonentity in Canada - So why would they give me a tour complete with TV slots?

It took a while, but Ronnie eventually gave me the details. Apparently it was all to do with a song called 'Before you've said goodbye' I'd written some time ago. I'd made a demo tape and sent it to Ronnie who said he'd send it to Brendan O'Donnell, a popular Irish country singer. I heard nothing about it, and after a while, forgot all about it.

What I didn't know was that my demo had been used as the backing track for a big TV advert in Canada, and it was then released as a single and it somehow got into the Canadian hit parade.

I told Ronnie we'd discuss Royalties later - and his reply was quite typical of the man.

"Money, money. That's all you ever think about. Whatever happened to 'art for art's sake?'"

Then I recalled the Cruise-Liner fiasco…

"This trip to Canada - is it an Equity-backed booking - or is it one of your-"

Ronnie sounded as if I'd insulted him. "There's no need to be facetious, Sean. I know the American booking ended up a little unfortunately for you, but this one is the genuine article. I'll send you details and yes an Equity contract and you can browse over them … and get them back to me by the end of the week."

I still wasn't convinced he wasn't having a joke at my expense, then I accepted that - where bookings and potential commissions were concerned - agents, and Ronnie in particular, had no sense of humour.

The original of the contract document duly arrived, and after I'd gone through it carefully, I could see no faults, or hidden catches, so I signed it and sent it back to Ronnie. Normally, there's a reasonably long delay between signing the contract and actually going on the booking, but in this instance I didn't have to wait longer than a month.

A fortnight after I'd returned the contract, Ronnie got in touch with me. He positively enthused over the telephone.

"This could be the start of a really long association with the Canadians. If they like you - and who wouldn't like a man as talented as you - they've hinted that there could be a whole series of one-night TV broadcasts, along with a number of one-to-one 'in depth' interviews ... Who knows - they might even go as far as to offer you your own TV series ... Look what happened to Val Doonican."

"Let's not get too carried away, Ronnie."

"All right ... but if you do treat this engagement seriously, I can see that it could open up a whole new vista for you."

"Don't worry ... I'll do my best not to blow it ..."

"It'll be the last time, if you do." I couldn't tell if Ronnie was joking or not, and I felt a little annoyed at him after I'd rung off. All right, there'd been a problem on the cruise ship, but it hadn't been my fault, and it seemed as if Ronnie blamed me for it.

There and then I made up my mind to avoid

anything that could lead to 'complications' when I was in Canada. Like Ronnie had said, it could be the start of a whole new market for me - if things didn't go wrong.

Canada is a big country, and the cities I visited were awesome. Everything seemed to have been built with a total disregard for the space used ... but it certainly gave you a feeling of open uncluttered airiness. I seemed to have wandered along great wide boulevards as wide as football pitches, staring up at immaculately clean sprawling buildings. No, that isn't quite right. The buildings weren't 'sprawling' they just gave the impression that, like an undercooked cake, they'd just spread out as far as they could before they solidified.

Vancouver was my first date and the show was as perfect as I could have wished. I felt as if I was in great form, and the audience gave me a really thunderous reception, and applauded my performance long after I left the stage. I was treated almost like a celebrity at the hotel and at the studio.

I was due to appear on a live chat show the following night, so I had the chance to look at the reviews in the morning papers. I don't often read reviews, but on this occasion I was tempted.

Although one critic didn't exactly rate me as highly as Celine Dion, they did quote me as being 'a bright and very entertaining personality' and recommended that their readers should take every opportunity to watch me that night. Another wasn't quite so enthusiastic, but did say that I was 'a personable and not unpleasant sort of swinger who didn't offend the ear'. The final review was the worst, but even so the critic admitted that my kind of music was not his specialty, and as such he found me barely tolerable. In all I wasn't too disappointed by what I'd read, and when I prepared for the 'live show' I was quietly confident that I'd not fall flat on my face.

The make-up girl admitted that she'd never heard of me, but made up for that by being very friendly. She had relatives in Birmingham and was disappointed that I wasn't too familiar with Smethwick. But she did ask me that when I was next in the midlands, to 'say hello' from Christine.

The show was a simple affair. The interviewer, an apparent cult figure in TV, asked a few pre-determined questions designed to bring out humorous incidents and provide a light-hearted atmosphere. After the interview, the guests were then invited to perform. The schedule I was given indicated that the interview would last no longer than ten minutes, and I'd been allocated a four minute slot to deliver my latest song, 'May I borrow you.'

Everything had gone really smoothly. I felt comfortable with the interviewer, and he seemed to be quite happy with the stories I'd told him. I'd estimated that there was enough time for one final question before he would invite me to move to the small stage to deliver my song, and my mind was already preparing for the performance. I only half heard the final question, and was about to deliver my pre-prepared answer when I realised the question was not the one I'd been expecting. I gaped at the man and he grinned back at me.

"Come on Sean, don't be coy about it … Isn't it a fact that you've not long been divorced, and are on the market again? Would you say that you are open to offers right now?"

I sort of blustered, forgetting all about 'camera image' as I fought down an urge to tell the guy it was none of his damned business. I did manage to come out with a civilised sort of reply, but I was still annoyed when I walked onto the stage and waited for the taped orchestra to begin the introduction to my latest song.

It was 'form' to attend an after-show party, but I broke the rules by leaving the studio as soon as I'd finished my slot. I guessed that there'd be some kind of reaction, both by the host company and by the newspapers. I couldn't have cared less.

My next date in Quebec, to do a short appearance on a music programme, then appear on a live chat show. I hadn't been in the hotel more than an hour when I got a telephone call - from Ronnie.

"You did it again, Sean, after all that I told you … You went and screwed up on TV of all places. What the hell were you thinking of? Or were you just not thinking at all, as usual?"

"Take it easy, Ronnie. You'll blow a gasket."

"I'll blow more than a gasket! Do you realise that you could have blown everything, just by being

311

thoughtless. What came over you?"

"Sanity…"

Ronnie wasn't listening. He thundered on. "It would have been bad enough to put on a poor performance … But you … Oh no! You have to go and insult the most popular TV interviewer in the whole of Canadian TV."

"I didn't insult the man … I just didn't go to his 'drinkies' party after the show."

"That isn't how the papers see it. I got a call from a friend of a friend of a leading critic, and believe me, tomorrow's papers will crucify you. I doubt if the rest of your tour is going to go on. I'll do my best to smooth things out … and in the meantime stay in your hotel. Don't speak to anyone - especially any reporters - and wait for me to call you."

Ronnie's pessimism proved to be a little unfounded. Yes, some of the critics did give me a bit of a slating because I upset protocol by avoiding the party which of course they all attended…but some others discretely gave me a boost, and referred to me as 'the man who goes his own way'.

The outcome was that I was still invited to appear in Quebec, and afterwards in Montreal. Ronnie was conspicuous by his silence …

The TV format in Quebec was much the same as I'd experienced in Vancouver, with the exception that during the 'chat' part of the show, the presenter concentrated on my previous verbal and social 'performances'. Since I'd been expecting something of the sort, I was prepared, and I'd decided to look at the funny side of the situation.

Fortunately the presenter was no great admirer of his counterpart in Vancouver, and treated me with some sympathy and support. I got the feeling he would have liked me to really poke fun at his Vancouver colleague, but I decided not to ruffle too many feathers.

The interview went better than I'd anticipated, and even before I began my song, I received a prolonged and ringing applause from the audience. Even more satisfying was their reaction once I'd ended my song. They gave me a standing ovation.

With only one more TV appearance to negotiate, I was feeling quite good when I arrived at the hotel in Montreal. This feeling was boosted when a couple of people in the foyer recognised me and, like a lot of North Americans, came up to me and, as if they already knew me, told me I had their full support for privacy in my personal life. They said they were looking forward to seeing me again on TV and wished me luck for the performance.

The receptionist too adopted a familiarity that I'd not often experienced. She flattered me with her single-minded attention, making me feel as if I was the only person in the hotel at the time. Even the way she smiled at me as she handed me my key-card was more than just a professional courtesy. She smiled as if she really meant it. I couldn't help but smile back at her as I turned away. Suddenly her voice rang out..

"Mister Clarke. You have a message …"

I turned to find her holding out a card. Frowning, I took it from her and glanced at it, expecting to find that Ronnie was fretting again, or crowing because of my recent success. The note was not from Ronnie. It was a simple request.

"Please contact Betty …." followed by a Montreal telephone number.

I looked at the receptionist and saw a hint of anxiety in her expression. "If there's a problem, sir, we could have somebody 'deal' with it for you. I guess you get pestered all the time?"

"Er … No. It's quite all right, thank you. If the lady is who I think she is … she's someone I knew in Manchester sometime in the past."

"Oh." The receptionist tried to hide a crestfallen look as she forced a smile. "Well, Mister Clarke, if there is a problem, or you need anything at all, please call me. I'm Rebecca. I'll get the porter to collect your luggage."

"Thank you, Rebecca."

The room was like any other modern hotel room, only bigger. It had a decent private bar and a comfortable looking easy chair, along with the bed, cabinets and a built-in wardrobe. The bathroom was spacious and spotless, and the view from the window was interesting but not spectacular.

I unpacked and fixed myself a drink from the

private bar before I looked at the card again. To be honest I was intrigued, and a little apprehensive. Could it really be the teenager I'd met in Willet street police station … and how would we react if I did return her call. I couldn't even figure out how I would feel, let alone guess how she would be.

I put the card down on the bedside table and drained my glass. I went to the bar and poured another Brandy then sat in the easy chair and stared out of the window.

I gave a start and almost spilled my drink when the telephone interrupted my dream-like state. I picked up the receiver and heard a polite telephonist asking if I would accept a call from a … Betty Walker. The hairs on my neck stood up and a wave of gooseflesh ran over my arms. I took a deep breath.

"Yes, I'll accept the call."

"Mister Clarke? Mister Sean Clarke?" A female voice, husky and resonant, sounded in the earpiece. The accent was unmistakably Canadian with hardly a trace of the Mancunian I remembered.

"Yes, that's me. What can I do for you?" I was quite calm. I probably expected her to sound exactly as she'd done in nineteen sixty four, but she was a woman now and in a way 'foreign' into the bargain.

"I don't know quite how to explain this … "She hesitated and I waited. I could hear her breathing and to me it sounded as if she was agitated.

"Can I help you?" I asked.

"I hope so. Are you the singer who's been in all the papers during the last couple of days?"

315

"Yes, that's me."

There was another long pause. Her voice seemed to tremble when she spoke, and she seemed unsure of herself. "I don't know how to put this … but were you arrested on Christmas Eve nineteen sixty four? I don't mean to offend you, or anything … and if you could just …"

"It's all right, Betty. It is me … I sat next to you, and we shared my sandwiches."

"Oh My God! It *is* you!" This time I could hear her half-laughing, half-crying, and I waited for her to speak again. She was a little cautious when she spoke this time. "How … How old are you?"

"I'm forty-eight in a few weeks' time."

I could almost picture her bewilderment as she tried to face the fact that when she'd last seen me I was, in her estimation, about forty five. I could tell that she was really becoming disturbed. "I … I don't understand this, Mister Clarke."

"I can understand why, Betty. Look, we can't do this over the phone. If it will help you, I'm prepared to meet somewhere while I try to explain what happened that Christmas. Do you know anywhere discrete, where you'd feel comfortable?"

"I'm not sure … It's shaken me a little." There was a pause and I waited patiently, not wanting to influence her decision. I heard her take a deep breath. "All right, Mister Clarke. Do you know the Old Village Eatery?"

"No, but I'm sure I could find it."

"Would you meet me there?"

316

"What time?"

"Two o'clock. Would that be all right?"

"I'll be there."

The Old Village Eatery proved to be as update and modern as all the other establishments sited in a quiet corner of a wide tiled square at the centre of which was a shallow rectangular concrete pond fed by water cascading down a series of irregular steps. People were sitting on a low wall bordering the pond sunning themselves in the warm afternoon; and a few pigeons lurked close at hand hoping for a handout. Neither the birds nor the people paid any attention to me when I got out of the taxi and walked across the square to the 'eatery'.

Fronted by an enormous stainless steel framed glass window and a simulated 'olde worlde' sign hanging above the door, the restaurant looked as if it had been transported from a showroom. Through the window I could see randomly-spaced glass-topped tables with stylish chrome-plated scrolled legs and matching chrome legged chairs. Beyond a long curved stainless counter I could see an area which seemed to be more secluded, hiding behind a metal fret-worked screen, and it was there I guessed I'd find Betty.

I went in and walked to the screen where I paused and surveyed the half-dozen tables nestling in the less brightly lit corner. Two were unoccupied and three were taken up by couples. Only one table, situated in the far corner, had a single female occupant. She

317

started to rise as I walked towards her.

I felt my breath catch in my throat as I looked at her. She was beautiful. I'd remembered her as a pretty teenager, but the intervening years had added depth and character. She was tall and slim, and wearing a tailored pale green skirt and jacket beneath which was a matching silk blouse. Her hair, I remembered as being a pretty but nondescript shade of brown, was now a deep rich chestnut, and styled to frame her tanned oval face. Sparkling grey-green eyes looked at me with disbelief. The sparkle faded from her eyes and the colour drained from her cheeks. She seemed to waver then sat down quickly. I hurried to the table and sat down facing her.

"Betty?" I asked, even though I knew it was her. "You look as if you're just seen a ghost." I forced a smile.

"I have just seen a ghost." She shook her head and took a calming breath. "I don't believe this." Her voice was soft, softer than I recalled. "It really is you!"

"Yes. You're not imagining it, I promise." I could see that she was trembling, and I noticed her slim hands were shaking as she held them tightly on the table top. I waited, giving her the chance to compose herself, but before I could speak I was interrupted. An efficient smartly dressed waitress came to place small menu cards in front of us, and we both ordered coffee.

"You're looking well," I said.

"You look exactly as you did that evening when …" She frowned. "Why didn't you come back for me?"

"I did … This is going to sound incredible, Betty, but I swear it's the truth." I gave her a reassuring smile before I began to explain what had happened to me on the night I'd taken her to the hotel in Manchester.

"…. and after the 'vision' of the little boy vanished, the room became different. It had all changed. You were gone and everything about the place was unrecognizable in other words I was still in the room but in my own time 1994."

The waitress arrived with the coffee, and I could see Betty considering what I had told her. Once the waitress had gone, Betty toyed with her spoon, making patterns across the surface of her coffee. At length she looked across the table at me. She stared into my eyes for some time then gave a slight shrug. "I trusted you all those years ago, and even when you didn't turn up, I still believed in you … "

"I really did my best to track you down Betty… but …" I shrugged. "It was so hard at first, trying to convince myself that it had all really happened. There are times, even now, when I find it almost impossible to believe that I 'lost' thirty years in an instant."

I noticed that Betty's hands were no longer shaking as she looked at me. "I don't know why, but I still do believe in you." She gave the ghost of a grin. "It would take a pretty fertile imagination to dream up anything as bizarre as what you've just told me … and even more gall to tell it to my face … Mind you, you have had the last thirty years to make up a story."

I was about to protest when I saw that she was still smiling at me. She took a sip of coffee, staring at me over the rim of her cup. After replacing the cup, she wiped her lips with a napkin then frowned at me.

"Can you explain what happened?"

319

I shook my head. "No. It was hard enough trying to come to terms with it." I hunched my shoulders. "The more I puzzled over it, the more confused I became … So, I just tried to forget about the whole thing, but that didn't work, and then I began to … sort of investigate."

She regarded me with a slightly amused expression. "Yes, I can see you as a 'gumshoe' … you have a sort of doggedness about you …" She gave a self-conscious shrug. "All right, I don't know you at all, but I suspect that once you set your mind on something, you won't be shaken off easily."

I smiled. "I'll take that as a compliment."

"Good. I meant it to be." She took another sip of coffee and I did the same. There was a silence that didn't feel uncomfortable, and then Betty's expression changed. She seemed unsure and a little embarrassed, so I looked directly into her eyes.

"Is there some problem, Betty?"

"No … I … er… I know you got angry when that TV reporter asked you about your marriage."

"Yes, I was annoyed with him, not only because the question was unscripted, but I wasn't prepared to talk about my private life 'on the air'."

"Are you still annoyed?"

"With him, probably. It was a painful period of my life, and it took me quite a long time to come to terms with being on my own after living for ten years with the same person."

Betty nodded. "I know what you mean." I looked at her and I could see the understanding and 'empathy' in her gaze.

I regarded her seriously. "From that, I gather that you've been through it too?"

"Yes. It was dirty and messy, and I could imagine exactly how you felt when that presenter tried to upset you. It was bad enough coping with it all in private, but as for being asked to bare your soul on TV I would have reacted exactly the way you did. Even at the best of times I hate people poking their nose into my affairs."

She gave me another soft smile as we lapsed into a slightly 'edgy' silence. I think we both welcomed the half-filled cups before us, and we sort of used the coffee to cover the slight tension of the situation. After a few minutes, Betty broke the silence.

"I think you're like me … you have two personalities. One is your 'stage' persona which you are quite willing to show the world, but your second is the important one, the inner one … I'm guessing, but I'd say that you reserve it for only a few special people in your life …"

It was with regret that I looked at my watch and saw that if I was to get ready for the show that evening, I would have to leave her. She saw me and gave me an understanding smile.

"You're going to be late for the programme if you don't go soon."

"Yes. I'm sorry."

"Then, we'll have to meet again, later this week perhaps? I couldn't make tomorrow because I have to travel to a business meeting, but I'd be free-"

I let out a sigh. "Sorry, love, but I'm leaving for Manchester in the morning."

"Oh." Betty didn't try to hide her disappointment

"I could get you into the studio for tonight's show ...?"

"No." She shook her head. "I wouldn't feel right. I'd rather remember the 'real' Sean Clarke - the one who hasn't changed at all in thirty years."

Sean paused for a moment to let the memory subside then got up from his chair and walked to the door that separated the kitchen from the hallway. "I feel like a proper drink. Would you join me, Andy?"

"Thanks." I followed him as he went into the front room and I sat in the usual place on the settee while he poured a couple of glasses of Brandy.

I waited until he'd given me a glass and took his seat on the armchair diagonally to my right, then I spoke.

"And that was it? You just saw her that once, before you came back home?"

Sean savoured the Brandy, inhaling the heady fumes then closing his eyes after he sipped the golden liquid. He smacked his lips in appreciation then looked at me with an amused yet quizzical expression on his face.

"It seems like my answer could be important to you."

I shrugged, and tried to appear undisturbed by

the accuracy of his statement. "I'm just interested, that's all."

He gave a slight smile then took another deliberate sip of Brandy. He then rolled the glass between his hands while holding my gaze with a cool long stare. "Oh? Then you would be 'interested' to hear that I didn't see her again unt-"

"I knew it!" I couldn't help myself, even though I did my damndest not to react.

"I don't understand." Sean frowned at me, taken aback by my interjection.

"I do." I suddenly became angry with him. "It might sound corny, but I expected you to say that you never saw her again."

"But ... I didn't." For an instant, Sean looked hurt. But I hardly noticed.

I'd reached my limit and I could no longer contain my disappointment and my annoyance with him. I got to my feet and he did the same, and we faced each other like a couple of belligerent schoolboys. I was in full flow by now, and nothing could have prevented me from speaking my mind. "Yes, I know - you don't have to tell me ... Betty was killed in a car crash, or a plane accident as she was flying over here to meet you ... Forget it, Sean, I've heard it all before, and to be honest, I'm not impressed. I expected far better from you!"

Sean's mouth dropped open. "I honestly don't know what you're talking about."

"Is that right? Then, I'll spell it out for you. Everything you're told me over the past few months

323

would stretch gullibility to the limit! You haven't given me one single fact that I could verify properly."

"What do you mean? I told you about the Hotel, the police station, I even told you about the headlines in the newspaper that Christmas Eve!"

"Anyone could have read up those details, and for someone with as good a memory as yours it would be a simple matter to pop them out like rabbits from a conjurer's hat whenever you wanted to make your story sound that little bit more convincing. I'm sorry, Sean, but it doesn't work anymore."

"Are you calling me a liar?" Sean took a menacing pace towards me, but I didn't flinch. Even though I was a little awed by his presence, I stood my ground and glared back at him.

"Call it what you will. Artistic licence, poetic adjustment ... or just plain tripe!"

"You self-opinionated, impatient, ignorant, arrogant little snot." Sean reached out and caught me by the shoulder. His grip was like a vice, and even though I struggled he was easily able to propel me out into the hall. "If you'd had the plain courtesy to listen properly to what I was saying - and allowed me to finish, you might have taken a different stance ... No! I doubt you would." He reached out to open the front door. "You'd already decided that I was lying ... Well you can take your narrow little mind and your 'superior intellect' - and you can get the fuck out of my house!" He shoved me onto the doorstep when I narrowly avoided falling onto the path.

Despite the tension in the situation, I was still

able to think clearly. I stared at him as he started to close the door. "What could you have told me that would have made any difference, Sean?"

I didn't think he was going to answer for a moment, then he took a deep breath and growled angrily at me. "I was going to say that, after my trip to Canada, I didn't see Betty again, for quite a while … Then we started writing to each other, and telephoning … Eventually she decided she was going to come back home to Manchester…"

It must have been a devil inside me. I smiled at Sean and nodded. "Yes, let me guess … She came back home, to you, and you married her and lived happy ever after…"

"As a matter of fact … I did!" He slammed the door in my face.

*   *   *

FIFTEEN

Everything Sean said led to a dead witness and thinking back to Sharon Hanson's funeral I thought this is where I came in. I was utterly disappointed as I drove home to my flat. Disappointed, that Sean seemed to be as much a charlatan as all the other sensation-seekers who'd tried to fool me. I was annoyed that I had wasted months on what had proved to be a useless and irritating exercise ... but even that didn't justify my own behaviour. I don't know what had come over me. When I arrived at his home the last thing I intended was to create any aggravation, and I certainly had no intention of 'squaring up' to Sean the way that I did ... For some unknown reason, I acted totally out of character and I definitely did not want to upset him as much as I'd obviously done ...

I treated myself to a can of beer from the fridge when I got home. While I drank it, I contemplated what I'd done, and it became evident that I had destroyed whatever empathy that had existed between Sean and me. That was it. End of story.

I'd forgotten that Amanda had told me she was starting her new job, so I was puzzled when I got no answer when I telephoned her late that afternoon. She called me later, after I'd finished a ready meal and was settling down to watch TV.

327

I was careful as I spoke to her. I avoided telling her exactly how disastrous the meeting had been and told her instead about the 'meeting' Sean had had with Betty in Canada. Having successfully side-tracked her, I was comfortable enough to tell her how Sean had told me that Betty had come back to Manchester. Since I knew I was no longer going to pursue the matter, I even told her that Sean had admitted that he and Betty had got married. This appealed to Amanda's 'romantic side', and she was in a pretty good mood when we rang off. I didn't feel the slightest pang of remorse at having misled her, and was sure that when we next met I would be able to flannel my way out of any awkward situation that might develop.

I made myself comfortable on the settee and thumbed the remote control, switching channels to find something worth watching. I settled on a drama but within minutes a familiar face came onto the screen. Sean was playing the part of a small-time villain and he was convincing - convincing enough to make me turn off the TV. In other words I couldn't even face him in any shape or form.

I turned on the radio, and hoping not to hear Sean's lilting accent, I began to file away all the notes and tapes I'd taken during my meetings with the mercurial Irishman.
It took some time, and after I'd finished, I had another drink and took myself to my bed.

Having little or no conscience is a great boon. I slept the

sleep of the innocents that night and woke up refreshed and ready for anything. The 'anything' turned out to be a new investigation project, suggested to me by an editor friend who'd had an idea that his magazine sales could be boosted by a 'startling revelation' showing the number of marriages of convenience taking place in the region. He gave me some direction as to the line he wanted me to adopt, then left me to it.

Since there was no pressing time-scale on the project, and I didn't expect to see Amanda until she'd settled in her new job. I guessed she wouldn't contact me until the following week, so I took a couple of days off. I thought I might take advantage of the mild late autumn and take a drive out of the city.

I hadn't been to the coast for some time, so I decided to take a trip to Blackpool. The town wasn't exactly heaving and I had little problem in finding a vacant spot in a car-park close to the sea front. I spent the whole morning just wandering along the promenade invigorated by the gusting breeze that blew in from the sea. After a decent meal at a restaurant close to the tower, I visited a conventional 'Council park' and watched half-dozen old men playing bowls until late afternoon.

By the time I got home in the early evening I was totally refreshed and quite tired. After a couple of cans of beer I went to bed and slept like a baby.

On my second recreational day I drove to Chester and parked up close to the centre of the city - not far from the race-course. I walked into the heart of the 'old city' and just mooched. I went into the

Cathedral and absorbed its beneficent calming atmosphere. Mid-morning I had a 'luxury cream tea' which was far from luxurious, but staved off a few hunger pangs before I began a light-hearted trek through the cluster of shops lining the old cobbled main street. I didn't buy a thing, but nevertheless I was in a pleasant mood when I treated myself to decent meal on a barge which sailed up and down a short reach of the canal. I ended the day by parking up alongside the river Dee, and spent a dreamy hour just sitting on a grassy bank watching the wildlife.

There was a message from Amanda on the answer-phone when I got back to the flat. She'd been asked to spend a few weeks in Brussels, on business, and would not be home again until the end of November. She hoped I'd miss her - as much as she'd miss me - and she promised to get in touch as soon as she came home.

I was getting hungry, but didn't feel like 'cooking' so I trawled off to the local Kebab house and stayed to enjoy a decent four courser. There was nothing on TV when I got back so I turned to Sean's notes.

I re-read some of the earlier stuff then listened to a section of one of the recordings I'd taken at his home. There was no doubting the sincerity in his voice, and as I listened I could visualise how his expression used to alter with each shade of his ever-changing moods.

After re-filing the notes and the tapes, I got myself a can, and half lay on the settee, drinking and pondering. I had liked Sean, but I couldn't figure out what he'd wanted from me. I'd sensed that he'd needed someone to hear his tale and I'd been a willing listener. He'd been good ... most of the frauds I'd met in the past were so transparent I'd dismissed them before the end of the first session. Sean's story was compulsive listening. It had the ring of truth about it ... maybe that was what had held my interest for so long? But, at the end there was nothing that had truly convinced me that it was anything more than an interesting and elaborate fabrication.

I was still thinking about it when I went to bed but, unlike Sean, I didn't have any pertinent dreams, In fact if I did have any dreams I couldn't remember them when I woke up the following morning.

Self-motivation has never really been a problem. In fact, at most times, the difficulty has been in restraining myself, especially when I had a good line of enquiry and 'the bit between my teeth'. But, the prospect of looking into 'Convenience Marriages' didn't really excite me, and as a result I started my mission slowly.

In general, when faced with a task like the current one, I usually began by contacting a number of friends who helped me out with direct information or by steering me in the right direction. This time I was a little at a loss as to who I might contact. I thought long and hard before I came up with a couple of names that I trawled out of my list.

It wasn't straightforward. Neither of them were what you might call 'attention-seekers' and neither were easy to find. It took me two days to get in touch with them, and although interested in the project, the first of my contacts wasn't much help - which left me with an enquiry schedule of one.

Wilbur - not his real name - wasn't forthcoming at first, and I suspect that he thought I might have used whatever information he gave me to incriminate some of his friends and associates. Since most of them hovered at the edges of 'disreputable' society, and were not averse to dealing out a violent kind of justice, I could appreciate his reticence.

It took a long time to convince him that nothing I wrote would be specific to either him or any of his associates. Then, once he was assured that there'd be 'no-names-no-pack drill', he relaxed. For the next forty minutes he broadened my education and gave me enough details for me to have the basis of a rough draft of my proposed article.

During the rest of that day, and for a couple of hours the following morning, I worked on the rough draft. Satisfied that it was a strong enough base on which to build the rest of the article, I realised that I now needed some hard facts to shore up the bulk of the work.

Wilbur had given me a collection of names ... it was up to me to sort out the fact from the fiction; and to do that I needed to have some official confirmation. There was only one place I was going to get it.

It seemed like I'd spent a lot of time at the Offices of

Registration for Births Marriages and Deaths recently, and the receptionist gave me a really friendly smile of recognition when I went up to the glass lined counter. I smiled back at her.

"Hi Louise, it's me again. I have a whole new list of names that I'd like to check out." I gave her the sheet filled with the names Id managed to compile, and she gave me a look of mock indignation.

"Andy Priest, do you think I've nothing better to do than act as your researcher?"

"It keeps you off the streets, Louise, my love. " I winked at her.

"It may take some time…"

"That's all right … I've nowhere else to go right now." She started to turn away then paused and turned round to look at me. "One of these days it's going to cost you more than just money."

"Oooh I just can't wait. How about, you and I jet off to the Bahamas this afternoon after you finish work." Louise gave a theatrical sigh. "I'm sorry, I can't make it. I have to wash my hair." She grinned at me then turned and walked away.

While I was waiting for her to come back to me, I took a seat and watched the arriving 'customers'. It wasn't difficult to separate the Births from the Marriages, and Deaths, and in the half hour or so that I was sitting there, I got a potted version of Manchester life. Young and old, rich and poor; happy, and sad; here was a procession of people proclaiming their news, their emotions raw and open to the world.

As she'd hinted, Louise was some time before she'd gathered all the information I was looking for, and when she returned I went to the desk to meet her. She was holding a sheaf of papers, and she was still smiling. Placing the papers on the counter, she looked at me. "You know, almost single-handed, you've managed to fund this office for the next two days with what this little lot is going to cost you."

I hunched my shoulders in a good-natured shrug. "I wouldn't want you to get bored."

"Let me know the next time you're coming in to do some research. I'll book myself a couple of day's holiday. "She glanced down at the papers. "Is everything all right?"

"That's just fine ... You've maintained your usual high standard."

"Happy to oblige." Louise gave a coquettish little curtsey.

I smiled at her as I collected the papers in exchange for a handful of notes and coins and she sighed. Her expression was severe but I could see a glint of humour in her eyes. "No doubt I'll be seeing you again."

"You can bet on it." I waved the papers at her in salute, then turned and headed for the door.

I got to work on the information when I got back to my flat. But, as I pored over the certificates I started to think about Sean and Betty, and after a while it was all I could think about. In an attempt to distract myself, I forced myself to get a can from the fridge and sit on the settee. I opened the can, took a swig, and then started to study the copies of the Marriage Certificates that I really needed to work on for my story, but I couldn't. I really needed to find out...

After half an hour, I gave up and went to the telephone. I hesitated for a moment then dialled the number of the registry office. It was Louise that answered and I tried to keep my voice light-hearted as I spoke to her.

"It's Andy here ... I know I've just seen you, but could you do me a favour?"

"I told you ... I'm washing my hair tonight."

"No. I'm serious. I need to find out if an Elizabeth Walker Married a Sean Clarke in nineteen ninety five or nineteen ninety six."

"You are joking, aren't you? Do you know how long that could take?"

"Come on Louise ... I'll love you forever if you'll just do this for me ... and I will take you out for ..."

"Don't make promises you've no intentions of keeping ... All right, but I'm really busy right now ... I'll see what I can do for you ... Now what were those names?"

"Elizabeth Walker ... she was born in Tameside around nineteen forty seven, and emigrated to Canada and came back here in ninety five or ninety six to get married. The man's name is Clarke, Sean Clarke."

"I can't promise ... but I'll do what I can, I have your number so I'll ring you back if I find anything."

"Thanks and-" I shut up when I heard the soft click followed by the gentle burring sound in the earpiece. It was almost an hour and a half later when Louise called back. She spoke quickly and almost furtively.

"The supervisor is on the prowl so I might ring off suddenly. Right, I think I found what you're looking for … There were six Elizabeth Walkers married around the time you were interested in. There's only one who could fit the details you gave me."

"And?" I couldn't' keep the excitement from my voice."

"She married somebody called, let me see … a Joe Lynch. That's it, Joe Lynch in December nineteen ninety five. Sorry, got to go … hope it was useful?"

"Thanks." I gave a heavy sigh and put the telephone down. "I knew it!" I couldn't stop myself from shouting out loud.

Even though the information had vindicated my suspicions I was left with a sickened feeling in my stomach. I'd already told myself that Sean had been lying to me, but it was a different matter when I was confronted by irrefutable proof that he hadn't been telling me the truth.

So 'Sean's Betty', had got married … in nineteen ninety five … but the fact is she hadn't married Sean Clark and that's all that mattered.

*   *   *

SIXTEEN

Amanda called me a couple of days before she was due to come back from Brussels. She told me when she would be arriving at Manchester airport then refused my offer to collect her. She and her new boss would be picked up by a chauffer-driven limousine and taken directly to their office.

Amanda did promise to speak with me as soon as she was able but I waited in vain for her call. So, as things worked out, I didn't have the opportunity to see her until mid-way through the first week in December. When she finally did give me a call she explained that she was busy keeping pace with her new job, and so tired at the end of each long working day that all she wanted to do was sleep.

I told her I was busy too. I mentioned that the article about the convenience marriages went down well with the magazine editor and that he'd given me a couple more commissions which had kept me well occupied. I told her that, having finished the latest of these, I'd chosen to have a few days relaxing. Being relatively financially sound, I could afford to indulge myself. We agreed that my R and R and her 'break from the new grind' should coincide and we fixed up a rendezvous.

I hadn't told Amanda, but I'd decided to embark on a wild spending spree. It was unusual for me, but I did feel a growing compulsion to throw most of my caution to the wind and treat myself to at least one decent piece of new furniture. That was the reason I'd suggested we meet somewhere in the city centre. I'd always respected her opinion on 'fabrics and furnishing' basically because, in that department, I have what is commonly viewed as a total lack of taste.

On the morning of our meeting, nature had decided to show some sympathy. In contrast to the recent bout of icy winds, and freezing driving rain, the day broke with unseasonal warmth. The sky was a delicate shade of blue and fluffy white clouds drifted slowly eastwards propelled by a gentle breeze. It made me feel good as I left the flat, and even better as, after I'd parked the car in the multi-storey, then walked down High street.

Amanda was waiting for me at the corner of Debenhams. She didn't see me at first and it gave me the chance to 'look her over' as I walked towards her. She looked different somehow, and I don't just mean the really smart coat. She had an air of confidence about her, and she appeared to be exactly what she was - a professional working girl - no longer a student and drifting even further out of my league.

When she did see me, her face broke into a beaming smile. She almost ran as she came to greet me; and I was startled when, without hesitation, she flung her arms around me and gave me a more-than-sisterly hug.

"Andy. It's great to see you again. I have a million things to tell you …" She spoke rapidly, almost breathlessly when she stepped back to look at me. She frowned. "Are you ill?"

"I don't think so - why?"

"You look thinner ... Have you been eating well?"

"I've not been on a diet."

"I know your habits too well ... you had a cup of coffee for breakfast - right?"

"Well ... err ..." I hunched my shoulders and gave her a weak grin. "I didn't want to be late."

"Come on. We get some food inside you while we talk. Fancy anything special?"

"*Yes you*, I thought, but out of my mouth came, "No, not really..."

"Right. She grabbed my arm, turned and marched me to the junction then crossed into Fountain Street and up to Pizzaland. I glanced through the large plate-glass window as she hauled me inside, and noted there were only a few mid-morning customers.

We chose a table close to the far wall, and Amanda unfastened her coat to reveal a pale blue silk blouse and a matching scarf loosely draped around her neck. She did look different. Even before I had a chance to sip my coffee she aimed the question at me. It wasn't as if I wasn't expecting it, but even so it caught me off guard...

"How's Sean? Have you seen him this week?"

I made a play of wincing as I sipped the coffee and blowing on the surface to cool it while I tried desperately to think of an answer that wouldn't send her into orbit.

"No, I've not seen him for a while. I've been working on two or three commissions and I haven't had any spare time."

339

Amanda did not even try to hide her disappointment. She gave a deep sigh and her shoulders slumped. "I've thought of little else while I've been away and I can't wait to hear the end."

"The end of what, for God's sake." I said, not meaning to raise my voice.

"The end of Sean's story, that's the only way we can evaluate the whole thing. I suppose I'll just have to wait. When do you plan to see him again?"

"We never had any strict schedule, and there isn't any timetable. I still have a deal of tidying up to do before I'm free."

"Andy it's less than three weeks to Christmas ... You're not going to leave it too long, are you?"

I gave an evasive shrug. "I can't promise anything."

She frowned at me, but before she could say anything, the waitress arrived with our orders. I took the opportunity to busy myself with my pizza which gave me a natural excuse to avoid speaking to her for a while. She ate slowly and spent a lot of time just staring at me, and I could feel myself colouring under her gaze.

I was still munching when she spoke.

"Andy ... you're hiding something from me."

I swallowed a great lump of pizza and it stuck in my throat. Gagging fiercely, I took a mouthful of coffee in an attempt to wash the blockage away. When I did finally succeed in clearing my throat I gave her my best innocent look.

"I don't know what you mean, Amanda."

"Yes you do Andy. Hiding. It means telling a person something but leaving bits out, for example

340

being evasive, you know not telling the full story. Fucking hiding." Her hand was poised in front of her mouth and the slice of pizza in her hand was starting to look like it might connect with my face at any moment. Deep down I knew I couldn't carry on with the charade for much longer but I was aware of what I had to tell her and what it would do to our relationship. Here was I, a champion of 'the truth', dithering like a frightened schoolboy at the prospect of doing exactly what I had condemned others for not doing.

My head told me to have the courage of my convictions and tell her outright that Sean was nothing more than a cheat. But my heart disagreed.

I knew that I'd have to say something, and say it soon, as in now, otherwise; Amanda would guess the worst and castigate me for saying nothing. The piece of Pizza in my mouth felt as large and as digestible as s a sack-load of straw. I drowned it with coffee, letting it soak for a few moments before I took a deep breath and screwed up my eyes as I forced it down my throat.

From the look on Amanda's face at that moment, I knew I'd lost whatever chance I had of coming out of the situation with some credibility. I had a sudden brainwave …

I told her the truth …

Amanda listened, enthralled, as I reminded her how Sean had been given the opportunity to go to Canada, and how Betty had contacted him at his hotel. I had spoken slowly and could see the growing misty-eyed sentimentality in her expression. So, when I came to the conclusion I delivered the blow as softly as I could. For a full second I thought she hadn't heard what I'd said. Then realisation crept over her face, and her excited expression crumbled.

She stared at me with an uncomprehending frown. "What do you mean, Andy?"

"I'm truly sorry, but it's the truth. When Betty Walker came back here from Canada, she did get married ... to a guy called Joe Lynch."

"You know that - for certain?" Amanda held me with a piercing gaze that would have made Torquemada proud.

"Yes. Well, I'm as convinced as I can be that the Betty Walker was the one that Sean was speaking about. I have a friend, Louise, who works at the registry office and she checked the details for me. She was quite definite - no mistake - Betty did not marry Sean."

"Did he ever mention that he had remarried?"

"As far as I can recall, Sean has never mentioned having a wife until now ...I've never *seen* her. So maybe he's made her up as well."

"I can't believe you. What ever happened to a journalist's curiosity?"

"Amanda, I didn't look into every little thing he told me - only the things I thought were relevant in proving that he did -or did not go back in time."

"You were interested in Marianne!"

"For God's sake, Amanda! Marianne is news. She's beautiful, she was a dancer, and now runs the biggest dance school for miles. But I never went to interview

342

her. Know why? Because she, never witnessed anything unusual. The people I needed to talk to were the desk sergeant, Jack Hargreaves, Stanley Fisher who lived on Sefton Avenue, Sharon Hanson - even the Boswell Brothers."

"Didn't they both commit suicide at the same time, in prison?"

"Yes, they did … and all the others are dead too! That only leaves Betty to vouch for his story… and he's just told me now that she's his 'wife'. The wife, I might add, whom I've never met and who he has up until now, as far as I'm concerned, never mentioned. But he slipped up there. He'd given me the name of a real living person - and coupled it with a detail that I could check out. Now that I have … I know that he's been stringing me along!"

"Before you go any further Andy, can I just say something?"

"Sure, of course."

"When Sean tells you his story does he tell in in sequence? You know, tell it like it happened or does he jump back and forth?"

I thought for a moment before replying. "Yeah, you could say that it was pretty much in sequence as he claims it happened. Why do you ask?"

Amanda paused like a Barrister about to deliver a line that would win the case,

"Well then Andy is it not possible that the reason Sean has never really mentioned his wife Betty up until now is because she is the end of the story."

"Amanda dear you could have a point there but, you are

forgetting that what you are saying is only relevant if she is his wife, who she is definitely not."

As a means of completely deflating an occasion, my statement was perfect. From that moment Amanda shrank into a kind of shell, and although she still spoke with me, her conversation was desultory and her attention was quite plainly elsewhere.

We finished the pizzas and I told her about my plan to buy some new furniture. She agreed to come with me and offer her advice, and this she did, but the whole morning was something of an anti-climax. I ordered a new settee and coffee table. Thanks to Amanda they'd enhance the 'ambience' of my flat and give it a touch of class that it didn't deserve.

I'd planned on taking her for dinner, but once she'd helped me choose the furniture she said she would sooner go home. She gave me an unenthusiastic kiss on the cheek and turned away. I watched her walking down Market Street, and I could see that she'd lost all her natural sparkle. I felt guilty that my 'news' had been the cause…

The days dragged on, and the weather changed in line with the advance of the year. Each day broke with dark leaden-grey skies and sharp bone-cutting winds. I had no new contracts and to be honest I didn't feel like searching for any. I had a lethargy that matched the dull dreary days as December slowly approached its close. I'd spoken with Amanda a couple of times, but I hadn't needed to be a genius to sense that her feelings towards me had definitely chilled. It was like she had just been told there is no such thing as Father Christmas. She spoke with some feigned enthusiasm about her work but her words carried no conviction.

It was, therefore, with some surprise that I answered a call from her on the morning of the twenty third. Her voice was bright and chirpy and she virtually bubbled over the line.

"Are you doing anything tomorrow morning, Andy?"

"Not to my knowledge."

"Good, then you won't have to cancel anything. We're going out. I'll call for you about nine thirty, so don't slouch about in your flea-pit. Right?"

"Yes, all right. Now just where are you-"

"See you in the morning, Andy. Bye."

The morning of Christmas Eve broke with a sullen grey light that barely penetrated the damp mist that clung to the ground and swirled gently in a ghost of a breeze. I awoke early, showered, dressed, and downed a quick coffee and a couple of slices of toast.

Amanda gaped at me with wide startled eyes when I answered the doorbell within seconds. She blinked and shook her head.

"Did you sleep behind the door, or something?"

I grinned. "You know damned well your message intrigued me. It's a wonder I slept at all last night." I closed the door and followed her onto the pavement as she strode towards a flame-coloured Celica. I was impressed. Her last car had been much like mine, held together by faith hope and sealing wax.

345

I slid into the passenger seat not able to suppress a Cheshire-cat grin.

"You know, Amanda, I could easily get used to this. Now - where are we going?"

Amanda gave me a secretive smile as she started the engine. "Wait and see. It's a surprise. So just sit back and enjoy the ride."

I knew better than pursue the matter. I enjoyed her company so much that I just followed her instructions and relaxed into the comfortable seat. She turned on the CD-player and a soft wave of instrumental music flowed over us. I was so comfortable that I hardly noticed where we were going, until she turned from Oldham Road onto Broadway. I frowned.

"Amanda. You aren't taking us to-"

"Just keep quiet." Amanda smiled as she slowed for the traffic lights and signalled that she was about to turn into Bathurst road.

I sat upright. "Amanda. If you're thinking of going to Sean's house - forget it. I am *not* going to see him ... and that's my final word!"

*   *   *

SEVENTEEN

Amanda parked outside the house on Sefton Avenue and turned off the car engine. I sat stiffly in the passenger seat, my arms folded defensively across my chest. I stared straight ahead and could sense Amanda staring at me.

"Well, Andy… are you going to sit there all day, or are you coming in with me?" She unfastened her seat-belt and opened the door.

"I told you, I am not going to see him again."

"Not even to wish him a merry Christmas? I thought you said you liked Sean?"

"I did - I do … oh." I turned my head and saw that she was stooping to stare at me. She had a gentle smile on her face and my resolve weakened. After all, as she said, I did like the man - even though he had tried to sell me a three legged pig.

"Oh, all right Amanda, Christmas the season of good will to all men, I get it, lead on." I unclipped the belt and opened the door.

We stood side by side on the doorstep and Amanda pressed the bell-push. There was no sound coming from inside the house and I wavered.

"Perhaps he isn't up yet … maybe we should call back later?" At that moment I heard the sound of footsteps coming down the hall. Ah well, I thought, I don't have to stay too long, and I can maintain a veneer of civility for a few minutes - just to please Amanda who I believed was now using Christmas as a means of coercion.

Sean stood in the doorway and beamed at us. "You're right on time ... come in the both of you."

I stepped inside, striding over a scattering of envelopes lying inside the doorway. I saw Amanda stoop to gather them together then pick them up.

"Close the door, please." Sean had turned away and was striding down the hall way. I waited until Amanda had done as Sean had asked, then I jumped as she slid her hand into mine. It was some time since we'd held hands or anything else for that matter and it felt rather strange, but good. As we moved down the hall and we reached the door to the living room, Sean's voice came from within.

"Don't hang about, come in."

As we turned into the doorway, Amanda gave my hand a squeeze and pulled me, turning me slightly towards her.

"Here," she said slipping the envelopes into my hand, "I think it would be a friendly gesture if you gave them to him."

I frowned at her as I took the mail from her hand. She didn't wait for me but stepped into the room leaving me in the doorway. I don't know why, but I glanced down at the half-dozen letters I was holding as I followed Amanda.

The three of them were standing in the middle of the room and they turned to face me as I entered.

Amanda was smiling broadly, Sean had a slightly severe look, and the woman beside him looked at me with a faintly amused expression.

Sean smiled at me. "Andy - you haven't met my wife, have you …"

The woman moved forward extending her hand. I took it and felt the warmth of her gentle grasp as I stared into her deep golden brown eyes. She was certainly attractive with an aura of tranquillity and love about her that melted me to the core. She smiled and I was taken by a feeling of encompassing tenderness when she spoke in a soft husky voice.

"Mister Priest - or may I call you Andy. Somehow I feel like I know you."

"Please, please do." For some reason at that moment I was half tongue-tied.

She continued to smile at me. "Joe has told me ever so much about you, and I've been dying to meet you face-to-face."

"And I've-" I frowned at her. "Did you say *Joe*?"

"Yes." she turned to grin at Sean, "My husband, Joe."

I knew my mouth had dropped open and I was gaping, but I couldn't help it. I gave a start when Amanda called softly to me. "Why do you think I gave you those letters … Look at them, Andy."

Still perplexed I looked down at the letters in my hand … I shrugged as I read the top one, addressed to Mr. and Mrs S. Clarke. I slid it aside to look at the one beneath it … Then I caught my breath.

Mr. and Mrs J Lynch
1 Sefton Avenue
New Moston
Manchester.

I lifted my head and stared at Sean then his wife, and finally at Amanda. They were all grinning at me as if I was the village idiot. I frowned at Amanda. "You knew!"

Amanda nodded. "Last week I was watching a late-night quiz show on TV and one of the questions was …What was John Wayne's real name …The answer was *Marion Morrison*. It set me thinking, so I went to see your friend Louise at the registry office. She told me she'd phoned you with the name of the man who married Betty, but she said that was all you'd asked for. When I asked her, she let me look at them in black and white … Once I'd seen the address on the certificate, I got in touch with Joe, or should I say, Sean, and Betty and they invited me to come round. We all thought it'd be a nice surprise if I brought you here on Christmas Eve."

"Well …" I shook my head. "Fuck me; the word surprise is totally inadequate. I'm a journalist completely lost for words."

Sean let out a great laugh and the others joined in. I felt more than a little foolish for a moment then I had to smile. Sean came to me and clapped me on the shoulder.

"Can you imagine me trying to make my way in show business with a name like Joe Lynch? Didn't you realise Sean Clarke was my professional name?"

350

"I … I never really thought about it."

"And you call yourself an investigative journalist?" He grinned at me. "Changing names in my business is like putting on make-up. We all do it, or most of us … Like Englebert Humperdinck."

"I know, Gerry Dorsey."

"Ha!" Said Sean. "Even that is not his real name."

I realised what he'd said was right. Most of the really well-known 'stars' had changed their names to something a little less mundane to help their careers … now I was thinking clearly, I could bring to mind hundreds of others. Even though I knew it was only his stage name, I still thought of him as 'Sean'. I mean in my defence, does anyone think of Cliff Richard as Harry Webb?

Amanda squeezed my arm and gave me a 'sorry for the poor wet spaniel' look. "When Louise told you the name of Betty's husband, Joe Lynch, you heard confirmation of just what you'd been looking for all along." She shook her head. "Unlike you, I still believed in Sean."

I turned to Sean and his wife with a hangdog expression. "I just don't know how to tell you how sorry I am that …" I frowned when Betty started to smile at me.

"I told Joe all along that you wouldn't believe his story which is why I stayed well out of it." She gave a little laugh. "Even though I'm a part of it, even I sometimes wonder if I've been imagining it all." She reached for Sean's hand and gave it a squeeze as she turned to look at him. "You could say that ours really was a 'dream

351

romance'."

An hour later we were all sitting in the living room, Amanda and I on the settee and Betty in one of the armchairs, while Sean was perched on the arm beside her. We were drinking Sean's excellent Brandy and chatting amiably. Betty had explained how, after that one meeting in Montreal, she'd made up her mind to follow Sean back to Manchester at the earliest opportunity. Sean too had been affected by that meeting, and while Betty was making arrangements to come to England, he was organising another visit to Canada.

Neither had admitted their plans when they'd spoken on the telephone - as they did frequently during the months after their meeting. Fate had taken a hand and had organised another meeting for them at Manchester airport. Sean had arrived early for his flight and was whiling away the time by sitting in the observer's lounge watching the incoming flights. Unknowingly, he'd seen Betty's flight arrive just as he was making his way to the car park to collect a book he'd brought to read on the flight but left in his car. As he was making his way back into the terminal he had - in his own words - the most marvellous shock of his life. Betty was standing outside the arrivals lounge in a line of people waiting for taxis...

The mood was interrupted by the shrill chirping of the telephone. Betty jumped up and vanished into the kitchen, and a couple of minutes later reappeared with a broad grin on her face.

"Michele and her little girl will be here in about fifteen

minutes, and she's told me that Jason will be here tomorrow for Christmas dinner."

"Oh. In that case ..." I started to get to my feet.

"What do you think you're doing?" Sean frowned at me.

"Well, I ... you don't want us here when-"

"You and Amanda are our guests ... Right?" He looked at Betty and she nodded firmly. "And that means that - if you can put up with the noise of an exuberant grandchild, you're welcome to stay."

I looked at Amanda and she smiled, nodding slightly to me. I shrugged. "In that case, Sean, we'd very much like to stay. Thank you."

Sean went round refilling glasses and beaming at us. Having made sure we were all well supplied, he returned to sit on the arm of the easy chair where his wife was sitting. He looked straight at me as he raised his glass. "Here's to your good health, Andy ... and to the disappearance of all your scepticism."

As I acknowledged his toast and lifted my glass along with the others I noticed that Sean appeared troubled. "What's wrong, Sean?"

Sean shrugged. "There are times when I even doubt my own recollection of the past."

Even though I lived through it all, and have the concrete evidence of this smashing lady by my side, I still can't understand what happened to me. "

Amanda leaned forward a little and looked directly at Sean. "Maybe I can help? Ever since Andy told me about you and your, let's call them, experiences, I've been formulating a theory about the events you described. Don't get me wrong, I'm not offering a set of cast iron facts that can't be disputed … but if you're agreeable, I can put forward my own views to try to explain what happened?"

Sean glanced at Betty and she smiled up at him before he turned to stare at Amanda. "If you can make some sense out of it, then I for one am more than willing to listen."

Betty and I nodded our assent.

Amanda took a deep breath then began to speak. "There are millions of people around the world who firmly believe that this 'conscious life' we are living is not the only form of human or spiritual existence. There are documented reports from hundreds of people who have undergone 'out-of-body-experiences'. Of course, there are a lot of sceptics who dismiss these reports as little more than sensational attempts to gain some attention … But on the other hand, there are enough of these 'believers' to assert some kind of credibility to their claims."

Amanda paused, looked around at us, and then gave a small smile. "Right, now that we've established that we don't have any sceptics amongst us …" She turned and raised an eyebrow at me, and I just grinned back at her. "I'll explain what I believe.

Time-travelling is something about which reams and reams have been written, but credible explanations have always been vague. In your case, Sean, I think that we have to look at another mystical phenomenon. When Brian Thompson was murdered in December nineteen sixty four, you were in a Belfast hospital with pneumonia, hovering between life and death, probably closer to death and close enough for you to have entered the spirit world.

I believe that somewhere, outside your body, your spirit met with young Brian on some sort of Astral Plane and he asked you to help save the life of Sharon Beckett. He knew that she was about to be murdered by the same people who had murdered him and-"

"Just a minute!" Sean interrupted. "You say that little Brian knew that somebody was about to murder Sharon - how could that be? It was after he had already been killed."

Amanda shrugged. "I don't really understand it myself and yes this could be speculation... but I believe that 'time' has no real meaning to a spirit and it was his spirit who had knowledge of the forthcoming murder. Brian was able to travel to the past or the future in order to accomplish his mission to save Sharon Beckett from the same fate as him... and you were the ideal person to help him."

Sean frowned. "In that case - how come I couldn't save the other kids that were murdered?"

Amanda smiled at him. "Your 'spirit' can only be at one place at any one time ... while you were in a coma in Belfast your spirit was free to travel to wherever Brian Thompson wanted it to be ... but once you regained consciousness in The Royal Hospital Belfast you returned to your own time in The Portland Hotel Manchester, you had to return to your physical self."

"So - why didn't I go as I was?"

"I don't know what you mean." Amanda frowned.

"I was seventeen when I was in hospital ... so how come I was forty seven when I met those brothers on the Moors?"

Amanda shrugged. "I suppose Brian felt that you would be more effective as a full gown man than as a teenager, hence the jump in time from 1994 back to 1964."

"Age has no meaning to a spirit. A ghost, if they exist and a lot of people believe they do, when they appear to someone do not necessarily appear as age they were at the time of their death."

Sean pulled a face then frowned. "All right ... supposing we can accept what you've just said ... how do you explain the fact that I dreamed about being on the moors thirty years after it happened? Remember I was on the plane in nineteen ninety four when I fell asleep ..." He paused then nodded. "I see! I probably recalled some of the details in Sommers' book that I had told the CIA girl and fabricated the dream around them." He frowned when he looked at Amanda.

Amanda shook her head. "No, Sean, I disagree. I don't think you were dreaming ... I think you were remembering or maybe reliving what you'd done thirty years ago. You see to 'go back in time' - you must have *been* back in time. Even time travel must obey logic. For example if you went back in time and tried to shoot your father the gun would jam, or you would miss, because if you killed him you would not be here to do so."

Sean looked blank for a moment then hunched his shoulders and smiled at Amanda. "All right, it might only be a theory, and we'll never have any way of proving or disproving it … but it does offer a logical explanation for what I went through and you have certainly done your homework."

Betty gave him a playful slap on the arm. "That's enough of theorising. Let's have another drink."

Sean got up and gave her a swift kiss before he began to collect our empty glasses. He paused in front of me and smiled. "Now Andy you have the whole story - what are you going to do about it?"

I smiled directly at him. "I don't know about you, but I think it would make a pretty good novel."

"Now, that's a thought." Sean winked as he took my glass.

We were finishing our second drink when we heard the sound of the front door opening followed by the sound of someone walking down the hallway. A tall blonde-haired girl, carrying a miniature version of herself came into the room. The girl smiled at us, but her daughter was beaming at Betty.

Betty hugged them both and gave each a kiss, while Sean did the introduction.

"Andy, Amanda. This is my daughter, Michele, and this is our granddaughter, Sophie."

By now the little girl was standing on the floor, hiding behind Betty and clinging to her skirt. Betty picked her up and gently stroked her cheek. "Don't be shy … This is Andy and Amanda. Say hello."

We got no more than a guarded glance from beneath the tiny girl's lowered brows.

It took a while but eventually Sophie accepted us. She settled down to play with some small toys Betty brought from one of the cupboards, and it was obvious she'd forgotten us as she played. I couldn't help but smile as I heard her 'baby voice' making excited sounds as she moved the toys around. I looked up and saw that everyone was smiling too.

Fortified with drinks we all talked easily, and I found Michele to be a delightful person. Witty and confident, she was definitely her father's daughter, though she confessed to having a voice like a bullfrog and no sense of rhythm. While we were talking, she occasionally glanced at Sean and, when he returned her glances, I could see the justifiable pride in his eyes.

Amanda spoke with her and I got the impression they had more than a little common ground. While they were engaged in conversation, I glanced across to Sean and he raised his glass to me. "You know, Andy, Michele has the one really concrete piece of evidence that made me realise that all that happened to me wasn't just my imagination. Michele, have you got your purse handy?"

"Why Dad?"

"I just want to show Andy something."

"I think I know what you want, Dad. Now, let me see."

Michele opened her purse, fished about inside then produced a key. Sean then came over to me and placed it in my hand "That's it, Andy."

"Is this what I think it is? The key to your door?"

Sean looked straight at me and said. "I prefer to think of it as a Key to Yesterday!

EIGHTEEN

It was the end of January 2005 before I was able to sort
myself out and settle down to work on Sean's story.
Amanda had gone off to Portugal with her boss at the
end of the previous week and I hadn't been in the mood
to work while she was still in Manchester. I got the
feeling that, sometime in the future, she and I might
embark on a relationship that was less casual than the
one we'd enjoyed so far but that would rely on me
saying something like "I love you "and I cope better
with what might have been rather than take a chance on
total rejection … Still, that was the future.

It was a typically dismal Manchester morning
and in keeping with the weather, I was feeling dismal
and lethargic. The wind was hurling fifty pence piece
raindrops against the window when I dragged myself
out of bed, and it was still hurling them when I went
into the kitchen and made my first coffee of the day. I
forced myself to toast a couple of slices of bread and ate
them in the kitchen. Refilling my cup with a fresh brew
of coffee I slouched into the living room and opened up
the computer.

I sat, just staring blankly at the empty screen. In
the past few days I'd had several attempts to begin the
novel, but none of them gave me the slightest
satisfaction. Even though I'd drunk a couple of cups of
coffee my only inspiration was to make myself a third

rather than begin another abortive attempt at a first chapter.

I was halfway to the kitchen when I stopped and turned round. I surveyed the untidy collection of notes which were spread over the table and the settee, and I realised that there *was* a story here, waiting to be told if only I could begin to tell it and more importantly will anyone believe it enough to publish it. A good start would be if I could find a decent title as I'd already dismissed three so far. Then it hit me as I remembered something Sean had said, and I thought 'of course, it's obvious.' I went back to the computer still holding the empty coffee cup, raised it in the air as if it were Brandy and said "Cheers, Sean", took a deep breath, then started battering away at the keyboard.

*   *   *

KEY TO YESTERDAY

CHAPTER ONE
The Year 2004, the place Manchester, England.

Fate is truly fickle. I'd spent a whole day chasing after a story, only to have all the main protagonists refuse to speak to me. I was tired and hungry and thoroughly pissed-off ....

Printed in Great Britain
by Amazon

48740846R00210